9/24

Bro. Barney O.P.
O2C BOOKS

Dear Oliver & Briege,
There is life beyond
Alliance — great though
it is.
Great to see both of you
Michael
June 2010

The Blackfriars of Mediaeval Europe!
- in England since A.D. 1221 - and the latest member of the Order of Friars Preachers is young Joe Coyle – aka Brother Barnabas - just arrived from London with all his worldly possessions in a tin trunk.

    Barney is serious, intense, determined – but to his amazement he finds monastic life is *fun* – despite a freezing winter that lasts from December till March, life without women, and only a small drop of alcohol on major feast days.

    Despite the little sip of alcohol, or perhaps because of it, Bro. Barney's monastic life style could have a curiosity value in the minds of one and a half billion Muslims, bearing in mind a thousand years of what might be called 'ardent theological debate' between Muslim and Christian. And then there's more than a billion Hindus, Sikhs and Buddhists who might have an interest, while a billion Catholics will certainly appreciate Brother Barney's life-

forming experience, as will a further billion fellow Christians and some of earth's agnostics and atheists (a billion is the estimate) - who may find it difficult to avoid the temptation to take a peek – just to see what the hullaballoo is all about!

This book could be a winner! - maybe even an 'International Best Seller' - like every other book you pick up in a bookshop these days! ... Hmm ...

Opinions / Reviews

"Provocative, sometimes infuriating, and always entertaining ... I particularly enjoyed and agreed with the short chapter 'Sex, Love, Marriage, Divorce, Nullity and a Caring Church.' I don't expect you will agree with all Br. Barney's musings but you will be stimulated into musings of your own. Thank God the Br. Barneys of this world still have a voice. Long may it be so."
 - Brian D'Arcy, C.P., Priest, Broadcaster & Writer

"... [an] intriguing and humorous story..."
– Joanne Fleming, Down Recorder.

Overheard in the Office:

"So – the Pope didn't reply to your Open Letter"?

"Looks like it – or maybe his letter is still in the post."

"You don't think the word 'troglodyte' has anything to do with it!"

"I don't see why! I mean, I didn't hold it against the writer who said of one of my short stories that I should hang it up in the Jacques! It was an apt comment - fair and truthful."

"How many people did you send a draft copy of 'Barney' to?"

"Let's see - the Pope, a Cardinal in Rome, a Cardinal Archbishop, an Archbishop, two Bishops and a few other notable people - thirteen in all."

"And only Father Brian D'Arcy stuck his head over the parapet wall - to let you know what he thought. Do you not see anything strange about this?"

"Not at all. They are all very busy people!"

"And Brian is not?"

"Are you suggesting there may be another reason for not writing to me?"

"It's possible!"

"Well – I dunno. I only wrote what was in my head! There's nothing wrong with that! It just means that I'll have to wait for proper reviews ..."

"From the professional reviewers?"

"Yes .... And from people who buy my book."

"How many do you think?"

"Oh – it could be as many as a couple of dozen!"

"And it's their view that counts?"

"Absolutely! The voice of those who buy the book is the one to listen to. And they can email their thoughts to me from my website at www.o2cbooks.info. "

"I look forward to that!"

"Me too! Tell me more ... why you think the pope and the bishops didn't write! What's this about a parapet wall ... is there a war on?"

IMAGINED REACTION to 'Brother Barney':

"**HH the Dalai Lama reminds Brother O'Shea** that upon reincarnation HH could possibly fly like a butterfly or sting like a bee and in the latter capacity may visit County Down – even if he *is* considered quite likeable." – *PA to HH*

"**Hey Man! That's my line about butterflies and bees**. You ain't supposed to plagiarise like that!" – *Mohammed Ali*

"**On behalf of the Londonderry / Derry Branch of the Orange & Green Order of Muslim Brotherhood** we strongly object to the statement that Muhammad, Peace be Upon Him, was illiterate. It might be true but to mention it in such a callous fashion offends our sensibilities. At our AGM/Ard Feis we will consider the imposition of a *fatwah* on the grounds of insolence, irreverence and lack of respect. A number of our Brethren, converted from membership of both Real & Continuity IRA deeply resent this evidence of further interference by an agent of British Imperialism masquerading as a Christian."
- *issued by 'Sean/Muhammad' on behalf of 4th Brigade Muslim Orange & Green Brotherhood, Stroke City*

"**His Holiness the Pope** rejects the accusation that those who give church leadership in Rome are a bunch of 'atavistic, muscle-minded, troglodytes'– a certain proportion possibly, but not the whole lot!

He also states that the charge that he forbids people to think is not accurate. They must just think more carefully, the way he does.

In the case of his old friend Hans Küng, Professor of theology at Tübingen University, the professor was merely silenced and forbidden to speculate about Infallibility – even if We do make a mistake now and again in our private capacity.

The various nuns and priests who propounded notions about married and women priests fall into the same category and had to be similarly silenced, for the good of all.

The Congregation for Doctrine of the Faith must protect the children of God from error, and in the twenty years the present Pope coordinated this office he assiduously did his duty, among other things forbidding some priests and nuns to minister to homosexuals and their families, thus avoiding the danger that such people may be left with the impression that the church condones homosexuality.

He assures *Urbe et Orbe* that there is absolutely no question of returning to the mediaeval practice of creating an altered mindset through physical torture, nor of silencing neo-Albigensians, Catharists and other erroneous thinkers by burning them at the stake if orthodoxy cannot be achieved. This never was desirable, as our venerable predecessors Innocent III and Gregory IX made clear at that time – despite the murder of a papal legate by these abominable heretics. All that they established was an *Inquisition,* an Inquiry! Incensed local people took unauthorised action. Today we are intent upon achieving much more control.

As regards the Nullity plea in the unfortunate case of the lady with seven children who was deserted by her husband we simply cannot do anything about it, as the evidence does not comply with the requirements of Canon Law. Jesus might allow such a plea out of love and compassion but we cannot be sure of His attitude, so we must proceed according to Ecclesiastical Law.

We cannot allow the impression to be created that nullity is divorce by the back door. We must be firm about this if we are to maintain respect and control. Sentimentality and exaggerated notions of love and pastoral concern cannot be allowed to rule the day.

- *Hon. Sec.* ~~Holy Office~~ ~~Office of the Inquisition~~
Congregation of the Doctrine of the Faith.
PS: A letter is on the way to Michael O'Shea's local Ordinary

"**What an odd little book!**" – *Anon*

"**I quite like it**. It's a bit funny here and there…" – *Anon Too*

"**Intriguing nonsense**. What sane person believes in angels?
- *Member, National Secular Society*

"**A fascinating insight** into modern monastic and religious life; a simple story that raises big questions about the mystery of our creation; well told in sometimes beautiful but always clear language. A great read, pervaded with a sense of humour that refreshes and stimulates. I recommend it to anyone with an interest in how we live – and die.

Interestingly, the author personally confronts the leader of his church with perceived defects in the organisation of the Catholic Church.

Can the ordinary Catholic really talk to the Pope, like to an ordinary human being, and expect him to listen?"
- *A Real Reader.*

Author's Note:

'Bro. Barney O.P.' was originally written as a screenplay. It was only after eighteen years of failing to persuade film makers, or raise the cash required to make it myself, that I decided to re-write the screenplay as a novel. I am, as I confess throughout the book, a slow learner.

I must come clean. 'Bro. Barney' could well have been written as a straightforward autobiography, but as it was already a screenplay I found it easier to continue to tell the story as if I were writing about someone other than myself.

This meant that I could be objective, and the use of an alter ego in the form of Joe Coyle means that I can permit modest creative licence - telling the truth but moderately embellishing certain events and altering the names of people who might not relish an invasion of their privacy.

Here and there I have used real names, those that I remember, and of people I trust not to be embarrassed about association with me - plus some who have died and cannot be embarrassed, for they have explained themselves to the living Lord.

The story is 90% factual - and 100% true!

The O'Shea family motif is *Vincit Veritas* - truth conquers - and I bless the unknown ancestor who created it, for in great or small things truth is vital. Without it life becomes even more perilous.

So believe me, all the central events I relate actually took place, especially those that seem strange and inexplicable.

Thank you for reading my book - if you do - and if you don't I'm sure God will forgive you - even if I don't!

Ah, come on! That was a joke!

By the way, if you think you recognise yourself it well may be - unless you intend to sue. In which case you are definitely mistaken.

Michael O'Shea

P.S: It is not clear how Angel came to control the form of this story.

Dedication

Tom and Margaret Mary (Madge, *née* Mulheron) O'Shea, loved me into existence, and continued to love and care for me in company with my brother and sister and a few dozen uncles, aunts, cousins and family friends, all of whom made me feel very welcome to the world.

I was a cheerful but dreamy little lad, rather given to hedonistic extremes, and as I grew older some people began to say, "Michael O'Shea is quite a nice fellow but it is a pity he is so wild!"

The first time I became aware of this was when my mother, red faced and rather annoyed, just back from a shopping trip to Belfast city centre, told me she had been sitting behind two women on the Falls Road bus, shrinking down in her seat as she heard them agree the point, in the exact words quoted above. It was the most severe criticism she ever levelled at me.

Other family members began to say, in a friendly way, that I was eccentric. "Ah!" I would ask, "But where is the centre?"

At that time I would have been unsure where it was, but after some years of erratic investigation and painful experience I discovered where it really is, and within it is the love of family and friends, especially the love of my three beautiful sons, Raymond, Tomás Ruairí and William Conor.

To all of these this small work is dedicated.

Michael O'Shea

Ardglass, County Down, Summer 2008
– and a grand wet one it was.

The making and unmaking of
Bro. Barney O.P.
An autobiographical Novel

Michael O'Shea

Plus
Addendum
'Sex, Love, Marriage, Divorce, Nullity & A Caring Church?' (p. 195) - including an open letter to Benedict XVI

O2C BOOKS

ISBN 978-0-9558878-0-2
Copyright © Michael O'Shea 2008/2009
FIRST EDITION – finalised April 2009
- amended 2010

The right of Michael O'Shea to be identified as the author of this work is asserted by him in accordance with the Copyright, Designs and Patents Act 1988.

All rights reserved. With the exception of modest quotes for review purposes no part of this publication may be reproduced, stored in or introduced into a retrieval system, or transmitted, in any form, or by any means (electronic, mechanical, photocopying, recording or otherwise) without the prior written permission of the publisher. Any person who does any unauthorized act in relation to this publication may be liable to criminal prosecution and civil claims for damages,

A catalogue record for this book is available from the British Library and from Trinity College, Dublin.

This book is sold subject to the condition that it shall not, by way of trade or otherwise, be lent, re-sold, hired out, or otherwise circulated without the publisher's prior consent in any form of binding or cover other than that in which it is published and without a similar condition being imposed on the subsequent purchaser.

Cover design & typographical layout by O2C Books. Main text 11pt. Georgia
****

'Brother Barney O.P.' – an autobiographical novel - is available through bookshops and public libraries worldwide.
To order Quote ISBN 978-0-9558878-0-2.

It can also be ordered online at Amazon, Barnes & Noble, Waterstones and other stockists, and from O2C BOOKS at https://www.o2cbooks.info

The Story

1 Angel 1
2 Joe 5
3 West 19
4 Brothers 31
5 Prior 39
6 Novitiate 47
7 Matins 57
8 Work 65
9 Clothing 71
10 Questions 75
11 Latin 81
12 Fieldmouse 89
13 Love Song 91
14 Cold Dawn 93
15 A Local Rule 97
16 Mouse Encore 99
17 A Sorry Venia 101
18 Chapter 105
19 Winter Beauty 113
20 A Hard Winter 117
21 A Frozen Traveller 123
22 Crown of Thorns 127
23 Easter 131
24 Visitors 135
25 Dragonfly 145
26 Sex 151

27	An Old Hen?..	159
28	Visions	161
29	Vigil	167
30	Decision	169
31	Albert...	173
32	A Tear for The World..	175
33	Angel Again..	181

ADDENDUM

Thinking? Cogito ergo sum? 189

Trust Thinking?..191

Sex, Love, Marriage, Divorce, Nullity and a Caring Church?
.... 195
Open Letter to Benedict XVI 206
Afterthought 223

Troglodyte?..225

The God Search 231

The Incarnation...233

Mary, Mother of Jesus...237

Authority.. 251

Questions About Authority: How my Great-Grandmother Went to Heaven and My Grandmother Went to Bradford - leaving me with .. Questions About Authority & Parish Priests
.... 261

Predestination? 275

The Face of Jesus?...285

Spirit 289

The Trinity 293

Evil 299

Life & Death... 307

Heaven, Hell & Purgatory 315

The Story

1 Angel

Darkness. Silence. Time is not yet.

Then, from the immensity and glory of his being God creates the physical universe, and it is good - a mere reflection of eternity, but good.

It is infinite, for it reflects eternity, but it is not eternal, for time and matter are contained within eternity.

I was there – astounded at the glory that was becoming - not equal to that of God, He who Is, but an astonishing reflection of his greatness and goodness.

At the dawn of the making I was there, as of right, for I am an angel of the Lord, he who makes all things.

I too was created, resembling him in that I can know and love. I did not know fully why or how I was brought into being, except that I was begotten in love, reflecting his glory.

But when your universe came into being I began to realise a further meaning of my existence, beyond sheer goodness. It appeared that I had a purpose, hidden until time began.

I was to have a special task.

I was to become the guardian of a child of man, from birth to the change that you call death.

I did not always know this. I had no need to know.

I accept my place, content in the wonder and glory of Yahweh, He Who Is. I know him and I am caught up in his love. But I do not know him as he knows me. I know him only in part, as befits a marvel of his creation, for I am a marvel if you could see me, become aware of me, with clear mind and full knowledge.

There are others like me, some of whom did not accept the reality that we are dependent upon a power beyond us, outside us, upon Yahweh, the maker of all things.

The greatest of these was the angel of light - no longer bright, become a dark monster of hatred and tortured pride, an advocate of despair... changed for all eternity, unlike the groaning travails and constant changes of your developing world.

You know of him as Lucifer - because of the Latin language that once ruled in a part of your world: Lucifer, the bearer of light, but he has had many names throughout time: Beelzebub, Satan, the Devil, Legion, The Deceiver, all of them inadequate to describe his nature, the malevolent dark brightness of his being, and his greatest wish is to hide himself from men and continue to destroy, lead people to destruction because they are not aware of the need for faith, love and the discipline of self control... You can recognise him by his works.

He was the first and greatest of Yahweh's angels; amazing in his likeness to God, and as with all of us free to think and begin to know himself. But as he came to know that he was most like God in his power he began to believe that he should be equal to him, or even greater.

A sad and foolish state - to refuse to accept, to resent, to wish to be the centre, to be adored. What simple derangement! What dread error! What untruth! And as the father of lies dark Lucifer's proud thoughts transferred to others of my kind, directly in the spirit - insidious, powerful, deceptive, to those who choose to hear, who wilfully chose to be deceived.

We who are pure spirit, like Yahweh, are free to choose, as you are. We would not have been like Him if the gift had been withheld.

So we chose, before and during the process of creation of your universe, though these changes are different to the changes that you know in time.

We made our choices, fateful to all of us and to you, so that Lucifer and those who followed him, inflating their importance because of their nature and the tasks they were given, and the freedom that led them to believe that they were far removed from the jurisdiction of their creator, exaggerated and distorted their power in a monstrous way.

I was not numbered among these. I resisted the lie.

I looked upon myself and Yahweh, and remained an angel of light, pure in mind and spirit.

I am one of many, greater in number than those who fell.

We are given freedom in an untrammelled way. We are aware of the wonder and beauty of origin, of he who is. We love him and know him, in the way given, from a distance it seems; though this is not entirely true, for we are caught up in His Love, rejoicing in it, reflecting it, made glorious by it, accepting our status, acknowledging the gift that is given.

But we are not part of Him. We are distinct, as the rays of your sun are distinct from the glory and fire of the sun itself; warmed by his presence, dancing and singing ever in the delight of knowing him, but always distinct; living with him in a union of eternal light, whereas we were once capable of dying into deep, dark death – rebel against light; lose ourselves in darkness. But we made our choice, and it will never be taken away from us. We live in joy, in eternal glory.

I would ask you to note with special care our relationship with Yahweh - the exact quality of it: that we are not part of him, that we are distinct. It has a bearing upon the story that I am about to tell.

We live with a life given to us but it is not His life. I ask you to remember this. I have a reason for asking this.

Remember also what happened to the greatest angel of light and to those who chose to follow him, adopting pride in place of reality, choosing destructive power in place of creative purpose, exchanging hope for despair, returning hatred for love, never to be released from an eternal choice - freely made, never to be undone.

Even now these dark angels would not undo their choice if they could.

False greatness, power, anger and destruction are what they worship – and as they had much to do with creation of time and matter they affected all that they touch. They affect you, and therefore me.

The story that I have to tell?

It relates to my task as an angel, for I am a messenger, as all angels are, but I am also a guardian.

Many men and women find it difficult to believe that such as I exist, tend to think of me and my kind as rumours that start in the nursery to delight, entertain and comfort your children.

Would that you would dwell upon this at greater length, that you would ask where this rumour started! If you did you would find that the knowledge came from a chosen people, and finally from He Who Is, living among you; this Jesus who said of himself, I am he Who Is – he who is without cause – Yahweh, in the Hebrew language.

Would that you would listen to him!

The information about guardian angels is but a small part of what he came to reveal to you.

But in my function as a guardian angel, also a messenger, I have a small story to tell. I am given this privilege, quite unique.

I must begin.

2 Joe

It was near the end of the glorious summer of 1962. Well, you would label it thus, but as you do not fully understand the concept of time - except as a mark of change - and as there have been errors in the past, this time base is not accurate.

However, we are here concerned with truth, not with mathematics or physics, so we will accept that at the time we speak of it was approximately one thousand nine hundred and sixty-two years since Jesus entered his world, the Year of the Lord, Anno Domini in the Latin language that many spoke at that time.

But now, in AD 1962, on the third floor of a terrace house in the place called Pimlico, in the city of London, on the island of Britain, Joe Coyle, in his late twenties, was almost finishing packing a large metal trunk - bought in the Army & Navy Surplus store in Vauxhall Bridge Road, round the corner from Victoria Station.

He had spent a long time deliberating, in his habitually meticulous way, between traditional leather trunks bound with wooden straps and this silver painted metal object, deciding eventually that a metal trunk would last longer. It was, after all, to be the solitary container of all his earthly goods, for all time, and only the best would do. For him everything had to be the best, even in your transitory world.

Now, in the dingy apartment he inhabited from time to time, with faded linoleum and a length of worn carpet at the side of a cheap divan bed, he was nearing the end of his packing.

"Four sets of underwear," he read from a typewritten list perched on the edge of the partly open drawer of a flimsy chest of drawers.

"Four pairs of white socks. Two pairs white shorts. My God! You'd think I was going to play tennis!"

He ticked the items on the list and slammed the trunk lid shut, fastened and locked it and dragged it into the hallway.

He went back into the apartment and looked round the poorly furnished, empty room. Everything done! A life wrapped up!

He took the jacket of his grey business suit from a hanger at the back of the door, shrugged into it as he looked round the apartment, bare except for a cheaply framed black and white photograph of himself and a beautiful, dark haired girl - an enlargement of a holiday snap: Joe, pale and serious, with his arms round the smiling girl, her eyes lit with happiness.

Dolefully he looked at the photograph and shook his head.

"I really am sorry Joli," he murmured, in a moment of heartfelt sadness, pale and determined.

It had taken him weeks - no, months, to make up his mind. She was so beautiful, so normal, so deeply committed, while he had always been uneasy and tense, heartened and delighted that such a girl had liked him - loved him, he knew.

He had been deeply attracted at the first sight of her during a one-day retreat in the Sacred Heart Convent at Hammersmith.[1] She was the most beautiful, the most wholesome girl he had ever seen; saw her and wanted to meet her, and had been delighted when they had met and talked, easily, naturally and spontaneously, a sparkle in their relationship right from the start.

The initial attraction had been mutual, and despite the thoughts that haunted him of another woman and another time they had gone out together, and he had learnt that she was as warm hearted and as merry as she was beautiful, with a smile that lit her face, coming from deep within.

He also began to appreciate the ability that had promoted her to a senior job in a government ministry – and then become aware that she was looking for a Catholic husband! It was strange that he had not realised this!

"My God," he muttered to himself. "If only I had known! If only I had been better prepared."

Looking at the photograph of Joli he compared her dark haired beauty with the corn coloured hair and green eyes of the young girl he had been about to marry, four years earlier.

When she called off the marriage the grief had almost destroyed him.

He sucked in his breath at the recollection. A year of sorrow, when bright hope had turned to black ashes, starting from the moment he had received her letter, as his ship docked at Cape Town:

"I don't love you. I don't think I ever loved you," Catherine had written, in her childish, schoolgirl script.

A dark cloud had descended as he read, and remained with him till he reached London's King George V Dock, swarmed down the ship's side and jumped clear before she was tied up, almost running as he made his way to the Underground and then to North West London to confront her; tense and impatient with the pace of the slow-moving underground train.

But there was nothing he could do. She had made up her mind, was resolved that marriage was not for her – not to him at any rate, and in his mind he could not help but instinctively link the decision with her boss, the owner of the business where she had started to work. He had seen her once with him, and it was clear that he was a rival, a predator to his mind.

At White City he had landed into Catherine's mother's house as usual, trying to control himself, talk rationally, clamp down on emotion, and resolve the situation with a reasoned, calm approach. But it had been impossible. He had found Catherine emotional and distraught, self critical and despairing - partly over her treatment of him but also, it began to emerge, because of her relationship with another, older man.

The businessman?

He never found out. She would not, could not, talk about her changed attitude. There was no meeting point, no hope – and then he had made matters worse by joining one of his shipmates and his girlfriend for a meal, as a distraction - and had ended up drinking too much wine.

Sometime after midnight the taxi had dropped him outside the block of apartments where Catherine and her family lived. As her fiancé he had always felt part of the family, accepted with a warmth that made him feel totally at home.

Now, on the verge of losing that warmth, the love that he had found, anger swept through him. It was an emotion beyond control, and in despairing fury he smashed a half full bottle of wine against the brick wall of the apartment building, blood red wine and broken glass splaying against the yellow brick. A dripping wound.

He made his way up to the flat and in the corridor of the quiet apartment put his shoulder against Catherine's bedroom door. It crashed back and she shot up in bed, clutching the bedcovers to her chest.

"The next time you say to someone 'I love you' make sure you mean it!" he blurted, and slammed the door shut, hard.

Starting to pack he found Catherine's young sister at the door of his room, alarmed and wide eyed.

"What are you doing? Where are you going? You're not leaving!" She was deeply concerned.

"Have to! Got to get away. It's all over."

"You can't go anywhere at this time of night," she said. "Stay! Wait until morning. Bitch! How could she do this?"

"It's just happened. She's not happy herself."

"Oh God. I don't like this!" She was almost in tears. "Please do stay! This is no time to be going."

And he had allowed himself to be persuaded, spending the next few hours in half drunken, despairing slumber, on the living room settee.

At seven o'clock he left the flat, and later in the day found a room in a large house along Holland Park Avenue, near Notting Hill - and lying on the bed he died - or appeared to be about to die.

He had been lying in the dim light filtering through tall windows that were partly curtained against the sun, and had drifted into a sleep that was more like a coma.

He became aware that he was floating near the ceiling, looking down on the young man on the bed – himself, he recognized - calmly aware that this young man was going to die.

Then suddenly he was back in his body, alarmed and horrified, struggling to rise and shouting aloud, "I am not going to die! I am not going to die!" - stumbling into a wash-basin, knocking it over and crying out aloud, his heart jumping in his chest, not ready to die.

The door opened and his new landlady appeared, wide eyed.

"What's wrong? What's happened?"

"I'm ill," he stammered. "I need a doctor!"

A taxi had been called and he arrived at a doctor's surgery, where the doctor prescribed tablets, for emotional shock he said, designed to calm and make sleep possible. But he had refused to swallow them, for he was afraid to sleep, for in sleep he could die, and he was not prepared.

He did not know what lay beyond.

He did not know where God was. He was a stranger in an unknown land, the pattern of his life and hope destroyed, a land of sorrow and tears, his love and his future gone.

He needed help but did not know where to find it. He felt like running home, to the comfort of his family, his mother, but pride kept him rooted in the city.

He found a cheaper room in a small house in the tangle of little streets off Shepherd's Bush, and then a job, the first one offered, on the night shift of Wall's ice cream factory in the North of the city, dragging heavy crates of ice cream into the factory deep-freeze, wrapped in layers of clothes and a woollen cap, working in hurt, emotional emptiness, tired with the effort of keeping alive; with occasional rest breaks in a yard that was piled high with thousands of shiny metal tins against dark concrete walls, and above the walls, like those of a prison, was the moon, a cold orb in a dark sky – where he wept, privately, until exhausted, or the moment came to re-enter the deep-freeze.

He knew that his workmates and the section supervisor looked at him strangely, but he could not talk to them. He was weary to the point of death, for he dared not sleep. He was without energy, lacking any motivation other than simple survival; his life's blood seeming to ooze away, filled with despair - and on the fourth day he found a dismissal note on the board where he clocked in.

Not a word was spoken. There was just a typed note and severance money in a small brown envelope. He was a non-person, a zombie, someone to whom real people did not speak.

He found another job – and he smiled in grim, exhausted humour at the change: to Joe Lyon's ice cream factory at Hammersmith, this time scraping and cleaning mammoth ice-cream vats during the night. At least it was warm inside the vats, with hot water streaming against polished metal as he scraped.

He found that he was just about able to work till dawn; bent over inside the metal vat, scraping and polishing as he sprayed hot water that swirled round Joe Lyon's rubber boots.

Then, as he emerged each day to empty streets at dawn he simply walked, without direction, racked by occasional weeping that he could not control, ambushed by grief.

He had lost, lost life and love and could believe in nothing human. The bleak thoughts in his mind were focused on a dark and dying world. There was no light, no future. Within himself he existed in sorrow, wasting away in the darkness, bone weary but afraid to sleep. If he slept he could die, go permanently into that darkness, know no more, never see the light.

He was afraid to return to the emptiness of his room, for there he might sleep.

In addition to his sorrow Joe became acutely aware of past sexual selfishness. Years of habitual pleasure, mostly alone, fed by feverish imaginings centered around naked women with voluptuous breasts, had, he now realized, created a barren wasteland in which he alone dwelt. When he had become aware of the love between himself and Catherine sex had paled into insignificance. He was entranced by her loveliness, the unique upturn of her mouth when she smiled, reflecting a sparkle in green eyes framed in corn coloured hair. Sex may have been at the root of the attraction but he was not aware of it. She was just beautiful, and on the one occasion when he had seen her naked he had been enthralled, entranced.

They had been alone in the family apartment late at night. He was sitting in the lounge when Catherine came into the room in her bathrobe.

She stood before him, and with her slight, crooked smile dropped her robe on the floor, revealing such naked beauty that Joe almost could not believe was possible. Spontaneously he took off his own clothes and put his arms round her, drawing her close. As he did so she glanced down and said in a low voice, "I did not know it would be so big," and indeed he was aware of an empowerment never before experienced, a deep sense of masculinity. He was overwhelmed by the wonder of being lovingly together with this beautiful young woman, naked and unashamed, capable of a love that embodied everything he had ever dreamt of sexually, plus a unity of mind and spirit he had not thought possible.

Gently he laid her on the couch, kissing every part of her body, worshipping and adoring, and when it came to the moment where he was poised over her, at the point of intimately expressing his love, he drew back, penis still massively erect, and said abruptly, "I want to wait till we are married," and she had nodded understanding, so that slowly, with many kisses, he was able to withdraw from her embrace, rejoicing in her beauty, deeply content that their relationship had risen to a new level of awareness. There was great sexual potential but it could wait, he could wait. There was something much more important. He simply loved the beauty of the whole person.

Now, because of his enforced separation from her he was not only full of sorrow but also aware of a state of mind, of soul, created by years of selfish sexual addiction. It was as if all the semen, the creative seed of life that he had gratuitously spewed out was congealed on the walls of his soul, like white bird spit hardened on dark cave walls - in the case of swiftlet nests useful for making soup, in his case a useless crumbling residue that in imagination had begun to flake off, revealing an empty nothingness. A state of soul that he viewed with horror.

In this spirit of sorrow and revulsion he wandered throughout the day, aimless and pointless. On one occasion, on a bus going along Kensington High Street, without purpose, just to be on the move, he felt a pain in his heart, as if this part of him was being squeezed by a giant hand. He was aware that the pain could kill him, but at this moment he would have welcomed death, for he would have died in daylight, not in the dark, and he would have escaped an agonizing experience.

The days passed, working throughout the night, and then during daylight hours, despite his despair, he began to look for a better job, eventually finding work in the publicity department of a company near Tottenham Court Road, preparing printing blocks and artwork. He had at one time worked in the print department of an advertising agency.

There, when he felt grief about to overwhelm him, he would go to the wash room and sit on the toilet, weeping; and when the spasm ceased he was able to return to his desk, acting as if life was normal.

At lunchtime, and sometimes after work, he found that swimming underwater in the local YMCA pool helped. The underwater pressure seemed to equalise the constant emotional pressure of mind and heart, neutralize a force that threatened to explode. At such moments he felt relief, a near normal stability.

The uncontrollable bursts of weeping became less frequent, but tortured dreams of the lost beauty of Catherine and the vision of their life together continued, and combined with the constant fear of sleeping brought him to the brink of total exhaustion, to the end point of endurance.

He took to reading the books of the bible, finding fellowship with Job:

"My eyes grow dim with grief,
and my limbs wear away like a shadow....
My days have passed far otherwise
than I had planned,
And every fibre of my heart is broken.
Night, they say, makes room for day,
And light is near at hand to chase the darkness.
All I look forward to is dwelling in Sheol,
And making my bed in the dark.
I tell the tomb, 'you are my father',
And call the worm my mother and my sister.
Where then is my hope?
Who can see any happiness for me?"

He had not read much of the bible before, only half listened to the readings at Mass during childhood and adolescence, not taking in much of the meaning.

The depth of feeling and experience revealed in books such as Job astounded him. As he leafed through the writings of both old and new testament he felt himself lost in a large world of ideas and experiences that he did not know, confronted by ideas that threatened to drown, raised questions beyond his comprehension, made him aware of his lack of knowledge and learning, heightened his feeling of being alone, living at the edge of life - abandoned and forlorn, with nowhere to go and no explanation of why this was so.

All that he was aware of was that he had lost love, that he needed help from outside himself, that he could not continue in such misery, that he needed aid, not from any human source but from the unknown God he believed existed but with whom he had no contact.

He needed help from a being in whom he believed in an intuitive fashion, and blindly accepted that only the man Jesus could help. But he did not know him, or where to find him.

He accepted that Jesus was God, probably was God, but he knew nothing of him, other than he had been cruelly done to death, and it was said that he had died for love. He did not know Jesus personally, but was prepared to believe that it was possible to do so. In him was his only hope, if he really was God. No human agency could relieve his sorrow.

In this dawning hope he turned to God in ardent prayer, an agonized, wordless plea for help from a source that he did not know, could not understand, but knew that he desperately needed.

In this mood of despairing hope he determined to dig himself out of a life of despond, make a last effort to return to normality, get away from sadness, sleep without fear.

So it was that one evening, in the cheap little digs at Shepherd's Bush he determined that he must make an effort to break from sorrow.

In the communal bathroom on the landing below his room he ran a hot bath and with utter determination to ignore grief he began to sing the hymn, "Nearer My God to Thee", though he only partly remembered the words: "... sweet shall my weeping be; nearer my God to thee..."

Following this blind act of faith, he climbed the stairs to his room and knelt beside the bed, wordlessly seeking succour.

"Our Father ...," he began, and without warning he found himself lifted by a force beyond anything he had ever known, a burst of energy that deposited him on his feet at the end of the bed, some five feet from where he had been kneeling – astounded and amazed – crying out, astonished by something so unexplained, so powerful and unexpected, filled by a stupendous force and a light of love beyond understanding – trembling and instinctively aware that the power that had lifted him was a tiny expression of something much greater, a tiny breath as opposed to an untapped gale that existed at the very core of the universe.

Along with his astonishment there came a new weeping, a new full-hearted emotion, a joy that overwhelmed, so that he thought he had gone mad. How was it possible that he could have been kneeling and then, without warning had been lifted and set on his feet, as if he was an athlete exploding into a somersault?

It was beyond comprehension. The force, the power revealed, was awesome, positively frightening except that at the centre of it was benevolence and a peace beyond anything ever dreamt of by man.

It took some time to control himself, to get over such a shock, before he could ease himself into bed, tremulous but thanking God with all his heart, for he was no longer grieving, no longer embedded in sorrow and despair, not afraid to sleep, for there was indeed something beyond, and it was love beyond all knowing.

When he awoke a few hours later he was immediately aware of joy and thankfulness, his heart light with love. He was still inclined to tears, but they were tears of hope and elation. For the first time in a full year he was happy, removed from dark sorrow, happy in a way that he had never thought possible.

"Amazing grace! It's true!" he murmured to himself, recalling the title of the hymn and remembering the phrase 'actual grace', from his Catholic education in childhood: 'Grace: a gift freely given by God to help the soul in distress, enable him to believe in and know the Creator' – something like these had been the words of the catechism.

Joe's work that day was a time of bubbling elation. Life had a sparkle and a meaning. One or two of his workmates commented upon his smiles, his cheerful good humour, and when he walked home along Holland Park, strolling and looking at the lights of family living rooms, he felt no longer excluded from the beauty of a loved life. Indeed, he was in touch with the centre of a loved creation, and for the first time felt at home in the created world, in the universe.

He reached Shepherd's Bush in the darkness, in the rain, and as the red double-decker buses swished by on each side of the green he leapt into the air, crying out in solitary exaltation and delight – for he had been found, discovered by the source of all life, lifted out of the mire, washed clean and made new. He felt like doing a somersault, but he did not have the physical ability.

The intensity of love and joy faded over the weeks and months, but he was aware of a deep feeling of content, a profound centre to his being that had been missing, a need to give thanks, a wish to serve, to be at one with the unseen Creator, through the power of Jesus and the Holy Spirit, to be totally at their disposal – and for the first time he wondered if he should become a priest.

"Nonsense!" he told himself. "You are an emotional wreck! You are absolutely and totally unfit to make such a decision."

But the notion stayed with him, and there came the thought that perhaps in three or four years - say three-and-a-half - he might become more stable and reliable. Yes, in about three-and-a-half years.

He consulted a priest in the Carmelite Monastery on Kensington Church Street, telling him that while he would really like to marry he thought that it might be selfish, that perhaps he should become a priest.

His confessor had laughed - a hearty laugh, bubbling with good humour. The spontaneous laughter was comforting, though Joe was a bit put out by such a reaction to his heartfelt problem. Nevertheless, the priest's good humour eased his self questioning, even though he found it difficult to accept the accompanying advice: "Leave it up to God! He knows who He calls, and who not!"

It was difficult to know where God's overall responsibility ended and his personal responsibility began. So it wasn't really an answer, but it would have to do! He was no clearer in his mind about what lay ahead, about what he should actually do.

Now, looking at the photograph of Joli, he questioned himself once more. Was he really called to become a priest, to celibacy – and to voluntary poverty and obedience within a monastic order?

"I can't believe that I am about to do this," he thought, "that I have chosen this way of life - going against everything that I once desired, and causing a lovely girl to weep."

"I really am sorry Joli," he murmured, "But I could do no other. I would always have wondered."

"Damnit! Damnit!" he swore, and taking the photograph from the frame tore it, lit the pieces with his cigarette lighter, and threw the burning paper and the frame into a metal waste basket.

"Dramatic! Over dramatic!" he upbraided himself. "But I had to do it – get rid of the memory, devote myself fully!"

His face was pale, the skin drawn tight over cheek bones, but he felt an inner freedom, a poised expectancy, facing the unknown, but aware that he was offering himself in the service of the God of love – learning how to love, how to leave self behind.

3   West

The train moved out of the station, heading towards the West Country, clacking slowly along the shining web of rails leading from Paddington mainline terminal, passing under a cobweb of electric cables suspended from a forest of metal supports, past a number of steady red lights - permanently warning - and a green light that offered safety and clear passage past factory buildings and small brick houses butting up to the track - followed by street after street of tree lined suburbs, heavy green foliage softening the outlines of semi-detached houses and lamp posts that curved and bowed towards each other in petrified unison.

'Restful expectancy' or 'composed tension' was how Joe would have expressed his mood. He had little doubt that he was doing the right thing, that he was following a path that could put his talents to use – such as they were.

Rather to his amazement he had discovered that he had talents, that he could think and communicate - that out of a strongly independent approach he could develop a theme and present an argument coherently.

He had begun to realise this in a hesitant manner as a new member of the Catholic Evidence Guild, located in a little schoolhouse at the side of Westminster Cathedral. There, on Tuesday evenings, he regularly attended lectures given by seasoned members of the Guild, especially Frank Sheed,[2] a man who had a marvellous gift of being able to encapsulate theological speculation in words that shimmered with meaning, enhanced understanding.

He and other speakers such as Cecily Hastings[3] laid out the central beliefs of Christianity in great detail.

On Friday evenings new and less able speakers attempted to speak about these teachings, on very specific topics, taking questions as if from a crowd at Speakers' Corner.

Only when they were ready were new recruits encouraged to take viva voce examinations, conducted by two licensed speakers and a priest who represented the Cardinal Archbishop of Westminster.

It had come as a surprise to Joe that he could think on his feet, marshal his thoughts and speak coherently.

At school he had not shone academically, had been regarded by himself and others as lower stream in all subjects. He had never shown any talent at anything other than a bit of English and, God help him, water polo!

Even with English it had been the sound and cadence of the words that had appealed, not the rules of grammar, which mostly left him confused; and when it came to understanding the construction of other languages such as Latin and French his wits deserted him almost totally, in this case confused by the strange sounds of the words, as well as unexplained endings that seemed to be required in order to make sense. Terms that were bandied about with aplomb by other class members were just stupefying. He never really understood what was an ablative absolute or a pluperfect subjunctive. He was, he began to think, just a bit dumb. The sounds of these languages were foreign to his Northern Irish ear.

He was equally bemused by physics and chemistry, and also privately ashamed to admit that he simply did not understand mathematical oddities such as cosines and tangents. He realised that such terms must have a meaning, but the sight of neatly arrayed tables caused his head to freeze. These things were not for him, and when he listened to the other lads chatting about quadratic equations on the bus taking them home up the Falls Road, he went quiet, silently admitting to himself that he might be a bit slow – well, stupid, though he never actually used the word.

So, in the years that had passed since the misery of his broken engagement he had been surprised to discover that he had an innate, unsuspected ability - able to think in abstract philosophical and theological terms - at a primitive level, he reminded himself, aware of his lack of academic learning.

Nevertheless, he rather astounded himself during Catholic Evidence Guild debates and practice speaking sessions, discovering an instinctive understanding of patterns of thought, of reason and logic, with a surprising ability to lead other people into greater awareness, greater discernment and perception.

It turned out that he was quick witted in debate, and he was mildly embarrassed by the discovery; but people were impressed, he realised; and upon stepping down from the CEG platform at Speakers' Corner on one occasion, following the usual sixty minute question and answer session, he had been approached by a woman from the crowd who told him that she had seen someone behind him as he spoke and that she wished to become a Catholic.

He had been vaguely impressed and intrigued by the thought of a mysterious, invisible person providing backup to his words – and was about to turn around and look behind him when he realised the witness could not be seen in the physical world. He was also rather tickled to learn that the lady's grandfather was a Grand Master of the Orange Lodge in the feared loyalist Village enclave of the Lower Donegal Road in Belfast.

The fact that he too was from Belfast was an obvious influence, but he could not discount the presence of an unseen helper. Faith came by hearing, it was true, but it was a direct gift from God, not something that he personally could give, and after a cup of tea across the road in Joe Lyon's teashop, and a few other meetings with the lady, he recognised that this particular call to faith was genuine, subsequently verified by the fact she had gone on to be received into the church.

Strange things happen when one is dealing with the unseen God, he reminded himself, and it looked as if God was blessing his witness.

It was his experience as a CEG speaker that had led him to the conclusion that he should become a member of the Order of Friars Preachers, the Dominicans, known in mediaeval England as the Blackfriars, because of the black outdoor cloak they wore.

Reflecting upon such things as the train reached open countryside Joe reassured himself that he had made the right decision. It had been costly. It had necessitated giving up the idea of married love, and he deeply regretted the hurt his decision had caused to Joli.

What a beautiful girl, he thought.

"You have only gone out with me so that you have something to give up!" she had said to him, wrapped in his arms on a dark night at Victoria Station, sobbing at the news of his decision.

Despite the sadness and sombre emotion of that moment he had burst into loud laughter. The notion was so ridiculous, so comical; and now, in reverie he smiled, remembering the laughter of the Carmelite friar when confronted with his own concern that he might be selfish because he wanted to marry.

It appeared that robust, instinctive laughter was sound medicine when confronted with idiotic ideas.

He began to recognise that Church teaching about the presence of the Holy Spirit, always with the children of men, pointed to a subtle, ever present reality, recognised occasionally by those who had faith and a mind open to what the bible called Wisdom, the spirit that moved among men, that occasionally delighted and held in thrall.

There was no doubt that truth could be revealed and consolidated by laughter - that joy and laughter were fruits of the Holy Spirit.

It was a comfort to begin to recognise that the demands of faith had compensations, that a willingness to leave all things and follow Jesus brought rewards of mind and heart; that the supernatural life of the world to come was actually present here and now, though only perceived darkly, as a reflection in a mirror.

"Shades of Saint Paul!" he mused.

At the same time, reflecting upon his own state of mind, his own faith, he recognised that he was under tension. In the darkness of a determined and continuous act of faith he was like a coiled spring, ready to launch into action. It was slightly scary, a deliberate act of faith and readiness, keeping himself at each moment of every day in a permanent and demanding act of awareness, an openness to reality that was occasionally painful. His life style now depended entirely upon faith.

In some ways it was a faith that did not come naturally to him, despite that amazing moment at the bedside of his digs at Shepherd's Bush. His attitude had developed into what was mostly a determined act of will. There was little consolation and a lot of concern about people – all of them brothers and sisters underneath the Father of all, and all suffering and deprived in many ways: many without faith or any kind of understanding of life's meaning and purpose.

People without faith must regard the idea of dedicating oneself to the unseen reality of God as a form of insanity - and the further step of embracing voluntary personal poverty and a life of sexual abstinence as total madness - an impossibility perhaps?

"You people depend upon a belief in a God who is a spirit!" – a jovial heckler had stated at Hyde Park on one occasion. "Your belief is as substantial as a puff of smoke!"

The heckler had clearly done some thinking, for he went on to point out that the description of a spirit is that it has no height, no depth, no width, no colour, and could not be touched or felt. "A great description of nothing," he had mocked. "Just not real! Does not exist."

Joe had enjoyed the subsequent discussion. It was beyond the usual level. He had pointed out that the nearest each of us could come to realising the quality of a spirit is to think about oneself; come to understand that each of us is a combination of matter and spirit, that in us the spirit is the animating principle of life, the *animus*, or soul, giving life and shape to the physical body, and having within it the greater spiritual power of intelligence, of knowing and loving.

It was demonstrably true that human beings had a capacity for knowledge and love far beyond that of any other creature on earth, and it was a power that would not be destroyed, could not go out of existence when the body fell away in death – because the spirit is not material, can not be broken into constituent parts, was everlasting, more permanent than matter.

It had been a long and complicated discussion, followed intently by the audience, but the heckler had not been convinced, carrying a section of the audience with him when he declared that Joe's opinion was simply a matter of faith.

"Faith and reason," Joe had declared, referring to the fact that men's power of reasoning had been affected by the sin of Adam and Eve in the Garden of Eden, and we should be aware of this.

Mention of Adam and Eve had provoked a roar of scoffing laughter among many of the crowd, led by the heckler, and had set Joe off on an exhaustive analysis of what theologians mean by the Garden of Eden and the Fall of mankind – in that it was necessary to describe something so unknowable in a figurative language, to pinpoint the truth that the first man, or men, had defied God and had eaten the fruit of the *tree of knowledge of good and evil* – not an apple tree in sight!

Adam, that first man, or group of men, were of the earth, *adamah* in Hebrew – and had set themselves up to be judges of right and wrong, in defiance of God's instruction; and as a result of this act of pride sin and death and suffering had entered the world, and man's capacity to reason had become dim – in some cases very dim, he had added, indicating the heckler with open hands, as if pouring out recognition upon someone who had achieved an apogee in the sphere of dimness.

There was a burst of laughter from the crowd and Joe immediately regretted his action. It was too easy to make fun of people.

'Shouldn't have done that!' was his immediate thought, but he was relieved to see that the heckler himself was convulsed with laughter. Not too much damage done then, even though he had offended against the CEG rule that one never attacked the person, always dealt with the idea.

Such discussions were a constant battle, often satisfying but always leaving Joe mentally and physically exhausted. Usually all he wanted to do was to crawl into a dark corner and sleep, allow time and nature to restore lost energies.

But he was good at what he did, and knew that somehow he had to persevere with his street-corner witness - until the thought of the priesthood began to haunt him, and the struggle between this possibility and the beauty of a life with Joli began to torture.

He smiled grimly as he recalled the months of investigative thought that had gone before his return to Christianity, before he had met Joli - twisting and confused, looking for explanation in many religions and faith systems, driving himself to study the religious beliefs of the world, especially those of Islam and Buddhism.

Reeling from the shock of being discarded by his fiancée, in a permanent emotional state, he had found it difficult to come to grips with many conflicting ideas.

Muhammad's Koran, or Qur'an, had been inspirational to begin with but ultimately disappointing and perceived as positively warlike towards the end of his reading. It was the product of a gifted imagination, creating and recreating facts and ideas garnered from Jewish and Christian sources, and all the more extraordinary in that it appeared that Muhammad could neither read nor write, that he had absorbed much of the core of the Hebrew and Christian religions through listening to other people.

Perhaps this explained Muhammad's failure to fully understand the person of Jesus and the claims that he made, classifying him as just another prophet.[4]

A further concern was that Muhammad's sayings, the 'recitation', had only been collected and written down three hundred years after his death. There was, therefore, room for inaccuracy, corruption of Muhammad's teachings, despite Islamic belief that to recite these words in Arabic was to recite the very word of God, given to the prophet: not that Joe undervalued the power of collective folk memory, especially in the case of Islam, where constant daily recitation is a requisite part of religious practice.

However, as far as Joe was concerned Islam did not have a satisfactory core, did not convince, regardless of the millions that found it a guide to the mystery of God. It did not have the sound, central challenge of the astounding claims by Jesus that *"He who has seen me has seen the Father"*, that *"I and the Father are one"*, and *"He who believes in me has eternal life"*; and again, *"I have come that you may have life and have it more abundantly,"* culminating in the extraordinary statement that all who believed in him would share in his resurrection from the dead: *"I will raise you up on the last day"*.

As Joe and other CEG speakers constantly pointed out - you either believed what Jesus said or you classified him as a madman – despite the fact that there was no hint of madness, just extraordinary claims made by an extraordinary man, a real person who spoke with an authority that one would expect from someone who really was and is God, teaching an extraordinary vision of life and death, promising everlasting life.

Those who recorded Muhammad's words in the Koran made no such claims, and although much of the general message was uplifting there was a threatening element that was upsetting, promising war against the 'infidel' and, despite fine rhetoric about equality of gender, went on to outline rules that reduced women to perpetual subjugation, second-class citizens.[5]

No such attitudes could be found in Christian scriptures, even though mediaeval people who professed to be Christian had waged bloody wars against Islam – some in legitimate defence but many unjustified - and had themselves perpetuated thoughtless notions of female inferiority.

Such attitudes and actions by people who claimed to be followers of Christ were the product of a crude, male dominated society, not far removed from paganism and invariably inspired by a primitive lust for power and territorial control.

It was quite clear that Jesus preached a way of life and love, of peace and forgiveness – forgiveness by a loving God to all who repented of wrongdoing, and a forgiveness that should be shown by men to each other.

To Joe, as he searched for meaning, Buddhism had appeared more attractive than Islam.

Buddha's teaching was poetically beautiful and imaginative but offered no solution to problems of existence other than a negative asceticism, a withdrawing from the world rather than providing an explanation of why evil existed.

It also postulated a brand of reincarnation that seemed to militate against the specific identity of things. Ultimately it merely reflected the universal desire for an improved form of life – in this case the state of Nirvana, which might have been identified as the Christian Heaven had it not been for the doctrine of reincarnation, which indicated a perpetual cycle of birth and rebirth.

In pursuit of detailed information Joe had joined a class in the City Literary Institute, conducted by Christmas Humphries QC, founder of the Buddhist Society [6], and discovered that a reasoned approach to questions of cause and effect, and the purpose of existence, simply did not exist.

Life, the universe, was simply to be accepted as a great, unexplained, amorphous whole, and though the life of Gautama Buddha bore an uncanny resemblance to the life of St. Francis of Assisi - both sons of rich men who abandoned everything to search for perfection - Buddha's way of life, of self denial, moving towards 'enlightenment', did not contain any reference to the possibility of a personal God, a putative creator of the universe.

Of course Buddha, living in India at least 400 years before Christ, did not have any input from Hebrew culture, never mind knowledge of the teachings of Jesus, so it was a tribute to his strength of character and humanity that he devoted his life to the search for an explanation of the ills of the world and ways to deal with them.

Not a bad effort, thought Joe, but no cigar, for the results were largely negative: escape from the ills of an imperfect world:

Regard this phantom world
As a star at dawn, a bubble in a stream,
A flash of lightning in a summer cloud,
A flickering lamp - a phantom - and a dream.

To Joe the world was not a dream. It was beautiful, but it could be a nightmare reality. Buddha's language was poetical, but not in any way offering a practical explanation of the origin and purpose of a suffering universe, merely a way of enduring it, peacefully, calmly and with dignity. As a way of life it had much to recommend it, but as a solution to questions about existence it had nothing to say.

It surprised Joe that Christmas Humphries, with a reputation as a skilful barrister, had not seemed to value reason in pursuit of such questions.

To Joe reason was vital in the search for truth.

Something more than reason was needed of course, to be able to accept the extraordinary claims made by Jesus that he personally was the answer to questions about existence.

To accept that he was and is the way, the truth and the life, that he was God incarnate, and that he had entered his own universe and endured suffering and murderous death in order to atone for the great sin of Adam demanded an opening of the mind that was only made possible by the gift of faith, God acting upon the soul.

"Thanks be to you, almighty God," Joe whispered under his breath, almost unaware of the sunshine that flickered across his face as the train sped into the West of England, through the beautiful green fields that led to the Cotswolds. "Thank you for gifts of faith and reason."

4 Brothers

The train began to slow and with a puff of steam pulled into a small country station, coming to a groaning halt.

"This is it!" Joe felt a deepening of alertness, a thrill of tension. It was the end of the line for him.

"Oakchester! Oakchester!" called the guard, descending from the van.

"Just you?" he asked, as Joe walked towards him.

"Looks like it," said Joe. "I have a trunk."

"Right," said the guard, and tucking his green flag under his arm he helped Joe to slide and lift the shiny metal trunk onto the gravel platform.

"Thanks," said Joe.

"Right," said the guard, and stepped back into his van, waving the flag and giving a sharp peep on his whistle.

There was an answering hoot from the engine and the train groaned prodigiously, spat out much steam and got under way.

Not a great line in rolling stock, thought Joe, and then the train was gone, a plume of smoke rising above tall, leafy trees as the square end and domed top of the guard's van disappeared round a bend.

Joe was absolutely alone, standing on the platform in his grey suit, sweating in the afternoon heat.

It was quiet.

Looking around Joe could see thickly planted trees that climbed up a hill, behind a red brick station building nestling in a small gravel car park.

He scuffed a shoe in the dust and walked around - waiting, and then sat down on the trunk, wincing slightly at the touch of the hot metal. He took off his jacket and folded it to make a cushion.

A trickle of sweat dripped down both cheeks and he loosened his tie. A business suit was not the best dress in this place.

In the silence Joe's perceptions intensified and he became aware of the sound of birds, and then the whisper of leaves as a light breeze ghosted through the tops of the tall trees.

A small bird ran and pecked at the edge of a flower bed. A fat bee buzzed and nuzzled a flower in a peaceful world of hot, somnolent beauty.

The roar of an engine and a squeal of brakes shattered the quiet and a battered estate car swept into the station car park, coming to an abrupt stop.

The tall, stout figure of a friar, clad in flowing white and black robes, burst out of the driver's door and leaving it flopping open bustled towards Joe.

Face plump and perspiring, red and apologetic behind large black framed glasses the new arrival gasped,

"Joseph Coyle? Sorry I'm late. That dammed estate car again! Will not start when it's needed! My heavens you have a load there," pointing towards the trunk and beginning to tug at it.

"Don't tell me you took all that nonsense about clothes literally! You'll have enough with you to last twenty years – if you survive!"

So saying he and Joe took each end of the trunk and deposited it in the rear of the car, the friar thumping down the folding tailgate door with such force that Joe was sure that he saw pieces of metal fly off.

Only then did the newcomer turn to Joe and say, "I'm Brother Edward. Glad to meet you. Let's get a move on," and he shook Joe's hand and dived for the driver's door.

"P-pleased to meet ... you," Joe stammered, overwhelmed by such dynamism.

"Oh what a day!" exclaimed Bro. Edward, slamming into a gear and pulling a starter at the same time. "Never felt a summer like it. It's beginning to get to me!"

The car jerked out of the station yard and they began to ascend a steep, winding road that mounted the hillside.

"We'll be in time for a cuppa tea." Bro. Edward spoke in a high pitched voice in an accent that Joe thought was from Lancashire.

"Only two more of you young men to come. Quite a good intake this year."

"How many are due?" asked Joe.

"The round dozen. You're Irish?"

"How kin y'tell?" asked Joe, putting on a broad Northern Irish accent.

Bro. Edward laughed, "You're not as broad as that!"

"No, I suppose not. I've been around a bit, travelled a bit, and I have probably lost a lot of the accent. Had to when I left the North. People couldn't understand me."

"It's always a problem," said Bro. Edward. "What made you come into this lark?" Bro. Edward seemed to have little difficulty in jumping from one topic to another.

"Conscience," said Joe. "It seemed the only thing to do. I eventually realised that all the things I had heard at home were true – the basic stuff I mean, not some of the external rubbish – and I had to follow it up."

"I see. A late developer. It's hard to do."

"Aye, you could say that!"

"I suppose you had to leave a girl behind?"

"Aye."

"Hard to do." Bro. Edward was sympathetic. "I had to leave a fella behind myself!"

"A *fella*!" Joe could not prevent his voice from rising.

"Yes m'old dear!" Bro. Edward was smiling. "We're not all as straight as you."

Catching the expression of alarm on Joe's face Bro. Edward burst into laughter, "Not to worry old thing. Don't worry! Not practising! Just a Christian now!"

Joe was looking at the large friar in amazement, "But how ...you ... I mean how can you live ...?"

"With a crowd of men you mean?"

Joe nodded weakly.

Brother Edward's eyes danced with merriment behind his large glasses. "Well, I could hardly join the nuns, could I? No matter how I might like to!"

"But, but ... does it not lead to ... to difficulties....?"

Bro. Edward laughed uproariously!

"Believe me; we have no time for ... difficulties!"

Joe could not help but join in the laughter. Edward's humour was infectious.

"My God! If people knew that ... if people knew that you were here it would confirm everything that they have thought about monasteries."

"Priories old dear. Priories! We're a priory. Benedictines and Cistercians and things like that have monasteries and abbeys. We Dominicans have priories."

"Well - Priories. If the Reverend Paisley knew that you ... were here ... he would be ranting and raving about the red whore of Babylon and all that jazz."

"Well. I have to be somewhere y'know," Bro Edward said gently, sounding apologetic.

"I know, but..." Joe was confused.

"... and this is where I have to be, to be saved, to be saved - to be shure to be shure!"

Bro Edward laughed delightedly and Joe could not help but join in - waving his hands in the air as if giving up.

Bro. Edward calmed down and concentrated on making his way round a sharply rising bend in the road.

"No. I have had it all explained to me. There are some people whose genes get all mixed up and they can't help themselves. Biologically they are women... or more female than male. We are all a mixture of male and female. Some peoples' percentages go all haywire. They can't help being born that way. That's me. So I have to accept it, and do the best I can to avoid the occasion of sin ..."

"... so you come to live with a body of men...."

"I know it sounds odd!" Bro. Edward was laughing again as he concentrated on another sharp bend.

"But here - in the Priory I mean - there's not so much time to think about normal things ... I mean normal to me!" Bro. Edward bubbled with laughter. "I just put myself in Christ's hands and leave the rest up to him. That's what you have to do!"

"That's certainly what I have to do," Joe agreed.

"And it's no different for me. If I were a raving, practicing homosexual - I mean had given myself totally up to lust and pleasure - I wouldn't be here. I wouldn't be able to stick it. It's the best place for me ... you see m'dear!" Bro. Edward acted like a fussy old aunt and patted Joe's knee.

In another situation Joe might have reacted violently to being patted with on the leg by a professed homosexual. On this occasion he could only laugh. He felt quite safe, and his laughter was tinged with respect.

"I see. You're quite a guy Brother Edward!"

Bro. Edward pouted. "Oh do call me Edwina! Big Ed!", and laughed so hilariously that the interior of the old vehicle filled and burbled with such a volume of laughter that it seemed to overflow and echo into the sky as the battered station wagon chugged round a final corner and drew up in front of an ancient stone building.

As they got out of the car Joe was aware of mellow Cotswold stone and rambling roses climbing high against the stonework of a long two-storey building, connected to a small but beautifully proportioned church, with a soaring spire.

Almost before the car stopped Bro. Edward was out and had the rear door open, tugging at Joe's trunk.

On his way to join him Joe heard a voice calling from on high, "Cooee! Cooee! Brother Edward! Have you seen that cat?"

Startled, Joe looked up.

Poking out from the open casement window, with its diamond-shaped leaded lights, was a three-foot length of garden cane. Tied to the end of the cane was a piece of string, and tied to the end of the string was a ball of paper.

Framed in the open window was the pale face of an ancient friar, black cowl drawn over his head and lengthy wisps of white hair projecting and curling round his face.

It was this apparition who held the other end of the cane in a claw-like talon.

"Haven't seen it Father. Probably up in the raspberry canes," Bro. Edward said in a matter of fact voice.

"Thank you Brother," said the ancient vision, and the cowled, aged head was withdrawn.

"What - who on earth is that?" gasped Joe.
Bro. Edwards was calmly lugging at the trunk.

"Oh... That's Father Valentine. He's going fishing for the cat."

"Fishing for the cat?"

"Yes. It's just about his time now. Just before tea."

"Fishing for the cat?!"

Bro. Edward realised Joe was perplexed.

"Oh, yes. He's got a special relationship with the cat. Been at it some months now - no, I don't mean that!" He laughed wickedly. "He's old and doddery - but don't write him off."

Just at that Fr. Valentine appeared at the front door, carrying his cat fishing rod before him.

He shuffled towards them - a weird looking figure in white habit, with black cloak and hood despite the heat.

"In the raspberry canes brother?"

"Probably," said Bro. Edward.

The ancient priest looked at Joe.

Seen up close the skin of his face was smooth and almost as white as the hair that curled from under the black hood.

"Hello young man. Joining us?"

"Er.... I think so."

"Good," said Fr. Val, with a twinkle in his eye, "Keep the faith," and he passed on his way, calling out, "Here pussy, pussy! Here pussy, pussy!"

He shuffled off in the direction of the garden, leaving Joe open mouthed, dumbfounded.

Bro. Edward, continuing to lug the trunk, looked at him and started to laugh.

"Don't underestimate him. He's engaged in some psychological experiments. He has published some very heavyweight books on religion and psychology - at least they look heavyweight to me - and now he seems to have gone on to cats' minds. The fathers are not too sure whether he is going to make some major breakthrough or if he is just doting - but don't write him off! One of the brainiest members of the Order they say, or used to be."

"I'll believe almost anything," said Joe faintly, looking after the departing figure, and then lifted his end of the trunk.

Fr. Valentine's voice floated back from the distance, "Here pussy, pussy! Here pussy, pussy!"

5 Prior

Bearing the trunk they staggered down a short flight of steps and into a hallway with a floor of uneven sandstone flags and walls that had been rendered and painted but were now showing signs of bost plasterwork and flaking paint. In one or two places lumps of plaster had fallen away, revealing random rubble stonework.

"We'll leave your trunk here in the hall and I'll take you up to see Father Prior," said Edward.

"Right," said Joe, and they mounted worn sandstone steps that dipped so much in the middle that Joe found himself tending to slip off the treads.

At the top of the stairwell Edward motioned towards a door on the left and said quietly, "That's Fr. Val's room."

He knocked on the door facing the stairs and a voice called out, "Benedicite! Come!"

Edward opened the door and announced, "One of the new novices Father. Just arrived. Mr. Coyle."

"Come in. Come in. Mr. Coyle – Joseph, isn't it?" said the Prior, rising from a swivel chair and coming from behind a desk littered with books and papers and a few leather bound ledgers. He extended a hand to Joe and removed a pile of papers from another chair.

"Thank you Brother," he said to Edward, and Bro. Edward turned to leave, giving Joe an exaggerated wink from behind shining glasses, with a kindly, conspiratorial smile.

Fr. Prior waved his hand towards the chair he had cleared and Joe sat down, looking around with interest.

Dilapidation and need of repair were words that sprang to mind.

The perimeter of the prior's desk was piled with papers and files, with only a small central island free from clutter. The room itself was lined with bookcases and what could be seen of the walls indicated that they had the same need of attention as the stairwell. Along the wall to the right of the prior's desk was a half open door. Through it Joe glimpsed an iron bedstead and a wooden chair

The lack of maintenance extended to the prior himself. He was small, had grey hair, probably in his mid-fifties, and wore an off-white robe, worn and patched and with a blanket-like texture that looked as if it had been washed and repaired many times.

The prior was unshaven and slightly worried looking. His right hand scratched fiercely at the back of his left hand. Eczema, thought Joe, looking at blotches of red and cracked skin on the prior's face.

"Welcome Joseph. I hope you don't mind me using your Christian name," said the prior, moving a packet of cigarettes and a cheap, old fashioned storm lighter across the desk.

Joe could not help noticing that the fingers of his right hand were heavily stained with nicotine. The cigarettes were Capstan full strength, untipped.

The prior was obviously a heavy smoker, and he had the slightly harassed, frustrated and shame-faced look of a man who was trying to give up the habit. Joe knew the feeling.

"Yes, welcome Joseph. The name will do in the meantime, until the robing in about three weeks. Then you will receive a new name - symbolic of a change in status, change of vocation, leaving the world etcetera - like Abram to Abraham, Simon to Peter, and Saul to Paul."

The prior moved the cigarette packet and lighter back to where they had been.

"You'd think that after two thousand years the church authorities might accept the fact that the name given to you at your christening is the one that counts!"

He toyed with the cigarette packet.

"But it's not so. I used to be John but now I'm Luke - which is good enough for me, even if I have a special affection for John the beloved disciple.... You've met Brother Ed - brother Edwina, as he would like to be called!"

Joe nodded and Fr. Prior smiled and scratched absentmindedly.

"Don't be fooled by the girlish act! He's a real man. Been here fifteen years and well on the way to sanctity. Great person - as long as he is not breaking the rule of silence and telling some of his silly jokes - but don't tell him that: not good for his humility."

He pushed the cigarette packet away from him.

"You will discover, Brother – better start calling you that - that we are rather a weird order."

He lifted his right hand from the cigarettes and scratched his left hand vigorously.

"Well, some might call it weird. It's just grown up like this in the English Province. Unlike any other group of brothers we don't grind people into a mould. Everyone is himself."

Again he fiddled with the cigarettes. "We've all got to follow the Rule of course, but we don't want everyone to be the same as everyone else - regimented. We've all got our part to play, and we should feel comfortable within ourselves, extended but not strained."

"If you feel strained you're not going to fit in, not going to be able to last the pace. So just be yourself, and be at peace. If you have any troubles come to me."

He pulled the packet towards him. "I may be able to help – or maybe not."

He pushed the packet away. "Have you got any questions?"

Joe had been partly hypnotised by the progress of the cigarettes across the desk and had to make an effort to switch his gaze back to the prior. "No - no Father, not at the moment. Fr. Provincial explained most of the set-up to me during our interview in London."

"Right. OK. Just one thing. What made you select this Order?"

"Well, I was speaking with the Catholic Evidence Guild in London - at Speaker's Corner - Hyde Park - and it just seemed natural - logical - that I should join the order of friars' preachers. Also, I admired Aquinas, though I'm a bit overwhelmed by him and his analytic approach - and I also admired what I heard about Fr. Vincent McNabb O.P."

"Fr. Vincent! He was from your part of the world I think. I have all your details here, somewhere."

The prior fiddled among some papers but gave up when the pages he looked for did not immediately come to hand.

"Yes, from Portaferry in County Down." [7]

"Well, if you do as good as him – or Aquinas!" - the prior smiled, "you'll not go far wrong. But don't try to do it all at once. You've got the novitiate year to get through, and then three years philosophy and four years theology. Plenty of time, God willing."

"Yes Father."

"Right. That's enough for the moment. I have to try and balance the books here," and rising from his chair he turned towards some open ledgers with a worried look, automatically opening the packet of cigarettes, and without thinking put a cigarette in his mouth. "How we are going to pay the coke bill - for our old central heating system - I don't know."

The prior became aware of the cigarette in his mouth and put it back in the packet, looking annoyed with himself.

"If you can find Brother Ed he will point you towards the novitiate."

"Thank you Father," said Joe. "I'll find it." And he rose and moved towards the door, the prior already beginning to flick distractedly through his heap of bills and one of the large ledgers.

"Thank you Brother," said the prior, and as Joe stepped through to the corridor and turned to close the door he saw the prior's hand stray automatically to the packet of Capstan and light one quickly, unaware that he was sucking at it as a thirsty man would suck a gourd of water in a desert.

Joe went down the uneven steps into the hallway. Looking through an archway he saw the sunshine playing along a colonnade and stepping through he found himself on a broad, tiled walkway, open to the fresh air along three sides of a rectangular grass lawn. The fourth side was occupied by the church, with its soaring, pointed spire.

He walked hesitantly along the cloister, expecting to see someone. But the cloister was deserted, a cool and profoundly quiet oasis.

Proceeding along the shorter stretch of the cloister walk opposite to the church, he passed by a stairwell on the left and then a large double door. Continuing along the walkway towards the church, enveloped by the pervasive silence, he came to a door halfway towards the church. He knocked timidly and opened it, finding himself on the threshold of a large sitting room furnished with deep, shabby armchairs and a couple of settees, plus an assortment of hard-backed chairs and a large table strewn with magazines and newspapers. The room was empty.

Further along he passed a solid varnished door labelled "Chapter Room" in stylised black script.

At the end of the cloister there was a wide arched doorway, with two leaves, each with a large, black doorhandle. He turned one with an effort and found himself looking into the church, a pleasant, grey stone interior with supporting columns stretching to the rear of the church and the main public entrance.

A rood screen fronted the main alter and on either side was a small altar. Halfway along the wall stretching towards the rear of the church was a further altar, slightly larger, containing a statue of the Mother of Christ. The whole was lit by the evening sun streaming through stained glass windows. The church was simple and beautiful.

He moved towards the rood screen and the altar rails and knelt, looking at a large figure of Christ crucified, suspended above the high altar. A burning lamp proclaimed the Presence of Christ. Looking earnestly at the figure of Christ he made the sign of the cross and whispered softly, "Dear Jesus. I give you my heart and my soul. Help me to know if this is where I should be."

After a few minutes he rose, blessed himself again and genuflected towards the high altar, towards Christ, mysteriously present in the form of consecrated bread. Leaving by the large door he had entered he noticed another smaller door, leading into the vesting room at the side of the main altar.

It was a simple church, beautifully proportioned.

An easy place in which to pray, he thought.

Going past the Chapter Room and the large lounge he knocked on the double door at the end of the cloister and opening it poked his head into what turned out to be a big kitchen, with steam rising round a red faced and very busy Bro. Edward, clad in a huge white apron.

"Hello brother Joe! Lost?" called out Bro. Edward.

"Yes. I'm trying to find the novitiate."

"I'll show you the way m'lad," said Edward, "as the actress said to the bishop," and he came to the door and pointed, "Up those stairs, turn right. You'll see a door on your right. That's it. I've had your trunk brought up."

"Thanks brother. That's very good of you," said Joe.

"Not at all, at all. See you later. Have to get on with the work or you'll get no lunch tomorrow."

"Is that what you do?" asked Joe.

"Head cook and bottle washer. That's me." Edward laughed, "and if you get poisoned you know who to blame!"

"I'm sure you do O.K. Thanks very much Bro. Edward."

"That's alright m'dear," beamed Bro. Edward, face red and dripping with sweat.

6 Novitiate

At the top of the stairs Joe opened a set of double doors marked 'Novitiate' in black letters. He found himself in a small reception hall and saw his trunk on the floor. Voices came from behind a door just in front of him and he knocked gingerly before opening it and poking his head round the corner.

"I think I should be here," he said, and the faces of eight or nine young men turned towards him, smiling a welcome, with a chorus of "Come in! Come in!"

A few of the novices were clad in the basic white tunic of the order – without cloak or cowl. They looked rather scrawny, as if only half-dressed. The remainder, like Joe, were dressed in ordinary civilian clothes. All looked quite happy and much at home, relaxed despite sitting on or straddling plain wooden chairs. A large square table occupied most of the polished wooden floor. There were no carpets.

There was a rustle of movement as Joe, much to his embarrassment, was ushered towards a solitary armchair, located at the side of an open fireplace at one end of the room.

The novice nearest to Joe wore a white tunic with a black belt from which hung a long rosary. He was studious looking, probably about twenty-three or four, quite handsome, with curling black hair and wearing a pair of thick, horn-rimmed glasses.

"Hello, welcome," he said, "I'm Phil". He had a slight West Country accent and a pleasant, quirky smile.

His smile seemed slightly mischievous and evoked an immediate response from Joe.

"I'm Joe... Joe Coyle."

They shook hands and Phil motioned to a large gangling youth beside him, also in a tunic, aged about eighteen or nineteen. "This is Alfie."

Alfie was awkward looking, with puppy fat that seemed to move in all directions at once, like a large jelly.

"'Allo mate!" said Alfie.

They shook hands. "You're from London," said Joe.

"Yeh – down the East End," said Alfie, "folks 'ave a greengrocer business there – wholesale."

"What happens next?" asked Joe.

"Cupper tea then a chat from the boss!" said Alfie, and turned to address everyone in the room.

"Anybody want tea?"

There was a general murmur of assent.

"I'll get it. I know my way around. No, no need to help. It's just a pot and some mugs," and Alfie flopped towards the door.

"Alfie has been here for three weeks, waiting for the rest of us," said Phil.

He and Joe continued to talk quietly, against a low hubbub of similar conversations, punctuated by laughter. There was a light, happy atmosphere.

"How long have you been here?" asked Joe.

"Three days, but I've been here before, so I'm fairly familiar with it. Convert you know. Met Father Matty when I was at university and one thing led to another. Parents were amused when I became a Catholic. Doing their nuts now that I have decided to become a frater."

"Mine are a bit stunned I gather," said Joe, "can't quite believe it! But they are Catholic and they just want what is best for me."

"What made you come ... if you don't mind me asking?" asked Phil.

"Not at all. Well, I started off by being pretty unsure about God - whether he is or not, and then I read Plato, *'The Symposium'* - don't know if you have read it?"

Phil shook his head.

"Well, Plato analyses the various types of love that there are: love of parents for children, children for parents, men for women, men for men - normal and homosexual - love of country - of truth, of beauty: a general analysis of the nature of love, and I was hooked."

"Don't know quite why, for Plato himself comes to no definite conclusion; just provides an analysis through discussion of ideas provided by other people, and ends up pointing out that all men agree on the existence of something called love but no one can define exactly what it is!"

"It hit me all of a heap. I remember reading it and putting the book down on my chest and saying, 'My God, there is a God'!" Joe's eyes lit up at the memory. "Couldn't quite see the logic of it, but couldn't avoid the experience - that's what it was. Couldn't get over it. Got uproariously drunk to celebrate the find!"

Phil laughed heartily.

"Not rotten filthy drunk, you understand. Just high as a kite. Couldn't explain it to anyone around me at the time. Hesitated to do so."

The reality was that Joe had drunk only two beers. He did not at that moment have time to tell Phil the full story: that he had spent a couple of years exploring the world, working aboard ships of the British Merchant Navy and had just finished reading Plato's simple discussion of the nature of love, in a Penguin book picked up in New Zealand.

It was only slowly that he came to realise that his experience was something similar to that recounted in the Acts of the Apostles, when the Holy Spirit descended upon the apostles, at Pentecost.

On that occasion Peter had to tell the crowd

> *"These men are not drunk, as you imagine; why it is only the third hour of the day.*** *On the contrary, this is what the prophet spoke of: 'In the days to come ... I will pour out my spirit on all mankind ... your young men shall see visions, your old men shall dream dreams.'"* (Acts. 2. 15)

Coming back through the swelling Pacific Ocean, swaying at ease with the slow roll of the RMS Rangitoto over unimagined deep, awed by midnight blue skies spattered with billions of bright stars, overwhelmed by the majesty of creation, caught up in an ancient Athenian debate, Joe found himself gradually growing into a new realisation of what love might be – arriving at such a profound and compelling perception that, as he finished his paperback Plato, he could not help but drop the book on his chest and exclaim, "My God, there is a God!"

It was a 'leap of faith' if you like, but in his case not a leap at all. He was surrounded by; enraptured by, glowing within, such an experience of love and joy - silver jubilance, gold delight - that it would have been insanity to deny the reality.

This was Joe's introduction to the mystery of God, the Creator of the universe. He had a long way to go before he realised that Jesus of Nazareth is the only person who can tell us more. He had to undergo much suffering and grief – partly related in this book - before he became aware of his total dependence upon Jesus and His Father, his smallness and their greatness.

The initial joyful intoxication of beginning to realise that there is a loving God had worn off by the time he arrived in the UK, and he had begun to ask himself if human reason can lead to such a realisation, a conclusion, that there is a creator. Did reason support belief?

---

* I cannot help smiling at St. Peter saying that these men could not be drunk because it was 9 o'clock in the morning. So they might have been drunk had it been 9 p.m.? Sorry. It's the way my mind works. I will apologise personally to Peter in due course.

On shore and searching through Foyle's book shop on the Charing Cross Road the title of Immanuel Kant's *"Critique of Pure Reason"* caught his eye, and although it proved to be heavy reading it at least led him to an understanding of how human reasoning may or may not be affected by extraneous influences, and, as far as Joe was concerned, we must trust reason, as long as we guard against such influences, against delusion. In fact we must go along with reason even if leads to almost unbelievable conclusions.

He judged out of all of this that there is a necessity to suppose a supreme being, the cause of all things; and this supreme being must contain within itself – Himself - a power of reasoning and love that is reflected in the created human capacity for reason and love - fully expressed by Jesus, the Word incarnate.

"It took me a long time to relate my experience to Christ," he told Phil, "because by this time I had virtually left the church, but by dint of reading and thinking and praying, and looking at other religions, I began to realise that he had something special, was something special – is something special - and after that I found that I couldn't avoid thinking about the priesthood."

"My experience was something similar," said Phil, "except that my approach was through science. I'm an entomologist - studying 'ents'," he laughed, "bugs I mean."

"The more I investigated the range of bugs that there are, I became aware of the marvellous complexity of it all, that there was a pattern behind it, something that you couldn't simply put down to a mindless evolution - though I agree with a god-directed evolution, even though some say this is incompatible with natural selection – survival of the fittest." [8]

"All the signs were of a creative intelligence far superior to ours, working to his own mysterious plan. Couldn't get away from it - like yourself - and then I met Matty   Fr. Matthew, who was Catholic chaplain to the university, and I couldn't ignore the implications of what he talked about. My parents think that Matty has done a

Svengali on me, but that's far from the truth. Matty doesn't impose, just raises questions in an objective way. Couldn't avoid the outcome."

"Weird isn't it!" said Joe. "Never dreamt for an instant that I would be here."

"Bloody ridiculous!" said Phil. "My mates think I'm cracked, and my former fiancée is away off weeping somewhere."

Joe shook his head, "Jesus but it's desperate! A weird thing!"

At that moment the door was kicked open and Alfie backed in, labouring under the weight of a huge wooden box-tray holding a variety of thick mugs that slopped amid the flow and ebb of spilt tea and milk. The tray also contained a huge metal teapot, brown enamelled and chipped, and a large, slopping jug of milk, along with a bowl of sugar into which was stuck a handful of teaspoons.

"Here we are brothers!" announced Alfie. "Brother Ed says, 'Don't get pissed on it, for it's strong stuff – and bring the tray back!'"

"You've met Brother Edward?" asked Phil.

"Yeh," said Joe.

"Quite a character," said Phil. "One of the most honest people I have ever met, though they're mostly all like that here. Just themselves. You can't help liking them - even if some are as nutty as fruitcakes."

Alfie poured milk into the mugs of tea and they were passed around. The brothers helped themselves to sugar.

"Can you smoke here?" Joe asked.

"Yes," replied Phil. "This is the only place: the novitiate recreation room – and it's only twice a day for a half hour each time."

Joe groaned, "I thought it might be something like that! And I'm an addict. Still, I suppose something is better than nothing."

He lit a cigarette and offered one to Phil.

"No thanks. Don't smoke. One of the vices I don't have."

The door of the recreation room opened again and a well-built, handsome friar aged about forty came in. He looked very fit, pleasant and smiling, unassuming and even slightly shy.

"Fr. Nick – the Novice Master," whispered Phil.

"Good evening lads. Good evening Brothers, if you don't mind me saying so. Any tea Alfie?"

"Yes. Brought a mug for you."

Fr. Nick took a steaming mug and wiped drips off with the flat of his hand. He looked around.

"We have one new recruit I believe."

He spotted Joe and came over.

"Joe Coyle, isn't it?"

"Yes," Joe murmured and rose to shake hands.

"You're very welcome. I see you are in good hands. You'll look after him Phil - Right?"

He turned to face the rest of the novices.

"Look: all hands. Can I have your attention! Joe here is not quite the last person to come. Two more are due tomorrow, so we'll save the full briefing until then."

"However, a few basics. The whole of this house runs to a rule - rule with a capital R. It's not absolutely inflexible. It's there as a guide - and you'll be studying it in detail - as well as Latin and the Divine Office, our way of prayer. In the meantime, a few pointers: first – we rise at 6.15 a.m."

There were some groans and Fr. Nick laughed.

"Sorry, but there it is. Each one of you will serve as knocker-up in turn. Alfie, you had better serve until we get a Rota."

"At 6.15 the brother on duty will knock on each door. He calls out 'Benedicamus domino' - your Latin is probably just about sufficient: 'Let us praise the lord'. You answer 'Deo gratias' – 'Thanks be to God' – and even if you don't feel like it it's a good idea to actually mean it. It's the sole reason for our existence, and if you mean it, even at that time in the morning, it makes the day go with a swing."

"You may thank God you are not a Cistercian, or your early call would be about 2.30 a.m. – with another at 4.30!"

"You wash - or do anything you have to do. Sorry, there's no hot water at that time. We don't run to that here, everything is on a shoestring. You just do the basics. Don't empty the po you'll find under your bed! That all comes during clean-up after breakfast, when you can get a jug of hot water for a shave."

"You don't talk at any time, either then or during the day - only at recreation and during classes. That applies particularly from the magnum silencium bell at 10 o'clock at night, when the day ends for us - the great silence - right through the night. That's why the po!" He grinned.

"Lights out at the magnum silencium bell. You have an hour from 9 p.m. till then for private study, reading or writing. All letters to go through me by the way – left open - not that I'm nosey, it's just that I have to know what goes on in your mind, so that I am able to help, able to judge how you are getting on. Anything private remains in here." He touched his breast.

"Don't be inviting parents or friends to visit you for the first six months, unless there is something absolutely urgent. You are being put to the test – for your own good. There is no point in remaining here unless you are fully aware of the type of life you will be leading - in all its rigours. It's not easy, but it has its compensations."

"Should anyone wish to leave, at any time, you are, of course at liberty to do so - but have a word with me first, if you don't mind!"

There was laughter and Fr. Nick smiled.

"Don't laugh! Some have been known to scarper during the night! Nearly did it myself! Right, that's about it. You'll learn all the rest as you go along."

"Oh, one thing that everyone has some difficulty with: the 'venia'.

"Should you be late for prayer, or for a meal, or offend against anyone, including breaking into their privacy by unnecessary conversation, you have to apologise, and this is how you do it. Clear the decks there."

He gave a further cheery grin and the novices cleared a space in front of him. He lifted the broad white scapular at the front of his habit, kissed it, and in one easy movement prostrated himself on the floor, his right hand outstretched and still gripping the scapular. He lay there for a moment and then turned his head.

"What happens then Alfie?"

Alfie rapped sharply on the table and Fr. Nick rose from the floor.

"That's the venia. It's from the Latin word for pardon. It may seem over-dramatic, but it saves conversation, maintains silence. You can practice it when you get your habits. O.K. lads?"

He laughed at the silence and the unbelieving look on most of the faces before him. "Don't worry brothers. It's not as bad as it sounds!"

There was a general hubbub of conversation as discussions broke out.

Fr. Nick turned to Joe.

"Well, what do you think so far?"

"Rubbish!" cried Alfie and Phil in unison and everybody burst out laughing.

"It can seem that way," said Fr. Nick, "but it has lasted for seven hundred years, from the time of St. Dominic, so it is well tested."

"I must go. I'll see you all shortly. Phil, will you find Joe a room?" Phil nodded and Fr. Nick moved off, exchanging laughing greetings with the brothers.

It was obvious that in a short time he had made his mark, had become very popular.

"Great lad Fr. Nick.," said Phil, "very easygoing and natural. Was a great rugby footballer before he came in here. Come on Joe and we'll find a room for you."

They went out of the recreation room. "I suppose I should take this along," said Joe, indicating his trunk.

"Right," said Phil, and they lifted it between them and carried it along a corridor covered by highly polished brown linoleum, with eight or nine inches of stained floorboards showing at each side.

Phil stopped at a door and holding the trunk handle with one hand he opened the door and glanced inside. "Yes. This one's free."

They deposited the trunk just inside the door and Phil said, "I'll leave you to it."

He stood aside to allow Joe to go in to a simple room, furnished with an iron bedstead, a washstand, a plain pine wardrobe and a small table with a bentwood armchair.

"By the way Joe," said Phil, still standing at the open door, "we do not go into each other's room. Part of the rule – to avoid booze-ups and parties - and even less savoury goings-on!"

They both laughed.

"This is your domain. Completely private!"

"Thanks be to God for some things!" said Joe. "I had visions of us living in each other's pockets."

"I'll leave you to it then," said Phil, and he shut the door.

Joe looked around. He went to the washstand and lifted an old-fashioned china water jug from the basin. Shaking his head unbelievingly he turned and looked at the bed. Under it was a china chamber pot.

He lifted it up and smiled as he held it aloft, and when he looked inside he burst into unrestrained laughter, his serious face transformed, for painted on the bottom of the pot was a picture of a horned devil, ferociously angry and raising its arms to protect itself.

Joe replaced the pot and took off his jacket. He hung it on a coat hanger at the back of the door and began to unpack the trunk.

7 Matins

In the choir stalls before the high altar the brothers recited the psalms in Latin, Joe and the other novices reading the Latin text and hesitatingly joining in the singing, bowing in concert with the professed brothers and fathers, for the first time participating in the prayer life of the community.

The novices were dressed in the long white tunic of the Order, buttoned to the top and stretching to the ankle, cinched in the middle by a black belt, from which hung a fifteen-decade rosary and crucifix. Until the clothing ceremony they would not wear the scapular and cowl that completed the normal friar's dress – a relic of the working clothes of the thirteenth century.

Joe had become aware that the scapular, a long piece of cloth just over twelve inches wide that slipped over the head and hung to the front and back of the tunic, was in matching white cloth for the priests and in black for the lay brothers.

Despite the fact that the lay brothers had, it appeared, little or no knowledge of Latin they seemed perfectly at home with the recitation of the psalms, those beautiful words from four thousand years ago, translated from Hebrew and Greek by St. Jerome in 385 AD:

"Beatus vir qui non abiit in consilio impiorum et in via peccatorum non stetit in cathedra derisorum non sedit," intoned the friars on one side of the altar.

Joe could just about understand:

"Happy the man who never follows the advice of the wicked .... or sits among the scoffers."

He then found himself stumbling to reply:

"... sed in lege Domini voluntas eius et in lege eius meditabitur die ac nocte" – "but finds his pleasure in the law of Yahweh and meditates upon it day and night ..."

And listened to the antiphonal response,

"*...et erit tamquam lignum transplantatum iuxta rivulos aquarum quod fructum suum dabit in tempore suo et folium eius non defluet ...*"

"... he is like a tree planted by streams of water, giving fruit in due season, its leaves never withering."

And so it went on, Joe's mind racing as he strove to understand. It would require a lot of work and study to bring usage and understanding to perfection In London he had taken a Latin O-Level course, but it was a tiny little foundation.

How the lay brothers could cope he did not know. He had accepted, instinctively realised, that the lay brothers were men who had abandoned education at an early age and only wished to serve in humble, practical ways, did not desire to be priests – probably considered the priesthood beyond them.

He might find himself in trouble about this, he realised, for one thing he knew about himself was that he absolutely abhorred and violently rejected notions of class. To find evidence of a hereditary class division in a religious order was disturbing.

At the end of Matins the brothers bowed low before Christ in the sacrament and each went quietly and separately to a place in the church, to devote the next thirty minutes to personal prayer and meditation.

Huddled in the dawn gloom at the end of a bench at the rear of the church Joe was aware of the deep silence, a time of waiting, an opening of self to the power and love of the unseen God.

Anything could happen: but probably would not, he smiled to himself. We are just to sit here quietly, he thought, separate but united, waiting upon the Lord, leave ourselves open to Him, hope that His peace will descend, that He will lead us into love, agape, the love of the spirit, where Jesus is and will reveal himself, will bring us into himself, take us into a love impossible to describe and only open to faith.

As he sat there he could not help but reflect upon a certain moment in the Pimlico flat, shortly after the amazing gift of grace given in Shepherd's Bush.

He had found himself living in Pimlico because he had started to attend CEG lectures in the little schoolhouse beside Westminster Cathedral. There he began to meet people, and commenced practice speaking classes, before nervously ascending a speaker's platform at Hyde Park.

A fellow speaker, a young South African lad called Sean Boud, had invited him to share accommodation in Pimlico, not far from Westminster Cathedral and only a mile from the new job he had found in Buckingham Palace Road, in the publicity department of the Cambridge Instrument Company, a scientific, industrial and medical instrument manufacturing company that had, amazingly enough, given his new life's interest, been founded by a son of Charles Darwin, the originator of the theory of evolution of species.

Equally amazing was the fact that his job was that of a technical copywriter, despite the fact that he knew nothing about science. The Sales Director who had interviewed him had been desperate for staff, and in the absence of the publicity manager had asked few questions.

Some weeks after he had started the publicity manager had returned from an extended illness and had talked to Joe in his private office, examining his credentials, and at the end of the interview, when Joe had returned to his desk, Joe could see through the glass partition the manager sitting with his head in his hands in an attitude of despair. It was a graphic commentary on his findings.

Nevertheless, Joe was constructively employed and industriously studying the mysteries of electric and electronic phenomena, process control equipment and medical instrumentation - blood pressure recorders, dye-dilution curve recorders and beautifully precise microtomes - slowly beginning to understand things that had baffled him at school. He was learning to think

Because of these unique developments Joe found that he could comfortably walk between home and work and finish off the day each evening by attending 6 p.m. Mass in the cathedral.

The house turned out to be almost totally occupied by CEG speakers, and for the first time in London he found himself surrounded by friends, a lively bunch of people much given to discussion and sharing trips to the cinema, to merry home cooked meals and a glass or two of cheap wine – the cheapest possible.

It was a pleasantly active scene, with many callers, but there were often private moments, and it was shortly after taking up residence that he found himself one evening sitting quietly before a bubbling gas fire.

Above the fireplace was a colourful painting that his flatmate [9] had hung. It was a primitive picture of an African veldt, as dry as dust, and in the foreground was a young man, a shepherd, carrying a lamb upon his shoulders, smiling and strong in the sunshine.

As he looked at the picture Joe recalled Jesus saying that he was the Good Shepherd, and he quietly thanked the unseen Lord for the gift of life, for being the good shepherd - for picking him up when he was lost and carrying him home, like the man in the picture, for releasing him from the prison of sorrow, for giving him peace and tranquillity.

In this quiet moment he murmured thanks to the good shepherd, to Jesus, this mysterious Lord of Creation, filled with quiet joy; and in the tranquil moment a voice spoke to him, in the spirit, saying to him, "I will take you into myself and burn you free of all things."

The sentence that formed in his mind was not a physical voice. There was no sequence of words as in ordinary human speech, just immediate apprehension of the complete sentence. It was not his own thought. It came from somewhere or someone else, with a cool, lasting clarity, a permanency of intent that became part of his soul.

He was not excited. He simply recognised a fact and pondered why it should be.

He continued to sit quietly, totally relaxed. It was a sentence that he knew he would never forget. It could have been the voice of God, a small whisper, but he did not necessarily believe so. Too many people are easily deluded, he said to himself. However, it could be a thought from the unseen creator of the universe, a positive intention. Amazing to think that it might be. If it was it was not an essential part of his faith, rather an unexpected gift; a consequence of faith.

He had never related the experience to anyone. He would have been embarrassed. People would think he was crazy - a nutter. A person who heard voices? He could imagine the sympathetic smiles, people looking at him strangely, saying politely, 'Oh, Really! How interesting!'

The incredulity, and the whispers to follow. His reputation shattered!

No way! Not for him! He was not going to make a fool of himself – but the voice had been real, had a lasting coolness, and despite his scepticism he was inclined to think that it did come from the unseen God.

'But why me?' he asked. 'I am no more important than anyone else. I am simply a poor ignoramus, a half-educated man recovering from a soul shattering experience - a hedonistic, selfish person, much given to romantic thought and to notions of sexual fulfilment – a sexual addict in fact, until recently.'

The only thing decent about him, he thought, was that he had loved one person inordinately, perhaps more than he should have, and had endured the loss of that love – learning that love can be exaggerated, is imperfectly understood, can be something greater than human, earthly love.

Now, in the lightening grey of the dawn, he meditated on these things, and immediately began to upbraid himself for dwelling on passing phenomena.

Surely he should be dwelling upon the Person of Jesus and the Unseen Father.

'Lord, forgive me for my distractions,' he prayed.

In the choir stall the prior rang a small bell and the brothers rose in unison, with a flutter of habits and the soft pad of shoes moved towards the sacristy to prepare for the first Masses of the day.

Candles were lit on the four altars within the church, and a priest went to each, accompanied by a brother or a novice. They bent low before the altars and began to celebrate the Eucharist, quietly and with devotion, at each altar a small bell tinkling at the moment of consecration.

Joe was not called upon to act as a server, so he sat and knelt in the nave of the church, listening to the muted words, rejoicing at the peace and prayerfulness. The candle lights at each altar and the sounds of the words were a hushed prayer that enveloped the soul.

In this early dawn Joe gave thanks for his being, for the fact that he was part of a wonderful, continuing act of love. His brow burned with fervour. He rejoiced to be where he was.

At the end of these first devotions of the day the brothers went quietly to the refectory, a long tiled room with three high windows looking over fields that sloped down into the valley.

On entering the room each friar went to a serving alcove and poured tea from a large teapot, or coffee from a huge urn, adding milk or sugar to taste. It appeared from the size of the coffee urn that this was the preferred beverage, and indeed Joe found it much to his taste, as well as to his sense of smell.

Thick slabs of brown bread and slabs of butter were the solid fare on every week morning.

"On Sundays," Phil whispered to Joe, "There is beautiful thick marmalade."

Joe nodded thanks, feeling slightly guilty about breaking the silence but accepting that some information needed to be communicated. He would have preferred to wait and discover what lay ahead as each moment unfolded.

The brothers ate in silence, each in cowled privacy, sitting on benches built into the perimeter of the room, with mugs and plates on well scrubbed tables.

Breakfast finished, each friar placed his dishes on a trolley beside the serving alcove and bowed before a crucifix fixed above a reading lectern.

Without further ado Joe made his way to the next scheduled activity: a shave with a small jug of hot water and a clean-up of his room, before preparing for the first class of the day – a study of the Rule and history of the Order and of basic Latin.

At midday the novices processed to the chapel, reciting a psalm, and there, in the stalls at each side of the altar the brothers continued to recite parts of the Divine Office before participating in sung High Mass, the central act of each day of prayer.

All members of the community and a sprinkling of local parishioners participated in this solemn celebration of the Eucharist, the commemoration of the last supper of Christ on earth.

To Joe, lost in contemplation of the life, death and resurrection of Jesus, the words of Jesus, repeated by the prior, was a moment of profound adoration of the man he believed to be God incarnate:

> *"This is the cup of my blood, the blood of the new and everlasting covenant. It will be shed for you and for all so that sins may be forgiven. Do this in memory of me."*

Very much aware of his sinful excesses in the past, Joe felt a profound gratitude to God for this continuing act of forgiveness, a sense of God's presence.

8 Work

In the refectory Joe and Phil, clad in aprons, were serving lunch to the brothers. The meal was coming to an end. It had been simple but substantial, again eaten in silence, and the two novices were clearing away the dishes as Alfie, perched on a high lectern, continued to read from the book stipulated by the prior - in this case a somewhat heavy tome: Darwin's *"The Origin of Species"*. Joe learned later that this was by way of an experiment. Normal choice would have been a biography of some sort, as near to light entertainment as the brothers ever came. There may have been a radio somewhere in the priory but there was no sign of a television set.

So Alfie was still reading from the introduction to Darwin's book, by a C.D. Darlington FRS, as they had learned.

Alfie was continuing to read, rather hesitantly.

". . . At the same time the foundation of Darwinism in the experimental study of evolution has largely been smothered in Darwin's own country. The Universities, with their museums and botanic gardens, are happy to forget what, in 1859, they were unable to resist. They contain no mem-oral . ."

Alfie was interrupted by the sound of a small bell rung by the prior. The bell hung over the prior's centrally placed bench seat. He was obviously irritated,

"...'Mem*orial*' Brother. According to Mr. Darwin you and I are at the pinnacle of natural evolution and our pronunciation must reflect this ..."

Alfie, blushing and embarrassed, continued,

". . . They contain no mem-or-ial of his work, and all the means of developing his doctrine they frustrate by an arrangement of teaching which the theory of evolution is not allowed to disturb. The old pedantic learning of botany and zoology, which Darwin treated as one subject they continue to cleave asunder, burying the halves under their ancient schedules of instruction."

The prior rang the bell again and Alfie stopped reading.

All the friars rose and stood in front of the scrubbed bare wood of the tables to begin grace after meals, intoned in Latin, with graceful bows at set moments.

Alfie descended from the lectern and despite the lack of a scapular did a belly flop venia, hitting the tiled floor with a loud smack.

The friars smiled as they continued to intone grace.

The face of the prior, unshaven and pallid, lit up in amusement and he clapped his hands.

Alfie rose awkwardly, his face aflame with embarrassment.

Joe, had the feeling, having listened to the reading from the introduction to Darwin, that without Alfie the 'Evolution of Species' would not prove to be such an entertaining read. Perhaps the prior would change his mind.

****

Joe was washing-up in the kitchen, soap suds up to the elbows.

Bro. Edward, resting from his cooking duties, came alongside and asked in a whisper - a wicked glint in his eye.

"Did you ever hear about the old lady aged about eighty?"

Joe shook his head.

"She was sitting poking the fire when the genie of the fire appeared and said she could have three wishes.

As a first wish she said that she wished she was young and beautiful again.

Kazaam! Immediately she became young and beautiful.

Next she wished that she lived in a gorgeous mansion.

Kazaam! The old house changed into a palace.

'And for your final wish?' asked the genie.

'I wish that I had a gorgeous young man,' she said - and her eyes lit on her cat curled up in front of the fire - 'that my old tomcat there could be changed into someone beautiful for me.'

Kazaam! The old tomcat was changed into a handsome young man, who strolled over and looked down at her, love and desire in his eyes."

Bro. Ed rolled his eyes at this point.

"The beautiful young man said to her, 'Aren't you sorry now that you had me neutered!'"

Joe sank his head close to the suds, convulsed with mirth.

Bro. Edward's eyes shone with satisfaction at the effect of his story.

****

Alfie and Joe laboured in front of a mountain of craggy coke. The lorry had just delivered it at the back door of the kitchen, facing the boilerhouse. The problem was that the coke was deposited on an area paved with round cobblestones, and given the jagged edges of the coke it was almost impossible to get the edge of a shovel under the fuel.

It was infuriatingly slow, each shovelful minute in the face of such a mountain. But it had to be done, for the first faint signs of autumn were evident, a chill air shifting the remnants of fallen leaves.

"Sorry brothers," Fr. Nick had said. "We have to be prepared. "You'll know all about it when winter hits us. It's a daily task, three or four times a day – on a rota of course."

Alfie's face and tunic were streaked with coke dust, as if he had personally dug the coal and burned it into coke. It appeared that he had the knack of turning every event into a near disaster. A real talent. He had begun to be called 'the master of disaster'.

Both brothers were delighted when the vespers bell rang.

****

The magnum silencium bell tolled and Joe switched out the light. He knelt in the darkness and stretched out his arms as Christ on the cross.

The moonlight flooded into his cell and lit up his earnest face.

"Father. Let me live and die with your son," he murmured, and then blessed himself and clambered into bed, where he slowly said the prayer that Jesus had recommended, "Our Father ... Our Father ..." Joe dwelt so long on these words that he fell asleep.

Sixteen hours of continuous activity used a lot of energy.

****

"This business of a change of name," said Fr. Nick, "what we usually do is ask each of you to write down three names that you would not object to use – to be called by. We can't guarantee that you will receive any of them but put your top choice at the top of the list! Is that enough guidance! A nod is as good as a wink ...!"

Nick smiled his usual friendly smile.

****

"Right," said Joe, "I know my first choice: Barnabas."

"Barney?" said Phil reflectively. "That's nice. Got a good ring to it. Barney the Bear! Why?"

"Barnabas," repeated Joe. "He was the only one in the new testament who stood up to Paul. Got fed up with his continual travels and constant pushing and told him he was not going on into Macedonia or wherever it was. Paul really was a know-it-all, and could be a bit over the top. Remember how that young fellow in an upper room went asleep during one of Paul's harangues and fell out of a first floor window? Paul didn't know when to stop – even told off Peter to his face - not that he didn't deserve it. Bit thick Peter. Slow to learn.[10] But Paul was definitely extreme, despite all his powerful writings – the beauty of some of them - and nobody else seemed to get a look in after he recovered his sight – and I just like the way Barnabas said: 'Halt! I'm going no further', even if Paul was a bit pissed off with him. Yeah, I like Barnabas! What about you?"

"Albert," said Phil. "Great mediaeval philosopher scientist and an O.P.: Albertus Magnus, a truly independent thinker."

"Right," said Joe. "What about you Alfie?"

"Ignatius, after the saint – not the soldier chap, the Jesuit fellow – I mean the one from Antioch, friend of the apostle John; got himself chewed up by lions in Rome. I remember reading about him when I was a boy. Nasty bit of work – not Ignatius – the fellows that threw him in. Very nasty. Hope I don't end up like that, but I must say I admire him."

"So there we have it," said Joe: "Barney, Bert and Iggy!"

"For God's sake," exclaimed Alfie, "I don't want to sound more ridiculous than I am: Iggy! My God!"

All three burst into laughter.

"Sacred Heart of Jesus: *Bert!*" said Phil, "sounds like a cartoon, or a plumber – and me wanting to be a distinguished scientist!"

"Isn't that what scientists are?" asked Joe, "Cartoons or distinguished plumbers, funny chaps who sometimes know how a thing works and sometimes don't? I like the sound of Barney, sounds friendly – of course he was known as a man of encouragement. So I'll be well pleased if I get it, even though I was very happy with what my mother called me."

9 Clothing

All the novices were spread-eagled on the church floor. They were wearing the full habit of the Order. Joe felt a sense of fulfilment as he lay outstretched. He was conscious of a sacred moment that was hugely satisfying, a moment in which he was making a total offering of himself to God, withholding nothing.

The prior stood over the prostrate novices, spread before him in an ever widening fan. He spoke with unusual dignity – almost majesty. Clad in fine priestly robes he was shaven and solemn.

"You have received these robes as a symbol of our Christian brotherhood, of having left the world and all its pleasures and concerns, in order to serve Christ's people, either here in England or in our missions in South Africa and the West Indies."

"The work of this Order is prayer and study: first prayer - for we can do nothing without this. Then study, for we are the order of friars' preachers – and to preach we have to know and understand."

"We own nothing of our own. We hold everything in common. At the end of the noviciate year you will decide, we will decide together, if your vocation lies here. It may or may not be. We must wish to do as God wills. Not our will, his. Not all are called: but," with a huge smile, "at least you have offered yourselves."

"You have each taken a new name, symbolic of your new vocation."

"At the end of this year you will decide if you wish to take vows of poverty, chastity and obedience. It is not easy, but it can be made light if we trust in Our Lord Jesus Christ, who said, 'You are not worthy if you do not take up your cross daily, deny yourself, and follow Me.' Very demanding, demanding in love and obedience to him, for he is very God incarnate. We must do as he has asked, remembering that he has also said 'My yoke is easy. My burden light.'"

"He will make it easy. Give generously to him and you will find yourself growing in stature, becoming more like him, for he lives in us through the power of the Holy Spirit - and it is his spirit that will lift us up and give us strength and joy, a joy that passes human understanding."

"We do not demand it. We accept that it is our task to serve without reward, in freedom and in love. There is no love without sacrifice, as he sacrificed himself on Calvary."

The prior scratched his hand fiercely.

"Greater love than this no man has, that he lay's down his life for his friends. Christ is our friend. Not because we are worthy of him, but because he gives himself totally to us, freely to us. In the spirit it is up to each one of us to return that love freely. If we do, we will be happy. If we do not, we will be less than happy. Walk with Christ, dear brothers. Serve him with all your strength. May the blessing of almighty God be upon you, now and forever more. In the name of the Father, the Son and the Holy Spirit."

He made the sign of cross over them and as rather squeaky exultant music sounded from the church organ shafts of autumn sunshine pierced the incense clouds around the altar and rood screen as the brothers rose and bowed.

The fathers and brothers solemnly processed off in pairs, in order of seniority, the date of profession - priests first, then lay-brothers, then novices, each pair bowing to Christ in the tabernacle.

Joe and Phil, the new Brothers Barnabas and Albert, processed together. The new Brother Ignatius and another young novice brought up the rear.

"Welcome to the Order of Friars Preachers Brother Barnabas!" Albert murmured quietly to Joe, with a smile of relief. "Thank God that's over."

As they bowed together Bro. Barney agreed. "Indeed Brother Albert! Two and a half hours of it!"

Behind them Brother Ignatius, stepping forward with his paired novice to bow, joined in, "Never thought I'd make it! I'm famished!"

"Guts!" said Albert in a sideways hiss.

"Well, I'm only a lad. I'm still growing," said Ignatius, bending down to bow.

He accidentally put a foot on the end of his long scapular as it draped across the floor, and when he straightened up and attempted to walk on the scapular tightened with a sudden jerk round his neck, so that instead of walking he pulled himself forward on his face before the altar.

Albert, quick to take advantage, looked back and knocked on the edge of a pew, proclaiming in a passable imitation of the prior's voice, "A disgrace Brother! Do that 'venia' again!"

All four brothers convulsed in helpless laughter – desperately trying to stifle the noise by stuffing scapulars into their mouths.

10 Questions

The door of Fr. Nick's study opened and Brother Barney's head poked round its edge:
"You wanted to see me Father?"
"Yes Brother." Fr. Nick was sitting behind his desk. "Come in. I just wanted to give you a little job - and find out how things are going with you."
"First, the job. It's the custom at the next Chapter meeting for a novice to give a brief oration - a bit of a sermon, a homily, and I thought as you have been speaking with the Catholic Evidence Guild you wouldn't mind doing it. Is that O.K.?"
"Whatever you say. What does it entail?"
"Well, you know that Chapter meetings are a kind of review of how things are in the community: a sort of company meeting. There is practical business - in this case it will be primarily how to keep the coke bill paid," Fr. Nick laughed, "and there is also an address on a religious theme – just to inspire us all to keep going, remind us what we are about. It's given by various people - in this case one of the novices: that's you! O.K.?"
"Whatever you say," Barney was quite cool.
"It's in Latin of course," said Fr. Nick.
"In *Latin*!" Shock and horror were written large on Barney's face.
Fr. Nick burst out laughing. He had anticipated the reaction. "Come on Barney. It's not as bad as all that!"
"But I've only got 'O' level Latin – and grade 'C' at that! I never could understand all that business about pluperfect subjunctive and ablative absolutes! I couldn't do it!" Barney was horrified at the thought.
Nick was still smiling.
"I'm not all that hot at it myself – but you do have a smattering, and we do have to try. It's a question of keeping the language alive, to a certain extent. It need only be three or four minutes: the shorter the better...."

"But...," Barney protested feebly.

".... and you have a month to prepare it...."

A resigned look came over Barney's face "...and when you have it written out I will check it for absolute howlers."

"Well, I suppose if I must I must. I'm not enchanted ... and I don't suppose anyone else will be when they hear it."

"That's the ticket! You'll enjoy the challenge once you get started."

"I suppose I might."

"It's just one of those things we do from time to time, to try and keep us familiar with lingua Latina. There are a lot of buried treasures written in that language. Good. Now - how about other things? How are you getting on generally? Is everything O.K.?"

"It's tough, but I'm coping – just about," said Barney, "I find the physical side of things very hard: getting up on the dot of 6.15 every morning and being on the go all day. After a nine-to-five job it stretches to the limit."

"Yes, I've noticed you looking rather tired - and a bit strained if I may say so."

"I suppose I am a bit strained. I might be driving myself a bit hard - but I'd rather do things well than just go through the motions: not that you could do that anyway. It's hard - but I can cope. I'm determined to."

"Well, don't drive yourself too hard. You have to be relaxed: kind of float through the day - give your all, but remember that it's only by God's power that we can succeed. Try and do it all on your own and you'll come a cropper."

"I know what you mean. It's hard to get the balance right between doing things yourself and leaving things up to God. I pray about that."

"Well, just do what you have to do and leave the rest up to him. We can't do anything without him: wouldn't even exist without him."

"Right!" said Barney.

Fr. Nick looked a little distracted for a moment,

"Everybody finds it hard."

He paused, "I'd better tell you now that Bro. James and Bro. Angus won't be going on."

"Oh," exclaimed Barney, "I am sorry to hear that! Just when we were all getting to know each other."

"It seems a pity," said Fr. Nick, "but of course that's what the novitiate is all about – finding out if it is for you."

"I suppose so. When do they go?"

"Already left. Went to catch the midday train."

"Good Lord! As quick as that!"

"Well, as the man says, if you've gotta go you've gotta go!" Fr. Nick smiled, "It's better to go quickly. Never mind. They'll find another way."

"Pity all the same."

"Yes - but we just have to accept these things. Now - is there anything else bothering you – apart from giving talks in Latin?" Fr Nick's face broke into a wide smile, and Barney also smiled, ruefully.

"Not that I can think of," said Barney. "One of the things I do miss is not being able to get up at night and make myself a cup of tea. That used to be a habit of mine in civvy street."

Fr. Nick nodded, "Yes. It's the little things that count. It's hard to give up one's freedom to do ordinary things."

"Not that I need cups of tea in the night these days," said Barney, "for I'm off to sleep as soon as I hit the sack. It's just the thought of not being free to do things I took for granted."

"What about the spiritual side of things, Barney? What about the personal isolation? Some people find it very hard not to talk – to live in silence with their own thoughts?"

"I love it," said Barney, his eyes lighting up. "Peace, blessed peace! I thought that I might be bored being locked up all day - in one's head I mean, as well as physically - but there is so much going on in terms of prayer and work and study that my problem is that I don't have enough time for private thoughts. Anyone who thinks that monks and friars spend all day lying around contemplating their navels needs his head examined!"

"A strange thing too: I don't miss television at all - except for the news; and I accept that it's all still happening out there, and that I'll hear about it eventually, if it's important enough."

"Yes. Life's busy enough in here," said Fr. Nick, "away from all distractions. You'll find after a few years that it gets into a rhythm, a pattern, and if you enjoy study you'll find theology and philosophy a great mental tonic." Fr. Nick paused. "So, there's nothing that really troubles you at the moment?"

Barney thought for a moment. "No - yes. It's a small thing – but I can't see the sense of it: going to confession every week. I know that I could be suffering from oceans of pride and all sorts of horrors that I am not aware of at the moment, but as far as I am aware I am not committing any grievous sins - and full knowledge and full consent is necessary to commit any - so I don't like having to go to confession when I have nothing to confess. It makes a mockery of what confession is for. Can it not be left to us to go when we feel the need?"

"Sorry Barney. I see what you mean – but its part of the Rule - and has been for nearly 700 years. It's unlikely to change."

"I'll have to accept it then I suppose: but I don't like it. I think we should have the same freedom as any other Catholic – the same right to mature self judgment. Isn't that what Christianity is all about - helping us to become mature human beings?"

Nick looked a bit uncomfortable. "I take your point Barney. If it were up to me I would grant a dispensation immediately; but it's a rule that is unlikely to be waived."

"Alright. So I have to put up with it. Oh - another thing I don't like. Excuse me being so critical. I'm just putting out my thoughts. I don't like the idea of lay brothers and priests having separate recreation periods – separate recreation rooms I mean. Seems against the spirit of Christianity. Should we not be all together?"

"I think if you were to ask the Lay brothers to join in with the fathers you might have a revolt on your hands. The brothers have different interests. What they want to talk about is not the same as the priests: a question of education and interest basically: a different sort of vocation."

"You may be right, but I still don't like it. What you are saying is that if Jesus were here now he would not fit in with the priests because he was a carpenter's son!"

Fr. Nick's face went red. He looked flustered.

"No - no! Not at all! Jesus was obviously quite an educated man for his day. He was able to confound some of the biblical scholars with his erudition - raise questions that astonished the official scholars - and not simply because he was God incarnate either. He would have played it fair in every way." Fr. Nick smiled again. "He was obviously very well read in the scriptures."

"It still doesn't alter the fact that as a carpenter if he were here now he would be expected to be in with the lay brothers – certainly his foster-father, Joseph, would be ...!"

Fr. Nick was squirming, but he was able to smile and come back sharply, "... and he would feel completely at home! Accepting that he had a different vocation! I understand what you mean Barney. The points you've made bear thinking about - but give yourself and us time before making a final judgment. One thing to be clear about is that we are not talking about basic worth and value. The lay brothers are equal to us in every respect. Many of them will be judged by Jesus to be very much more worthwhile than those who are priests: just as Joseph the carpenter was, just as many people living in the world will be, depending upon how truly they love and serve God in their own way. It's a question of different functions, different vocations. Can we leave it at that for the moment?"

Barney looked slightly embarrassed. "I'm sorry to be a bit prickly – but you did ask me, and these are things I am a bit unhappy about - oh, and another thing: I can't stand that curtain that is pulled across the rood screen every morning. It shuts us off from the people who come in to early morning Mass."

"That's just a local custom, because of the cold winds blowing through the church in winter."

"I still don't like it."

"You could bring it up with Father Prior if you like. It's only an organisational thing. Nothing to do with the rule."

"Alright," said Barney. "I'll think about it."

"Anything else?" asked Nick.

"Not that I can think of at the moment."

Fr. Nick laughed, "Thanks be to God! It's not often that I get such a grilling!"

Barney was suddenly alarmed. "Oh - I'm sorry. I didn't mean to ..."

"No," said Fr. Nick. "You have raised some fair points. They need answering. But I don't think either you or I can answer them fully at this moment. Alright?"

"Sure. Sorry to trouble you Father."

"My pleasure Barney. Not to worry."

At that moment the church bell sounded. "There's the bell for None. We'd better go."

"Right."

Both rose and Barney went towards the door.

"Don't forget about that talk, Barney! About three or four minutes – a couple of pages."

"Right Father." Barney smiled and went out of the room, closing the door behind him.

Fr. Nick dropped back into his seat. He rubbed his hands down both sides of his cheeks and emitted a breath as if to relieve pressure.

"Phew! Tough nut! Tough on us. Tough on himself."

11 Latin

On leaving Fr. Nick's room Barney was mostly concerned about Latin.

This could be a problem.

Latin had always been a bugbear, something that he found difficult; could have almost put him off the church.

He liked the sound of it, but since he had come back into the church as an adult he found it increasingly annoying that the Mass was in Latin, a language that he did not understand – and he could not accept the reason generally put forward for retaining it: that it was used throughout the Catholic world, promoting church unity.

'No matter where you travel you will be able to follow the Mass' was the mantra.

"Fat lot of use that is to me," Barney had often exclaimed. "I can't even follow the Latin Mass here in England - or Ireland! And how often am I going to be in Abyssinia, or Peru?"

Despite this, once he had made up his mind to volunteer for the priesthood he was determined to comply. For historical reasons in the Catholic Church to be a priest one had to understand Latin, to a reasonable degree.

When he had finally said goodbye to Joli, almost exactly at the three-and-a-half year recuperative deadline he had imagined, he had applied to the Westminster College for Late Vocations at Campion House, in the West of London.

He had felt particularly alone as he arrived at the seminary, much in advance of the appointed time, and as he sat on a park bench within the grounds, looking at the red brick college, he felt isolated, calm but determined, watching a small group of students a few hundred yards away, chatting and relaxed.

He was surprised when one of the distant figures detached himself from the group and walked towards him.

"Hello, are you waiting to see the boss?" the student asked. He looked to be in his mid twenties. Joe was touched by his concern

"Yes. I have an appointment with Fr. Tigar," Joe said. "I'm a bit early."

"You are O.K. then?" queried the student.

""Yes, fine," said Joe. "Good of you to come over."

"No problem. I just thought you might be lost."

"No. I'm fine. Not long to go now."

"Ok. I'd better get on then. Lecture coming up."

"Right. Thank you" said Joe. He knew he would never forget the young man's kindness.

A short time later Joe was ushered into the Director's office.

Fr Clement Tigar S.J. turned out to be a small, testy little man. He looked as if he was under pressure.

He scrutinised the letter and CV that Joe had written and then looked at him.

"How long since you masturbated?" he asked.

"Three months," Joe replied, not really put out by the frontal assault. He quite liked the directness. He accepted that a priest of the Catholic Church had to be celibate, and that meant no sex of any kind, even in thought.

Fr. Tigar looked again at the papers and said, "You are a disgrace to your father. You have wasted the time and money spent on your education."

Joe was stunned, in a remote kind of way. He did not reply.

Fr. Tigar continued in this vein for a further moment or two, Joe looking at him with growing amazement. The priest's abrupt approach began to seem less commendable. He made no enquiry about Joe's recent experiences, his personal development; showed no interest in what might have motivated Joe to think about the priesthood.

"You ought to be ashamed of yourself," continued the cleric. "I would not consider you as a student here."

Joe rose. "I'd better go then," he said.

"Yes. Go," said the crusty little priest, and Joe moved to the door, half stunned and half listening to a final fulmination.

"I would not consider you under any circumstance," were the last words Joe heard – and then, moving down the corridor, he could not be sure if he heard aright – "Unless you ...." something or other .... "in a year or two ..." and more words that Joe could not decipher.

"Unless *nothing!*" Joe said to himself. "If that's his way of putting me to a test he can *forget* about it!" He was beginning to react, with slow, deep indignation.

Under no circumstances would he ever participate in such childish psychological games, or accept such lack of courtesy. No way! *The* End! Westminster College for Late Vocations was definitely out.

Back at home Joe had no idea what to do. He would never return to Campion House. Who the devil did Fr. Tigar think he was? He had seen the priest's name on some Catholic Truth Society pamphlets, and presumably he must be respected. What Jesuit priest should not be?

But where was the marvellous sensitivity of Gerard Manley Hopkins' meditation on 'God's Grandeur'?

> *"The world is charged with the grandeur of God.*
> *It will flare out, like shining from shook foil;*
> *...... Oh morning, at the brown brink eastward,*
> *springs – Because the Holy Ghost over the bent*
> *World broods with warm breast and with ah!*
> *Bright wings."*

To Joe Fr. Tigar was one of the tired workers of the world that his fellow Jesuit depicted:

> *"Generations have trod, have trod, have trod;*
>   *And all is seared with trade; bleared, smeared with toil;"*

Tigar's heavy tread and toil was taking place in the vat of a pressurised ecclesiastical vineyard, squeezing out thinned down and bottled clerics – probably churning out priests with all thought and individuality squashed out of them, the chief product of their clerical education being an ingrained fear of offending 'authority'.

Joe did not like Fr. Tigar's attitude.

For a week or two he did not know what to do. He had broken off his relationship with Joli. There was no question of going back on that.

Then, in an edition of the Catholic Herald, he saw a small Ad:

St. Augustine's House, Walworth.
A Catholic Study House for Young Men in Business desirous of studying for the priesthood.

The wording was quaint. Joe was amused at 'desirous', but he thought he might as well investigate.

A week or so later he was interviewed by the parish priest of the Church of English Martyrs, Walworth, in the East End, not far from Labour Party Headquarters.

St. Augustine's House turned out to be a small residential house of studies in the Diocese of Southwark, located in an extended church presbytery. The parish priest was Canon Eugene Cottar, a fine looking old man with a ruddy face and a courteous, old-fashioned manner.

The interview took place in company with one of the curates, a Fr. Michael Bowen, who had the unglorified task of instructing young residents in Latin.

It went well and within a fortnight Joe found himself taking up residence, rather amazed and relieved that no accusations about his wasted youth had been forthcoming.

On the Saturday night he moved in Joe lay on a simple but comfortable bed in the House of Studies. As he fell asleep he thanked God for the change in his fortunes.

He wakened to the sound of loud voices and bottles smashing in the street outside. Saturday night people were making their way home after a refreshing night out in the local public houses.

What a way to celebrate the end of the working week! He felt regret, in a detached way, but was mostly grateful to God that he was safely tucked up in bed, embarking upon a course of action that would perhaps be more constructive than his own unruly past.

It emerged that a total of seven young men formed the student body of St. Augustine's House, all fine young fellows in their late teens or early twenties, with jobs in various parts of London.

Life proved to be much the same as the life he later discovered in the priory, except that after a half hour of prayer in the empty church before 7 a.m. Mass, followed by breakfast, all students went off to face a normal day of work.

Return via the District and Bakerloo Lines to Elephant & Castle station was followed by a meal prepared by the housekeeper for the seven students and four parish clergy.

Evening classes in Latin lasted for an hour-and-a-half, and at the end of each evening's formal study Fr. Bowen ordered all books to be closed and invited his pupils to engage in impromptu Latin conversation. Such periods were quite hilarious, and for the first time Joe began to realise that while the language was officially 'dead' one could actually use it to communicate. So much so that on his first summer holiday in the following year Joe was able to send a seaside postcard from County Down with a greeting that read

> 'Salvete omnes ex Hibernia. Hic volo.
> Sol fulgit et multum Guinnessium bibo'

which he hoped translated as

> 'Greetings to all from Ireland.
> Wish you were here.
> The sun shines and I drink much Guinness'

The card was a hit with the Canon, presumably because it demonstrated that Latin classes were reasonably effective, and also because, as Joe had begun to perceive, the Canon was slightly addicted to a wee drop of whiskey – which explained his ruddy complexion and veined nose.

Not that this detracted from the man himself, for he was a warm, kindly man, much loved by his parishioners.

He was, however, slightly irrational, as Joe discovered during dinner one evening, when all priests and students gathered round the large mahogany dining table, with the Canon in the chair at the top of the table, typically setting the agenda for that evening's table-talk.

"What do you think about this *'Lady Chatterly's Lover'* book?" he asked; the D.H. Lawrence book being much in the news because of the court case to decide whether it could be published in England.

Fr. Bowen, on his left, supping soup, tut-tutted something like, "O Dear me! Dear me!" smiled and lobbed the question to the student on his left, who muttered something condemnatory. And so it went round the table, all agreeing that a publication with graphic sexual content should not be tolerated, until the question arrived with Joe, sitting on the Canon's right.

"What do you think Mr. Coyle?" asked the Canon.

"Well," said Joe, aware of Fr. Bowen across the table putting a finger to his lips, indicating the need for caution.

But it was too late. Joe had already started, "I didn't think much of it as a book," he said, "not much life about it apart from the spicy bits! Not a great work of literature."

The Canon's face turned a reddish purple. His eyes opened wide and he stared in disbelief.

"You've *read* this book Mr. Coyle?"

"Yes," said Joe, "in an unexpurgated edition smuggled in from Sweden."

"*Mister Coyle!*" bellowed the Canon, bringing his fists down upon the polished wood of the dining table, on each side of his plate, setting cutlery jumping and jingling.

"*Mister Coyle! You're not a Christian!*" the Canon roared, fixing Joe with an incredulous glare.

"Of course - you were in the Merchant Navy," he exclaimed, "and I expect you were not as pure as you should be at that time!"

"True," said Joe. "But I have been forgiven...."

At this the Canon subsided, punctured by his basic Christian belief in forgiveness, and beyond him Joe could see Fr. Bowen raise his eyes to heaven, shaking his head. It was evident that Joe was not greatly valued for his diplomacy.

Subsequently the Canon tended to look at Joe with suspicion, but the Latin lessons continued.

It is also true to say that Joe, as he knocked on the Canon's door some days later and opened it to deliver a message, witnessed the priest caught up in a blossom of love, bowed over his desk in prayer and consumed by a holy fire that extended to Joe on the threshold, much to Joe's delight.

The Canon was a well tried, holy old man, with great faith in God and much love for God's people. In him a tiny *grah* for the whiskey was a small fault in a big man.

At the end of two years of study Joe and the rest took 'O' level Latin exams, and as far as Joe could ascertain all lads passed, at some level or other.

Joe's grade was very much in the middle, hence his concern about delivering a talk in Latin.

Mother of God! This would be a challenge!

12 Fieldmouse

Sunshine poured through the chapel windows to where Barney was squatting on the steps in front of the high altar, level with the rood screen, busily applying polish to a large number of brass candlesticks, spread out on newspaper.

Barney looked up and spotted a tiny fieldmouse sitting in the sunshine before the side altar on his right.

It appeared to be manicuring its forepaws, or perhaps chewing something. Barney looked at it, entranced by the beauty of the small body with its large ears.

The mouse was unaware of Barney.

After a moment Barney made a sound with lips and tongue, "Psst!"

The mouse took no notice. It carried on with the manicure.

Barney laughed at the sight.

Again he said "Psst!" and lifting a kneeling cushion he lobbed it in the direction of the creature. It took no notice.

Barney shouted "Hoy!" and the mouse paused and sat up straight.

Barney called out again, "Hoy! Mouse!" and lobbed another kneeling cushion in its general direction.

Fully alerted to danger the mouse took off at a run, Barney chasing it and laughing, lobbing kneeling cushions that were designed not to hit but to drive the tiny creature out of the church.

He succeeded, forcing it to streak out of the main entrance, leaving Barney at the entrance, smiling with delight and calling after it, "Watch out for that pussycat, Mouse."

13 Love Song

The church in twilight. The whole community stood in a single line in front of the rood screen, facing the altar.

In the body of the church a sprinkling of the regular congregation knelt in prayer.

The lay brothers and some of the novices, including Barney, held brass candlesticks, with candles alight.

Fr. Nick gave a slight nod to Bro. Barney, standing at the centre of the line, paired with Iggy.

Barney opened his mouth, nervously, to intone the opening words of the 'Salve Regina'. A low, strangled gurgle was the result and Barney flushed with embarrassment.

He opened his mouth again and this time emitted a high squeak. The candle he held wobbled and the novices nearby grinned.

He tried again, this time producing a high, shrill, note.

One or two novices giggled. Most of the priests smiled broadly.

Fr. Nick quietly intoned the correct note and Barney picked it up, managing to intone the required introduction.

The full community joined in, still half-smiling. In the candlelight beads of sweat trickled down Barney's brow.

Two-by-two the friars processed to Our Lady's altar, the hymn swelling and filling the church. The few faithful parishioners stood and joined in the singing. It was an impressive and moving ceremony: a love-song by candlelight.

Salve Regina, Mater Misericordiae,
Vita, dulcedo, et spes nostra,
Salve!
Ad te clamamus, exsules filii evae,
Ad te suspiramus, gementes et
flentes,
In hac lacrimarum valle.
Eia ergo, Advocata nostra,
Illos tuos misericordes oculos ad
nos converte
Et Jesum, benedictum fructum
ventris tui,
Nobis, post hoc exilium, ostende,
O clemens, O pia, O dulcis Virgo Maria

Barney knew the words by heart, and was easily able to translate:

Hail Holy Queen, Mother of mercy
Hail our life, our sweetness and our hope!
To thee do we cry, poor banished children of Eve,
To thee do we send up our sighs,
Mourning and weeping in this valley of tears.
Turn, then, o most gracious advocate,
Thine eyes of mercy and after this our exile
Show unto us the blessed fruit of thy womb, Jesus.
O clement, O loving, O sweet Virgin Mary.

The ceremony finished the friars begin the return procession to the high altar.

As the senior fathers passed Barney the sub-prior, Fr Sam, spiky black hair sticking up on his head and eyes glinting behind cheap round glasses, snuffled into a handkerchief, using it as concealment to lean towards Barney and mutter, "... and some make themselves eunuchs for the sake of the kingdom!"

Barney tried to avoid laughing out loud.
He loved the humour.

14 Cold Dawn

In the chill November morning a single electric bulb snapped on in the novitiate corridor, casting a faint light along its length. Knuckles rapped on Barney's door and a voice called out "Benedicamus domino!"

In virtual darkness Barney immediately whipped aside the bed covers and stood beside his bed as he sang out the response, "Deo gratias!"

Next door the knuckles rapped on another door and the same greeting was called, "Benedicamus domino!"

There was a silence, followed by a repeated greeting, slightly louder, "Benedicamus domino!"

Another rap and there came a sleepy mutter, "Deo ... grassias ..." Ignatius was awake.

Barney switched on the room light and poured water from the jug into the old fashioned china washbasin. The knocks and greetings were repeated, fading down the corridor.

Barney sluiced his face, dried his hands and face and pulled on the tunic of his habit. He had been sleeping in white shorts and singlet. He donned the scapular and cowl - the capula - and pulled it up to cover his head before going out to stand in the dimly lit corridor. The single bulb was the only thing keeping the intense early morning darkness at bay.

At intervals he was joined by brother novices, all bleary-eyed and shivering with cold, each engrossed in his own personal world.

The procession line formed, the novice who had been knocking on the doors intoned the opening antiphon of the morning processional prayer. As the brothers responded, alternating prayers and responses, the procession moved off, leaving the novitiate and winding its way down stairs and into the dark cloister, mediaeval hooded figures at the beginning of another day of prayer, as had thousands of brothers in hundreds of priory churches for more than seven hundred years.

Arrived at the church they bowed in pairs before Christ present in the tabernacle of the high altar and made their way to the choir stalls - where they were joined by lay-brothers and priests, entering quietly and singly, each bowing before the altar before taking his place.

A friar at the end of the choir stalls nearest the rood screen pulled a chord and curtains were drawn, separating the sanctuary from the body of the church.

Fr. Prior intoned the opening psalm and the singing of Matins commenced.

As they bowed during the psalms Barney's eyes strayed to the curtain and through a gap where the drapes had failed to meet he saw an elderly parishioner arrive, walking with the aid of a stick, and take a seat in the body of the church.

Breath from the mouths of the chanting friars hung in the freezing air. Again Barney's gaze strayed to the gap in the curtains, just in time to see another parishioner genuflect towards the hidden altar and kneel in prayer. Barney looked annoyed and distressed, and immediately Matins finished he reached over and pulled the curtain chord, opening the curtains abruptly.

The prior's eyebrows rose.

The community of brothers moved quietly from the stalls and spread throughout the dark church, pulling up hoods and huddling against the cold.

The only light came from the area around the high altar, just sufficient to show breath condensing, as friars and a small number of parishioners commenced the usual half-hour period of meditation.

At long last the prior rapped the wood of the choir-stall before him. Upon this signal he and the other priests got up and went into the sacristy to robe for the first Masses of the day.

Each priest was assisted by either a lay brother or a novice, who lit two candles at a side altar and accompanied a priest to it. Individual Masses began quietly.

The candles at each altar were the sole lights in the darkness and the silence was only faintly broken by murmured phrases and responses, and then the tiny tinkling of bells at uneven intervals as different celebrants arrived at the moment of consecration.

A small congregation of elderly people attended the Mass celebrated by the prior at the main altar, each intent upon the thanksgiving offering, devoutly receiving the body of Christ, lost in holy contemplation.

15   A Local Rule

"You cannot take the law into your own hands!" said the prior.

He was standing in his office, facing Barney, also standing. His face was stern.

"I know. But I simply could not bear seeing those elderly parishioners sitting out there on their own, cut off from us."

"I appreciate your motives - but it is not up to you to decide. It is simply a custom in this priory. The parishioners know it. They accept it."

"It's not a good custom - forgive me for arguing Father." Barney was anxious, "It separates the people from the brothers. It makes us look something special, and we are not. In God's sight we are all beggars - all imperfect."

The prior's face relented, and he smiled.

"Indeed – I agree. The curtain is only because of the fierce cold these winter mornings. I have to think of the brothers. It's hard enough for some of them - another of your fellow novices has just today decided he must leave."

Barney was distressed. "Oh - I am sorry. That's too bad."

He collected his thoughts. "I know you think me awkward Father. I really am sorry about that. I realise that the wind whistles into the altar from the rest of the church: but surely we can endure the same cold as those parishioners - especially the old ones who struggle up the hill to the church - on a morning like today?"

Fr. Prior stiffened again.

"I have to think of the welfare – every morning - of all the brothers of this community. Some of them are not as young and fit as you. I have to take this into account - and we simply cannot afford to heat the church, our income is so limited."

The prior's voice suddenly became full of kindness. "Look Barney, I know that your heart is in the right place. I know what you are saying. Please do not worry about it. The parishioners understand our situation. They have lived with it for many years. They contribute as much as they can. We do the best that we can – with contributions from our larger parishes and earnings from writings. We struggle on the best we can. We just put our trust in Our Lord. He will provide – but we are poor and we have to put up with it. Please accept the situation as it is: regard it as a cross to bear. We all have our difficulties, all have a cross."

He was deeply serious. "If we accept our difficulties and battle on, doing the best we can, things will resolve themselves – with God's help. We can't do anything about this problem just at the moment. Pray about it and accept it. Will you?"

"I suppose I have to Father." Barney was reluctant. He smiled wanly, "I just don't like it much. Please forgive me for annoying you. I know you have a lot on your plate. Thank you for seeing me."

As Barney opened the door to leave he glanced down and saw the prior's cigarette lighter and a couple of packets of Capstan in a rubbish bin. Unseen by the prior his intense face lit up. He went out and shut the door behind him.

16 Mouse Encore

In the early morning the friars ate thick hunks of brown bread and butter, washed down with mugs of tea from a large brown pot and coffee from a steaming urn.

Eating in silence the friars' heads were covered by their white hoods, each sitting in isolation at scrubbed tables bordering the rectangular refectory.

Just as he put a thick slice of brown bread into his mouth Barney looked up to see Fr Valentine's black cat at play with a dead fieldmouse in the centre of the tiled floor.

Bathed in early morning sunshine the cat, with a twist of its head, tossed the small corpse into the air and sprang after it, sliding on the red tiles as it re-enacted it's sporting kill.

Iggy and a few younger friars laughed quietly at the sight. An older friar smiled. Barney looked on, his face set hard as he remembered the beautiful little fieldmouse nibbling in front of the altar, and his laughing chase towards the church door.

Part of his mind appreciated the feline beauty and agility of the cat, but unable to endure the contrast with his memory Barney got up abruptly and strode towards it.

He prised the dead mouse from cat's claws and opening the window he dropped the tiny corpse into the field outside.

His fellow friars returned to eating without expression. Barney sat down to finish his breakfast, aware that he had interrupted a moment of enjoyment but deeply distressed at the death of the small mouse, whether it was the one in the chapel or not.

He bent over to keep his face half hidden by the white hood.

17   A Sorry Venia

Iggy burst into the novitiate recreation room, excited and spluttering. "I can do it at last! Come and see!"

The novices pressed to the door to see what was happening.

At the end of the long polished corridor, just outside the novitiate door, Iggy kissed his scapular and took off at a run.

Halfway along the corridor he took off in a diving venia, landing on the polished linoleum, hand still outstretched and gripping his scapular, face arranged in a seraphic caricature of supreme holiness and tranquillity.

He slid the remaining length of the corridor, smiling benevolently as his podgy body came to rest, just after he had banged into a prie-dieu set beneath a statue of the Virgin Mary at end of the corridor.

The bump dislodged the statue and as it wobbled and started to fall one of watching novices just managed to dive forward and catch the four-foot high plaster cast before it hit the floor.

Iggy's brother novices burst into howls of laughter and let a great, involuntary hurrah!

In the temporary silence that followed they heard the loud click of the novice master's door opening, and reacting like a flock of birds startled by gunshot escaped in all directions, diving for doorways and corridor corners, disappearing magically just as Fr. Nick came round the corner, expecting to find chaos.

All that he could see was a shining corridor and the statue of Our Lady mysteriously and inexplicably resting in solitary grandeur on the floor at the far end of the corridor, four feet below her normal level.

The corridor was empty of life, as the brothers shrank into doorways or quietly shut cell doors behind them.

Cautiously, unbelievingly, Fr. Nick moved forward, a half smile on his lips, wondering what work was at hand.

A shadow moved at one doorway and a novice gave a bark of laughter. This was too much for the rest and the loud laughter that had been cut short by the abrupt sound of Fr. Nick's door opening burst out with renewed vigour, until the novice who had first laughed dropped on the floor in a venia, followed by each of the novices, until the entire length of the corridor was occupied by nine prostrate bodies, each lying with one arm outstretched, gripping the end of a scapular.

Fr. Nick could not help but smile at the backs of the prostrate figures, but immediately assumed a stern expression.

He glanced at a large clock on the corridor wall. Its arms indicated exactly 2 o'clock.

He turned and walked quietly back to his room, went in and shut the door.

The novices remained on the floor.

Eventually Barney turned his head and looked at Bert, enquiry in his eyes. Bert managed to shrug his shoulders and both returned to looking blankly at the linoleum.

It seemed an age before they heard the sound of the novice master's door opening once more, and Fr. Nick returned. He looked at the clock. The hands showed five past two.

He clapped his hands together as sign that he accepted the apology, and all the novices rose, smiling sheepishly – all except Iggy, who lay spread-eagled near the statue of Our Lady.

Fr. Nick walked towards him, and as he did so there came the sound of a snore, echoed by a single high pitched shriek of laughter from one of the brothers, quickly snuffed out.

Arrived beside the sleeping figure Fr Nick pushed Iggy's shoulder gently with his foot.

Iggy blinked and woke with a start, looking up with unfocused eyes.

"Wakey, wakey Brother Ignatius," said Fr. Nick. "Kindly put Our Lady back where she belongs!"

Iggy scrambled to his feet and did so, face red and embarrassed. He then turned and prostrated himself at Fr. Nick's feet in an impeccable venia.

Fr. Nick, once more smiling broadly, clapped his hands and said, "A very good venia Brother. A distinct improvement!"

Loud laughter erupted from the other brothers, who then started to make further apologetic venias.

Fr. Nick held up his hands to stop them - horrified at the escalation. "Enough! Enough!" and he retreated once more to his room, firmly shutting the door.

In the corridor, silently drifting back to the recreation room, the novices heard a loud burst of laughter from behind Fr. Nick's closed door.

They smiled at each other.

18 Chapter

The entire community was assembled in the Chapter Room, each friar formally dressed in black cloak and cappa, sitting on the continuous wooden benching fixed to the perimeter walls of the room.

The black and white floor tiles seemed to echo the Dominican theme.

Fr. Prior sat in the middle of a row of senior friars.

He had been talking about practical matters within the community, and coming to a conclusion he said seriously, "So we must economise as much as possible: particularly on heating and electricity. We have to be as self-sufficient as possible. We must not waste our slender resources."

He continued with a smile, "The only thing I can say with great certainty is that we will not starve! We have Our Lord's word for that! Just be as economical as possible."

"Now, to other matters: Proclamations?"

After a moment's hesitation a grizzle headed friar rose and stepped forward.

"I proclaim myself for keeping the light on after magnum silencium on a number of occasions." He kissed his scapular and made a venia.

"Fr. Francis," said the Prior, "I know that you are engaged in vital study, but please do control it. Questions about the morality of embryo research are of great importance, but we must not be carried away by our desire to solve such problems immediately. In God's good time your research will bear fruit. We must all control our desires – even for a good thing."

He clapped his hands and Fr. Francis got to his feet.

A small lay brother, Bro. Giles, with a distinctly humped back, stepped forward.

"I proclaim myself for breaking the rule of silence," and then very quietly and in a rush, his face flushed with embarrassment, as if seeking to avoid the words being heard, "and of spending too much time reading cowboy stories." There were smiles all round as he did a venia.

"An understandable addiction Brother Giles," said the Prior. "You know what to do about it. Restrict yourself to one book per week."

He clapped his hands, and as Bro. Giles arose he said, "I recommend you broaden your reading: some Dick Francis perhaps – and Black Beauty. Then try something different: Helen Waddell's 'Heloise & Abelard' for example. A truly wonderful story - if you can fit it in."

Bro. Edward then stepped forward, his face red.

"I proclaim myself for breaking the silence and ...," with a rush of words, "... telling stories."

He prostrated his large frame in a venia.

Fr. Prior cast his eyes up to heaven.

"You really must control yourself Brother. There is no need to ask what kind of stories you have been telling."

At this Bro. Barney rose from his seat, his face flaming. He was very nervous.

"I proclaim myself for listening to Brother Edward's jo....stories," and on the side of the room opposite to where Bro. Edward lay he made a venia.

Fr. Prior spoke in good hearted exasperation.

"You see the effect you have on the community Brother Edward. It must stop. At least confine your jokes to recreation periods - and keep them tasteful - clean I mean!"

The rest of the community smiled broadly. The Prior clapped his hands and the two brothers rose sheepishly.

Fr. Prior appeared to be lost in thought for a moment, then, coming to a decision, he rose and stepped forward.

"I proclaim myself for listening to one of Bro. Edward's jokes..."

The smiles grew broader and the prior's face turned red as he growled, "... the one about the young lady and the cat."

He did a venia - much to amusement of all.

The sub-prior clapped his hands and the prior rose.

"You see what you are responsible for brother!"

Bro. Edward nodded in a half-bow – apology writ large on his face.

"Right! Enough of this Tom and Jerry show! - Father!" The Prior looked invitingly towards Fr. Nick and sat down in his place on the bench.

Fr. Nick nodded to Brother Barnabas who got to his feet once more. His face was still red and he nervously clutched a piece of paper, written on both sides.

Barney cleared his throat and tried to ignore the faces of the community, all looking towards him expectantly.

He began his dissertation quietly
"In nomine Patri, Filii et Spiriti Sancti."
In the name of the Father, the Son and the Holy Spirit.
He blessed himself and paused.
"Patres venerabiles. Fratri carissimi.
Venerable Fathers. Dear Brothers.
Opus non vobis dicere ego precem magnam dicesse.
It is not necessary to tell you that I have just said a great prayer.
De mysteribus dei patri, dei filii et dei sancti - interior natura dei interest.
It concerns the mystery of God the Father, God the Son and God the Holy Spirit - the inner being of God,

Unum sed Trinitas.
One but a Trinity.

De hoc Jesu solus narrare possest.
Jesus alone can tell us about this.
De hoc alius modus nescimus.
We cannot know of this in any other way.
Quando Jesu dixit, 'ego et pater unum sumus' -
When Jesus says, 'I and the father are one'

Barney looked around. He was beginning to get into his stride, forgetting his nervousness.
- et 'qui me vidit patrem vidit' – deus indicat."
and 'who sees me sees the Father' - he is indicating that he is God.

Barney made a long pause and looked around,
"Homo vere sed etiam deus esse."
Really a man but also God.
" 'Atendate,' Jesu inquit."
'Look to me,' he is saying.

Barney touched his own breast with both hands, one clutching the sheet of paper. He was passionately involved in the thoughts behind the words he uttered; obviously knew them by heart, for he had forgotten about reading the words written on the paper.
" 'In nomen meo petite, et accipiebitis'.
Ask in my name, and you will receive.
Jesu pater eique spiritum sanctum nos succurre mittebit:
Jesus and his father will send their holy spirit to help us:
In primo credite Jesu Patreque unum esse deus,
first to believe that Jesus and the Father are God,
secundo si paenitet nobis servabimur."
and second that we may repent and be saved.

He paused once more,
"Nisi spiritus sanctus mentes nostros illuminat credire non potest.
Unless the Holy Spirit enlightens our minds it is not possible to believe.
Facilitatem nobis 'Abba' clamare hic spiritus dat.
It is this spirit who enables us to cry out "Father".

Facilitatem nobis Christum vere deum hominemque cognoscere hic spiritus dat".
It is this spirit who enables us to recognise that Christ is true man and true god.

Barney paused and began to look more relaxed. He spoke more informally as he began to express the reality of his personal thoughts.

"In mente meo imaginem habeo – de anus exclamante in turba,
In my mind I have an image - of an old woman in a crowd crying out,

'Beatus venter qui te porterant et ubera quae suxisti,'
'Blessed is the womb that bore you, the breasts that you sucked,'

et Jesu ad eam vertens, adrisit dicitque -
and Jesus turning to smile at her and saying,

Barney himself began to smile, caught up in the scene he imagined,

- 'Qummo beati qui audient verbum dei, et custodiunt ille.'"
'Even more blessed are those who hear the word of god and keep it.'

Itaque nos -
So we,

Barney touched his breast again and his voice and manner expressed incredulity.

- bimpii imparesque nihilominus tamen beatores quam beatae Mariae, mater Jesu!
sinful and inadequate, are more blessed than Mary, the mother of Jesus!

Mater dei incarnati!"
the mother of God incarnate!

Again there was a note of incredulity.

"Jesu dixit! Vere est!
Jesus says it! It is true!

Totus humanitas -
All humanity,

Barney spread his hands wide

- cum Maria matro Christi, deo incarnato, inclusus - propter sum filium beatus est.
including Mary the mother of Christ, God incarnate - is blessed on account of her son.
Beati sumus est per fidem in Jesu,
We are blessed through faith in Jesus,
fidem quam ipse solus dare potest.
the faith that he alone can give
Liberamus per spiriti sancti."
we are saved through the holy spirit.

    Barney paused to deliver the final words of his talk.
"Est haec fides quae scientiam de patro, filio, et spirito sancto apportat.
It is this faith that brings knowledge of the Father, Son and Holy Spirit.
Haec est vita aeterna: deum patrem cognoscere et amare, in persona Christo, per donum spiriti sancti.
This is eternal life: to know God and to love Him, in the person of Christ, through the gift of the Holy Spirit.
Laud Jesus Christum, qui libere nobis dat societatem vita divina sua propiae!
Praise Jesus Christ, who freely gives us participation in his own divine life!
Adiuva nos, domine, ut in spirito sancto crederemus et viveremus.
Lord, help us to believe and live in your spirit.
Amen."
Let it be so.

    Barney bowed to the prior and backed into his allotted place to sit down.

The prior stood, beaming approval,
"Amen. Gratia tibi Fratro Barnabas.
It is so. Thank you Brother Barnabas.

Bene! Ex tiro orationem meliorem raro audivi.
Well done! I have rarely heard a better oration from a novice.

Tempus tuus cum –
Your time with -
- he paused to search for a phrase and continued whimsically -
'Collegio Catholico Testimonium'
the Catholic Evidence Guild
bene actum est."
has been well spent.
He looked around.
"Fratres, accipite bonum verbum.
Brothers, receive the good word.
Haec res in meditationibus nostris memorare debemus."
We ought to call to mind these things in our meditations.

    He began to speak in English. "And now dear Brothers we must to our duties."

    He shivered, rubbed his hands together, and as he turned his head he saw that in the deepening winter darkness a steady fall of snow formed an almost opaque curtain beyond the tall arched windows,

    "Nives hiemis accident!" he exclaimed.
    The snows of winter are upon us!
    "In nomini patri, filii et spiriti sancti!"
    He continued with a final prayer and blessing as all eyes focused on the thickly falling snow.

19 Winter Beauty

The priory and surrounding countryside were embedded in winter snow. The novices trekked along a narrow path at the side of the frozen lake, snow falling from branches onto black cloaks and hoods as they walked in single file.

Arrived at a spot giving access to the lake the brothers rushed for the ice with whoops and shouts and began to create a slide - lining up and running in the same spot until the surface snow was removed.

Iggy put on pair of ancient skates and wobbled about the ice.

"After you with the skates Iggy!" Barney called.

"Right! You can have 'em now. I don't think I'll ever get the hang of this," said Iggy, sitting down on the edge of what looked to be a snow covered boat, wedged in the ice. He began to unlace the skates and as he looked up he exclaimed, "Hey brothers! Do you see what I see?"

Further up the lake, a few hundred yards away, a flock of nuns from a nearby Convent, eight in all, clad in black, with small black bonnets trimmed in white, made their way out onto the ice. All were on skates. The brothers watched with interest.

"Why are the bunnies - the nuns – so well organised?" asked one of the novices. "Every last one of them has a pair of skates! – and this is all we have between . . . how many of us?"

Iggy tossed the skates to Barney, who started to put them on, nodding his head in the direction of each brother, "One, two, three, four, five....seven! Where's Paul and Terence? Nine if they were here."

"How do they do it?" The novice who had asked the question looked again at the nuns.

"Better at the housekeeping!" said Iggy, "Did you ever see a convent that wasn't spick and span, shining?"

He looked around. "Where are Paul and Terry by the way?"

"Left," said Bert abruptly.

Barney stopped lacing the boots.

"What! Left!"

"Afraid so, "said Bert, "Fr. Nick asked me to pass it on. Was waiting a suitable moment."

"Oh God! Did he say why?" Barney was clearly distressed.

"Just that they were finding it a bit tough. They each came to him independently."

"Too bad," said Barney, resuming his lacing of the boots. "Five down and seven to go! Did you ever get the feeling that you were next on the list?"

Bert and Iggy shook their heads, looking at him seriously.

"Only joking fellows. Watch this!"

He rose from the snow and struck out, wobbled a few times before settling down to a flowing skating action, leaning forward, his black cloak flowing behind.

He sped past the skating nuns and Iggy and Bert raced up the snow-covered bank to keep him in sight.

"There he is!" cried Iggy, and seen from afar his tiny, solitary figure sped across the lake, against a backdrop of trees and snow.

Then in the distance they saw his feet go from under him and his cloaked figure slide face down across the ice. They burst into loud hurrahs and laughs, jumping up and down.

"Serves the bugger right! Show off!" said Bert, laughing delightedly, and they slid down the snow bank to the lakeside, to where a few moments later Barney skated up, wobbling, a shame-faced grin on his face and frozen snow stuck to the front of his habit.

"That was great!" he said.

"Not from where we were standing," said Bert.

"Well, not bad for a fellow who hasn't seen a skate for twelve years! Great fun!"

"Brothers!" said Iggy, "we'd better get back! It's beginning to get dark."

As they reluctantly made their way back down the narrow lakeside path they heard the happy chatter of female voices, which died out as a double file of fresh faced young nuns caught sight of the brothers.

Each of the nuns carried skates, and the friars stood back along the edge of the path to allow the now silent nuns to pass.

In the fading light the faces of all of the young nuns, flushed with exertion, look beautiful and happy.

The friars and the nuns bowed slightly to each other as they filed past.

Ignatius was the only brother who spoke, "Good evening Sisters."

A single nun replied, "Good evening Brothers."

No one else spoke, but there was a smiling greeting on all faces, dimly seen in the fading light of the cold winter evening.

The friars resumed their trek in silence, each lost in his own thoughts.

20 A Hard Winter

"Benedicamus Domino," a voice called out as knuckles rapped on Barney's door.

Inside Barney struggled to become awake and slowly sat up, yawning and leaning on an elbow, half awake.

"Deo gratias," he proclaimed, his voice slow and devoid of energy, his expression empty.

Slowly he pulled aside the bedclothes and as morning greetings continued along the corridor he stretched, yawned, rubbed his back, shivered and slowly eased his feet out of the bed, standing upright and forcing himself into the normal routine by an act of will.

Outside in the corridor the novices lined up. No greetings passed between them. They stood in exhausted silence, hoods up, waiting for the first line of the antiphonal processional prayer to be intoned. It came and they moved off, heads bent forward and shrouded against the cold in the folds of cappa and cloak.

There were only six novices in the procession.

****

In driving snow Barney and Bert scraped snow aside and began to shovel coke into the boilerhouse. Their faces were grim.

They did not speak, and as Barney opened the boiler fire door he shivered and moved closer to the heat.

For a moment he hugged himself and then started to shovel coke into the fire.

Bert stood propped against boiler-house door, his head back against the door jamb, eyes closed, shovel resting on the ground, handle gripped in both hands.

As door of furnace clanged shut he turned with a wan smile to Barney, pushed himself upright, and deposited his shovel inside the doorway. Barney placed his alongside.

When Barney came out he closed and bolted the door and they walked past the snow-covered mountain of coke and plodded wearily across the yard, passing under a lean-to roof that abutted the kitchen, where two bedraggled tramps, each huddled in layers of overcoats, with scarves tied over their hats, hungrily devoured bowls of steaming hot food.

As they passed the tramps Barney looked at Bert and the tramps and muttered softly, "It's a great life!"

Bert rolled his eyes heaven-wards and the two tramps, wolfing into bowls of broth and potatoes, looked curiously over the rims of their bowls at the two friars.

"Good evening men," said Barney as he pushed open the kitchen door and passed out of the gloom into the light and heat of the kitchen.

****

Fr. Nick, at the head of the long table in the novitiate recreation room, outlined how the Rule of the Order had developed in the 13th century from the Rule of St Augustine , where all were to '*live together in oneness of mind and heart, mutually honouring God in yourselves, whose temples you have become*', and how every detail of dress and behaviour had been specified, firstly under the leadership of St. Dominic, born in 1170, and then, following his death in 1221, by Blessed Jordan, who was elected Master of the Order.

"The Rule is not the be-all and end-all of the Order," said Fr. Nick. "It only defines how daily community life is to be lived. The Order was initially founded by St. Dominic to combat the widespread Cathar heresy in Southern France, duplicated by the Albigensians in Italy, who taught that only the spirit is good, that the body is evil – to the extent that suicide was approved in principle."

"The popes at the time did not quite know how to handle the situation, and following the murder of a papal legate Innocent III appealed to the civil rulers to help stamp out a pernicious and growing sect. Things then got out of hand, with violence and murder directed by the nobles and kings, involving frenzied local mobs."

"Dominic advocated conversion by preaching and example, saying about the heretics that

'It is not by the display of power and pomp, cavalcades of retainers, and richly-houseled palfreys, or by gorgeous apparel, that the heretics win proselytes; it is by zealous preaching, by apostolic humility, by austerity, by seeming, it is true, but by seeming holiness. Zeal must be met by zeal, humility by humility, false sanctity by real sanctity, preaching falsehood by preaching truth.' **12**

And this is still what we are about, preaching truth insofar as we can understand it, and studying so that we may arrive at an understanding of what is true."

The remaining six novices had notebooks and pens at the ready but they did not take any notes. There would be no exam at the end of the year. They would be expected to become familiar with the Rule by living it.

****

The snow had started to fall at Christmas and from that moment continued to form deep drifts throughout the countryside. The temperature dropped to a permanent zero, so that the snow covered trees and hedgerows were wedded to the frozen ground, almost indistinguishable from the snow covered earth.

Here and there, where stormy winds whipped off the white cladding, a black tree emerged, like a weird multi pronged hand or periscope from the submerged and dying world below, seeking to grab air and vision. The short daylight hours with dark skies were almost inseparable from the winter darkness of night, and day after day passed in isolated, unchanging quiet, only disturbed by wild snow storms that battered the buried land.

News filtered through from the outside world, conveyed to the novices by the priests, that temperatures were the lowest recorded since 1740, that villages and towns were isolated, cut off by snow drifts that in places were up to eighteen feet deep.

For the novices the world of prayer and work continued in the same pattern, serving in the refectory, working in the kitchen and periodically shovelling coke during the day, in an unceasing effort to create heat - without success, for the rooms of the friary remained permanently as cold as the world outside, the inefficient boiler totally inadequate for its purpose. In the church, the voices of the friars at prayer echoed from frozen stone walls, as if the space they enclosed had been turned into an empty, icy drum.

Another novice left the petrified friary, and the work load of the remaining brothers increased.

Despite this the normal routine continued, even down to the regular weekend exercise trek, whereby the remaining five novices were required to go for a long walk, usually as far as five miles but sometimes to the Severn estuary and back, double this distance.

On one such evening, returning in darkness from the flat elevated level of Minchinhampton Common, caught up in a sudden wild flurry of snow, with winds of gale force hammering against tired bodies, Barney had an unusual experience that later he tried to relate to the brothers.

As they leaned into the wind, striving to protect themselves from the cold, swirling blasts, Barney felt himself suddenly removed from the intense fury of the storm.

He remained aware of the noise and din, aware of his struggles to remain upright, and of his brothers as they leant into the wind, but he was experiencing all of these elements directly, as if disembodied, looking at the essence of reality as if he were pure mind, pure spirit, not directly battered by the elements but aware of them as if from a comfort zone, removed from the physical reality but seeing into its core reality.

It was an odd experience, and although he realised it was probably caused by a unique combination of wind and weather acting upon his body he was deeply aware that this was how physical reality might appear to a disembodied spirit, remote and protected, but intensely aware of and directly understanding the essential nature of the physical world.

The experience lasted only a few minutes, and then he was back to being buffeted by the swirling snow and wind, trudging down the steep incline to the priory, at the end of the obligatory walk in the cold, deserted whiteness – a leaden sky above and the deep darkness of night descending. There was no sliding or skating as at the outset of the cold weather, just a determined trudge in the darkness, sheltering as much as possible beneath cowls and capes against the flailing snow, no communication possible.

As they entered the priory through the kitchen door, stamping their feet and shaking their cloaks to dislodge the snow, Bro. Edward lifted his head from the kitchen bench where he was working, his face ruddy and cheerful.

"Ah, look at what we have here. The last of the twelve dwarves – and every one of them Grumpy!"

The brothers manage to raise a wan smile as they continued through the kitchen, and as they disappeared Bro. Edward's cheerfulness was replaced by a look of concern.

"Bloody winter!" he muttered to himself, and he lifted a machete-like like meat cleaver and cut through ribs of beef with a strong blow. "Hard on them!"

****

As the brothers gathered round the fire in the novitiate recreation room Barney tried to describe this second out-of-the body experience.

Iggy said enviously, "God, how I would like to experience the world like that!"

"Yeah," said Barney. "If that is what it is like to know the world outside of the body, without a body I mean, it would be a marvellous way to know things."

They talked no more about it, knowing that they still faced the ordinary world of shovelling coke and washing dishes.

They were simply too weary for conversation.

21 A Frozen Traveller

Barney was working alone in the kitchen, cleaning after the evening meal, wearing a white apron wrapped and tied round his waist.

There was a loud knock on the hatchway beside the back door and he opened it, sending light flooding into the darkness. The startled eyes of a man, blinking in the sudden light, looked at him over a red nose. He had black curly hair, heavily flecked with snow and was silhouetted against the diminishing coke mountain.

"Hello," said Barney. "What can we do for you?"

"They said down in the village that I might get something t'eat 'ere." The man spoke with a soft West-Country accent.

"My God but you look cold," Barney exclaimed, reaching for a pot and ladling a large helping of stew into it.

The man was wearing only a light suit, with the collar turned up for protection. He rubbed his hands and blew into them. "Aye, it's pretty parky out t'nite."

The man was shivering, petrified with cold.

Barney put the pot on a ring of the cooker and exclaimed, "You don't mean to say you are walking in this weather!"

The traveller stamped his feet and flapped his arms against his body to generate heat. "Yah. Got t'get to Lunn'on."

"Where have you come from?"

"Bristol," said the traveller.

"You've walked all that way!" Barney was appalled.

"Nuthin' else I can do." The traveller smiled weakly, almost apologetically.

"That's dreadful," said Barney. He was deeply disturbed. "Right. Here we are. This should be warm enough now," and he took the pot off the stove, poured the thick steaming stew into a bowl and handed it through the hatch to the man, along with a spoon taken from a wooden cutlery container.

The man seized the bowl gratefully and began to wolf the stew down.

Barney looked at him again, taking in the light suit. "Have you no overcoat?"

"No," said the traveller, pausing briefly between spoonfuls.

Barney came to a decision. "Hold on there," he said and he half ran to the kitchen door that led to the cloister, peered out and saw that there was nobody about, and then sprinted on tiptoe to the stairs leading to the novitiate.

Arrived there he moved quietly to his room and opened the metal trunk, searched through it till he found a thick jersey, took it out and ran quickly and quietly back the way he had come, arriving breathlessly at the kitchen hatch and thrust the garment through as if getting rid of something stolen.

"Here! Take this! I haven't got an overcoat. It's a jersey. It'll help to keep the cold out."

The man stopped shovelling food from the bowl into his mouth and held out a hand, still chewing.

He looked rather bewildered as he swallowed. "Is this yers?"

"Yes, aye - I have two. I won't miss it. Take it now - and don't tell anyone I gave it to you. We're not supposed to give things away, in case we clean the place out - but I haven't taken vows yet, so it's O.K." He smiled with delight at the thought of the escape clause.

The traveller looked undecided, "Ye'r sure?"

"Certain. I'll never miss it."

The man looked unbelievingly at the jersey. "Grait! It'll certainly 'elp."

He put the bowl down and took off the jacket of his suit, slipped the thick polo neck sweater over his head and put his jacket on again.

"Tha's grait!" he beamed, running his hands down the front of the jersey with pleasure.

"Don't tell anyone where you got it," said Barney, "I could get into trouble."

The traveller's delight began to fade. "I dun want to cause no trouble..."

"No, no. There won't be. I swear. It's mine – until I take vows. You take it. I won't miss it, I swear. Will you have another bowl of stew?"

Convinced, the traveller relaxed and his face began to beam again, "Tha' would be grait!"

Barney took his bowl and refilled it. "Look. I have to go. I have Study. Will you be alright?"

"Sure. You're a grait lad. Thanks very much."

"Not at all. It's what we're here for. Just don't tell anybody where you got it. Okay?"

"No trouble, thanks again."

"Right. I'll be seein' you. Must go. Good luck!"

And as the man waved the spoon at him he drew the hatch door shut, cutting off the sight of man's beaming, chewing face.

"Jesus," said Barney, "I'll get myself into trouble!" and he took the apron off and stealthily slipped out of the kitchen.

22 Crown of Thorns

Fr. Martin, pale and severe of face, stood motionless, fully robed for Mass, hands joined in a stiff steeple of prayer, apparently absorbed in the white winter scene beyond the diamond shaped patterns of the sacristy window.

Barney stood silently behind and to one side of him, separate plumes of condensing air spearing out into the bitter cold as they breathed, blossoming out briefly before disappearing as they were absorbed and chilled by the air.

Barney swayed slightly, and for a moment caught the edge of the robing bench for support, before thrusting himself upright once more.

His face was pale and expressionless, head bowed over clasped hands.

Suddenly the priest moved, inclining his head to a crucifix on the bench before him. Barney started and belatedly did likewise.

The priest arrived at the entrance to the church before Barney and stood to allow Barney to slip apologetically past him.

They moved into the church, Barney walking with shoulders hunched forward. He swayed again - only a fraction, then righted himself purposefully. His eyes were dark in the white face, so tired that he looked as if he was not really present, not completely in touch with the chilled world.

Arrived before the high altar they bowed deeply.

Apart from the celebrant and his server the church was completely deserted, a consequence of the bitter weather.

Leaving the chalice on the altar Fr. Martin returned to the foot of the altar and bowing again he blessed himself and began the opening prayers briskly,

"Gloria Patri, et Filio, et Spiritui Sancto."
- *Glory be to the father and the Son and the Holy Spirit."*

"Sicut erat in . . ." Barney seemed to have difficulty in remembering the response.

His voice failed and Fr. Martin, his lips thin with annoyance, completed Barney's response*: ". . . principo, et nunc, et semper: et in saecula saeculorum. Amen.*
- *as it was in the beginning, is now, and ever shall be, world without end.*

Introibo ad altare dei," intoned the priest, and waited for Barney's response.

None came and he repeated the invocation,

"Introibo ad altare Dei . . ."
- *I will enter the altar of God.*

He looked sideways at Barney, waiting for the response, but Barney, head down as if he was under a great burden, seemed unaware that any reaction was required.

". . . Ad Deum qui laetificat juventutem meam," snapped the priest, totally exasperated.

- *to God who gives joy to my youth ....*

"Brother!" he snapped again, in an effort to get through to Barney, and as he turned his head in a fleeting moment of anger he saw that upon Bro. Barney's bent head rested a crown of thorns.

Below the crown Barney's face was ice white.

He lifted his head and looked directly at Fr. Martin, death and sorrow in his eyes.

The crown of thorns vanished.

Fr. Martin turned to the altar and looked at the figure of the Christ on the crucifix before him, his eyes wide in horror and self-reproach.

He struck his breast and murmured, "Mea culpa!" with real contrition.

In a new tone he proceeded with confession before Mass,
"Confiteor Deo omnipotenti, beatae Mariae semper Virgini,
I confess to God Almighty, blessed Mary ever virgin,
beato Michaeli Archangelo, beato Joanni Baptistae,
blessed Michael the archangel, blessed John the Baptist
sanctis Apostolis Petro et Paulo, omnibus Sanctis,
the holy apostles Peter and Paul, and all the saints
and turning towards Barney,
et vobis fratres: quia peccavi nimis cogitatione, verbo et opere;
and you brothers: that I have sinned in thought, word and deed;
- and he slowly and earnestly beat his breast three times as he said, more earnestly than perhaps he had ever done in his life,
mea culpa, mea culpa, mea maxima culpa.
Through my fault, through my fault, through my most grievous fault.

Ideo precor beatam Mariam simper Virginem,
Therefore I pray to Blessed Mary ever virgin
beatum Michaelem Archangelum,
Blessed Michael the Archangel
beatum Joannem Baptistam,
Blessed John the Baptist,
sanctos Apostolos Petrum et Paulum, omnes sanctos,
the holy Apostles Peter and Pau, and all the saints
et vos fratres,
and you brothers - bowing towards Barney -
orare pro me ad Dominum Deum nostrum.
Pray for me to the Lord our God.

By the time he had finished this prayer Barney had recovered somewhat and was able in his turn to repeat the formal act of confession, and then sit while Fr. Martin read the first Lesson, a reading from the first letter of St. Paul to the Corinthians, his voice echoing from the walls of the empty church,

> *"Didn't you realise that you were God's temple and that the spirit of God was living among you? If anybody should destroy the temple of God, God will destroy him, because the temple of God is sacred, and you are that temple."*

Had he been more alert, on another occasion, Barney might have thought that to read the word of God to people who were not there to listen could be considered a waste of time. At this moment he was content to listen to the Word, in preparation for the great sacrifice of the Eucharist.

> *"Make no mistake about it: if any one of you thinks of himself as wise, in the ordinary sense of the word, then he must learn to be a fool before he really can be wise. Why? Because the wisdom of this world is foolishness to God. As scripture says: The Lord knows wise men's thoughts: he knows how useless they are; or again: God is not convinced by the arguments of the wise. So there is nothing to boast about in anything human."*

More exhausted than he had ever been in his twenty-eight years of life, Barney felt that he had little to boast about.

23   Easter

The snows and freezing temperatures that had arrived so suddenly at Christmas departed with equal suddenness, on March 6th.

The transition in the South West of England, the worst hit area, was remarkable. Temperatures rose almost immediately to the norm for the time of year, the snow melted and disappeared within days, and within a further week nature seemed to be back to something like a normal schedule, so that people who had been surviving in a cold world of physical and mental isolation were suddenly released from a burden that had seemed would never end.

Now, on the Sunday following the first full moon after the spring equinox, in the complicated way that the Church had established the Easter date at the council of Nicaea in AD 325, the Feast of the Resurrection had arrived

In the darkness of the vigil night a new fire burned in a brazier in the church porch. There was no other light. Only the prior's face and the chest area and sleeves of his priestly garb were illuminated by the light of the fire, as he read from a large book held by Brother Ignatius.

Also in the darkness, like druidic shadows, were deacon and sub-deacon, two priests of the community, clad like the prior in flowing golden robes that faintly reflected the flames of the fire.

Nearby stood Brother Albert, holding a large candle, some five feet tall and about five inches in diameter. Also in the group was Brother Barney, holding a holy water vessel and a sprinkler.

The prior read in a loud, clear voice,

"Dear friends in Christ, on this most holy night, when our lord Jesus passed from death to life, the

church invites her children throughout the world to come together in vigil and prayer. This is the Passover of the Lord: if we honour the memory of his death and resurrection by hearing his word and celebrating his mysteries, then we may be confident that we will share his victory over death and live with him for ever in God."

He paused and taking the holy water from Barney he sprinkled it over the fire.

"Let us pray," he continued,

Father, we share in the light of your glory through your Son, the light of the world. Make this new fire holy,

He made the sign of the cross over the brazier.

and inflame us with new hope. Purify our minds by this Easter celebration and bring us one day to the feast of eternal light.
We ask this through Christ Our Lord.

"Amen," said all those who stood by, and Albert brought the candle forward and handed a stylus to the prior, who cut a cross in the wax and carved the Greek letters alpha above it, and omega below.

Christ yesterday and today, the beginning and the end, alpha and omega. All time belongs to him, and all the ages. To him be glory and power through every age for ever.
Amen.

The prior then lit the candle from the fire, saying, "May the light of Christ, rising in glory, dispel the darkness of our hearts and minds."

The Deacon took the candle, held it aloft and chanted

Lumen Christi!
Christ our light!

From within the church the congregation, quiet till then, chanted in response,

Deo gratias.

The deacon then led the procession into the church, which was in total darkness, paused halfway up the aisle and chanted again, on a slightly higher note, with the candle held higher:

> *Lumen Christi!*

And the congregation responded on an equally high note,

> ***Deo gratias.***

The novices and lay brothers lit tapers from the large candle and dispersed throughout church, lighting candles held by the congregation, and the procession continued to the high altar, where, as the congregation held their candles aloft, bringing light to the whole church, one could see that it was packed with worshippers.

At the high altar the deacon lifted the large candle and sang out on high, exultant note:

> ***Lumen Christi!***

and the congregation, equally exultant, responded with a final ***Deo gratias!***

All the lights in the church were suddenly switched on and the deacon began to sing, with swelling, heartfelt sincerity,

Gloria in excelsis deo
> *Glory to God in the highest*

immediately joined by the congregation on the second line of the glorious hymn of praise, with the church bells beginning to ring out in joyful celebration,

Et in terra pax hominibus bonae voluntatis.
> *And on earth peace to men of good will*

Laudamus te. Benedicimus te. Adoramus te.
> *We praise you. We bless you. We adore you.*

Glorificamus te …
> *We give you glory ……*

… tu solus Sanctus. Tu solus Dominus.
> *You alone are Holy. You alone are the Lord.*

To solus Altissimus, Jesu Christe.
> *You alone are the Most High, Jesus Christ.*

Cum Sancto Spiritu in gloria Dei Patris.
> *With the Holy Spirit in the glory of God the Father*

The sound of singing and bell chimes swelled to a crescendo of praise and thanksgiving.

"You have mourned for Christ's sufferings," said the Prior. "Now you celebrate the joy of his resurrection. May you come with joy to the feast that lasts for ever."

"This is the Lamb of God who takes away the sins of the world. Happy are those who are called to his supper".

24 Visitors

Black shoes clattered along the cloister, and Bro. Barney burst out of the front door of the priory, robes fluttering and face alight with pleasure as he greeted two young men, grabbing the outstretched hand of one of them and flinging his other arm round his shoulders in a quick, enthusiastic hug, exclaiming,

"Gerry, Ye'r a sight for sore eyes! How's Mum?"

"Hello there brother Joe - Brother Barney!" said Gerry, "She's fine. Sends her love."

He held Barney at arm's length, looking him up and down. "I like your skirts!"

"A bit windy in the winter; but great in summer!" said Barney.

All three men laughed, and Gerry turned to his companion, a handsome, bronzed Indian, wearing a white turban and dressed in a smart grey suit.

"This is Kiril - Kiril Kenada. He's a Sikh," said Gerry, "and you're not to start trying to convert him!"

"No fear. Everyone's got to make up his or her own mind about these things. How are you Kiril? Good to meet you."

They shook hands and Kiril replied, "A bit bewildered. It's not often I am dragged away at the weekend to visit a Christian monastery."

"Priory," said Barney, "but that's another story. You are very welcome. Great to see you Gerry. You've chosen a great day to visit - for it's a feastday. We even have booze! ... and I've fixed up with the prior for you to have lunch. Come on in."

He stretched out an arm and ushered them towards the priory, going down the steps and past the crumbling plaster of the hall into the cloister.

Kiril looked around curiously and asked, "What do you do here all day?"

"Survive - mostly!" laughed Barney. "Well - we do a bit of praying and a bit of study – preparing ourselves to go on to study philosophy and theology. I'm sure you have something similar in your religion?"

"I believe so - but I have no direct experience. I suppose I have been Westernised - since I left India. "I know we don't have monasteries - and we don't believe in celibacy either."

"I don't know much about Sikh's," said Barney, "are you the same as Muslims?"

"No. It's quite complicated – like everything in India – we actually grew out of Hinduism, not Islamism, but we believe, like Islam – like you do - that there is one God – and we are not too keen on religious images, unlike you lot!" There was a twinkle in his eyes.

Barney laughed, "Yes. I suppose it does look like we have too many images - and a lot of them not great art either - but we don't exactly worship them you know: more like paintings and statues of people we love who have gone away for a while. I think the greatest difference between us is our belief in Jesus?"

"Yes. You actually believe that he is God, don't you?"

"Yes, true god and true man."

"We would regard him as one of many prophets."

"Like the Muslims do. I remember reading the Qur'an, while I was searching for something – searching for clarity, and I discovered that Jesus is mentioned by Muhammad as a minor Hebrew prophet. I was quite amused...."

The three arrived at the priests' recreation room and Barney knocked briefly before entering.

Inside all the community, priests and lay brothers, were sitting and standing around, glasses in hand, talking and laughing. On the table was a stock of whisky, gin, wine and beer, and glasses.

"I'd better introduce you to the prior," said Barney, and he led the way to where the Prior was in friendly conversation with two of the brothers.

"Father Prior, may I introduce you to my brother Gerry and his friend Kiril?"

They shook hands. The prior was the soul of affability, "Pleased to meet you."

He looked at Kiril. "You're not Muslim? No - Sikh - that's right, isn't it?"

"True. How do you know?"

"Something about the headdress. I don't think Muslims generally wear turbans."

"That's right. Not that I know much about it. I'm more knowledgeable about electronics."

"Is that your interest too Gerry?" asked the prior.

"Yes. Kiril and I work together – in R&D at Coventry."

"Well, make yourselves at home. You come on a good day. This is one of our feast days and we let our hair down a little. Makes up for a long, hard winter - doesn't it Barney!"

"You can say that again Father. Never went through anything like it in my life!"

"It's not usually as bad as that," said the prior. "It was an exceptionally harsh winter - 67 days of snow cover I read, and a mean average temperature of minus one degree Centigrade! Now, Brother Barney, I suggest that you get our two guests a drink before lunch. We've got about a half-hour."

"Right Father. Come on you two," and they moved through the standing crowd of friars to the table, with many nods and smiles from the brethren.

"Right," said Barney, "What will you have?"

Kiril's eyes boggled at the display of drinks. "My heaven! I think this is the religion for me! A gin and tonic please."

Barney poured and asked, "Gerry?"

"Just a beer."

Barney handed him a glass and pulled the cap off a bottle.

"Thanks," said Kiril. "What exactly are you celebrating?"

"Tell him Gerry," said Barney.

"The Resurrection?"

"Oh yes. Christ's rising from the dead. I'm afraid I couldn't accept that. We believe in reincarnation - Well, I don't, but Sikhs generally do."

Barney said, "I'm afraid I couldn't accept reincarnation. The thought of coming back in some future life as a bird - or a grasshopper - is too much for me!"

"Me too," said Kiril, "but maybe I'll revert as I get older and have a bit of time to think about it all. It's hard to get away entirely from what you have been taught as a child."

"You can say that again!," said Barney, "I had to go half-way round the world and through a dozen philosophers before I came back to Christianity - though I must honestly say that if I had found something else - something more true – I would have stuck with it."

"Look you two, said Gerry, "If you are going to talk religion all day I'm going home to Mum. Give me another beer!"

A smiling Barney said, "Sorry Gerry. Here - help yourself." And he pushed a bottle and an opener across the table.

"Ah - come on Gerry," protested Kiril. "It's not often I have a chance to talk to a real live monk."

"Friar," said Barney, "but that can wait till later: Here! Would you like a Shankill Road Cocktail?"

"A Shankill Road Cocktail! What on earth is that?" Kiril was mystified.

"From the Shankill Road," said Gerry, "in Belfast, where some hard-line protestant loyalists come from."

"A Shankill Road cocktail?" Kiril was still mystified.

With one hand Barney lifted two bottles of 'Monk Export Ale' from the table, each showing a cartoon of a rubicund monk on the label.

In one hand he held both bottles by the neck and put on a broad Belfast accent, "Two monks by the th'oat!"

They laughed.

"That's another thing! What about you Christians fighting with each other? Look at Belfast! Look at Beirut!" said Kiril.

"Here we go again!" Gerry complained.

"Sorry Gerry," said Barney. "Just let us clear this up and then we'll get onto something else. You're right Kiril. It's a shame and a tragedy: the thought that groups of people who worship Christ, the prince of peace and love, fighting and killing each other. It's abysmal!"

He looked sad.

"The only thing that I can say about it is that they are not true Christians. They simply put politics and territorial claims - power politics - before Christ. They have a lot to answer for. We need to pray for them - that they will see the light - seek justice and truth. Don't judge Christ by the behaviour of some of his so called followers. It's been the same since the dawn of history: men killing each other over some false allegiance, some real or imaginary grievance. I don't think it will ever cease - to tell you the God's honest truth. I don't think men will ever learn to live in peace …."

"That's a bit defeatist!" exclaimed Gerry. "Surely if enough men of goodwill come together they can ensure peace - agree to something!"

"I hope you're right - and maybe you are about Belfast and Beirut. Eventually they may come to their senses - when the time is right and the men of violence see they are getting nowhere by slaughtering each other – but something else will start up in some other part of the world, look at the Philippines, look at Nicaragua, look at the Middle East, at some of the African nations. I'm afraid it seems to be man's nature to fight and quarrel - and kill each other. Look at the riots in our cities – over football, the colour of a man's skin: you name it: people will get into their little groups and batter hell out of each other."

"That's a terrible view for a man who's going on to be a priest!" said Gerry. "You are not giving civilisation a chance! Surely reason will overcome these things in time!"

"I hope you are right," said Barney sombrely, "but I cannot see it happening."

"I think Barney is right," said Kiril, "It seems as if nothing will get through to some people. Look at the ayatollah: urging his adherents on to kill for blasphemy! There's religion taking an active part in encouraging violence!"

"And he's not on his own," said Barney, "You only have to see and hear some of the hard, bitter, so-called ministers of religion at home to realise that!"

"Even take my own Order – the Dominicans, in the past – a group of people whom I think very highly of - love like my brothers. Seven hundred years ago they were part of the Inquisition, burning people at the stake because they were judged guilty of heresy - refused to accept the norms of the day. Abominable!" Barney shivered.

"There will be some reckoning at the end of the world - or when each one of us dies. If so-called religious people can offend so much against love and tolerance how can you expect some of the yahoos of society to behave?"

"I'm beginning to be sorry I came here!" Gerry exclaimed. "Can we not talk about something cheerful?"

Barney's eyes lit up in friendship and brotherly affection. "I am sorry brother! I don't know quite how we got onto this tack. It's not just as bad as I have said. There are some - a lot – of good people in the world. We must just pray that they are the majority. Have another beer young brother and then we will have something to eat."

He caught sight of a beaming Bro. Edward across the table and Bro. Edward raised his glass in greeting.

"What are you doing here Brother Ed! Are we not going to get any grub today?"

"Don't you be worrying your little head Brother Barney. It's all under control. Brother Ignatius is keeping an eye on things in the kitchen."

"Brother Ignatius!" Barney reacted in horror.

"Have some faith in your fellow men Brother Barney - you and your friends there!"

He leant over the table and looked owlishly at Kiril. "You're a bit sunburned for an Irishman, aren't you?"

Barney, Kiril and Gerry howled with laughter and Bro. Edward beamed with satisfaction, light glinting from his large spectacles.

"What would we do without you Brother Ed!" spluttered Barney, recovering from his mirth.

At that moment Fr. Prior clapped his hands and called, "Right - brothers and guests! Let's eat!"

On the opposite side of the table Bro. Edward gulped his drink down and made hurriedly for the door. As he passed the trio he muttered, with eyes cast up to heaven, "Ignatius and all the saints be with us!"

He went out of the door at speed, and most of the rest of the brothers drained their glasses and begin to make their way towards the door.

"Bring those drinks with you gentlemen!" said the prior as he passed by, in smiling good humour

"Thank you sir - Father!" said Kiril, and they moved into the cloister, which seemed to be full of friars, walking and chatting together, some with glasses in their hands. There was an occasional burst of laughter - in stark contrast to the usual silence.

In the refectory the benches were full to overflowing.

Iggy, Bert and a lay-brother were serving, and occasionally Bro. Edward poked his head out of the serving hatch to ensure that all was going well.

Large oval platters piled with roast beef, potatoes and Brussels' sprouts were strategically placed along the scrubbed wooden tables, along with bottles of wine and numerous glasses, into which Bert poured beer from a large jug where required.

Others helped themselves to wine. The Prior and one or two elderly priests drank orange juice.

In contrast to the usual silence there was a general hubbub of conversation.

"It's alright for some!" said Bert, pouring beer into Gerry's glass and looking at Barney

Barney motioned to Gerry, "My brother Gerry!" and then to Kiril, "Kiril Kenada!"

They nodded and bowed to each other.

"Great news!" Bert continued, "You're doing the washing up!"

In the middle of the laughter Barney said, "Not today Brother! Special dispensation! Thank God for little blood brothers."

At the end of the meal the tables were cleared and the prior rang the small bell suspended on the wall behind him.

Everyone rose and came round to stand in front of the long tables where they started to intone thanksgiving. It was in Latin as usual and although Gerry and Kiril joined the line of brothers they were necessarily mute and remained upright as the brothers bowed during the ceremony.

Gerry looked over Barney's bent back and then at Kiril, and they decided to assume the same bowed posture, but as they bent forward the friars come upright. Barney laughed heartily at the sight.

Grace came to an end and the prior led the way out of the refectory, nodding kindly to Gerry and Kiril as he passed by.

As Barney and the two visitors reached the cloister the sudden sound of a full orchestra burst forth. Kiril and Gerry looked at Barney in surprise.

"That's Father Vincent. He's a Mahler buff - The Resurrection - doesn't get much of a chance to indulge. Come on and I'll show you the novitiate."

As the music continued to reverberate through the cloister they made their way upstairs, chatting.

Arrived in the novitiate Barney showed them his room, holding up the po to the laughing visitors and turning it over to reveal the irate devil, creating much mirth.

Eventually Barney showed them the church, bowing before the main altar and pointing to the side altar where the fieldmouse had appeared. The story had to be told.

They emerged into the sunshine at the priory entrance and Barney said, "Well, it was great seeing you Gerry. You too Kiril."

"It was great to be here!" Gerry replied. "We certainly picked the right day, didn't we?"

"It was great indeed," said Kiril, "I'll have to give this Christianity serious consideration!"

"The way to every good Sikh is through his belly," said Gerry.

"By the way," said Kiril, "talking about bellies and things like that. What about women? How do you do without them?"

"Come on now!" exclaimed Gerry, "We've had enough of this!"

"I just wanted to know how they managed to do without!" Kiril shook his head. "I couldn't!"

"You just put it out of your head," said Barney. "Thanks be to God it hasn't bothered me at all. I'm a bit surprised. Must be the grace of God - or maybe it's dropped off!"

All three laughed, and then Barney said, "Well folks. I must be away. Brother Bert was only half joking about the dishes. I would be slaving away if you hadn't come - and I would feel better if I gave them a bit of a hand."

He turned to Gerry. "It was great to see you m'oul son. Tell mum I'm doing well, feeling great. I'm not too sure when I'll be able to get over to see her – perhaps after profession at the end of August. I might be able to persuade the prior that it would be a good thing. We'll see. Keep in touch."

They shook hands warmly and Barney turned to the Sikh, "Good-bye Kiril. We'll have another good discussion one of these days - when the brother isn't there to call halt."

With further handshakes the two visitors climbed into a car, and as it pulled away from the priory Gerry honked the horn and waved.

The smile on Barney's face died for a moment as he watched the car turn the corner and disappear. He stood for a moment, his face solemn, slightly sad; then he turned and skipped briskly down the steps into the priory.

25 Dragonfly

High summer arrived, almost a repeat of the heat of the previous year.
  The sun shone and the foliage grew heavy on the trees by the lakeside as the three novices walked along the narrow path - Bert sucking a long piece of grass, Iggy slashing at undergrowth with a stick.

All were sweating, and in the shadow of the overhanging trees, sun spattering the ground, Barney paused to wipe his forehead with the sleeve of his heavy habit.

"Do you know what would go well?" he asked.

"What?" said Albert.

"A swim."

"But we've no togs!"

"To hell with that!" said Barney, "Did you never hear of a skinny dip?"

He looked up and down the pathway, saw that there was no one about, and stepped off the track, quickly starting to strip.

Bert and Iggy looked on, amused.

"But what if the bunnies - the nuns, come by?"

"They'll just have to take their chances. I'm too hot to care."

Within a minute or two Barney was naked. He climbed into the prow of an old boat moored at the lake bank - the one that had been frozen in the icy winter - and dived off, swimming strongly for a few yards.

He turned and called jubilantly, "It's great! Come on in. It's really wonderful!"

Bert looked up and down the pathway and at Ignatius

"O.K. - but if we have a swarm of screaming bunnies fainting by the path I'm putting the blame on you! Are you game Ignatius?"

He undressed quickly and cautiously walked down the bank into the water, his body white and bony.

He swam out to where Barney treaded water, swirling his arms through the coolness.

On the bank Ignatius stood bemused.

"You're right! It's fantastic!" said Bert, "Iggy! Come on in!"

"I've always thought that swimming naked is the only way to do it!" said Barney. "It makes you feel so free - so alive. Must go back to the garden of Eden, before the serpent got loose."

They swam slowly; breaststroke, side by side – through a clump of lily-pads.

Iggy was still sitting fully clothed, propped on the edge of the boat.

"Iggy seems to be suffering the after-effects of the serpent's visit," said Bert.

"Iggy, come on in," he called "There's nobody to see you." Then quietly, to Barney, "It's a pity the old serpent did get loose - that fruit must have been really poisonous - making us so embarrassed about our bodies."

"As well as bringing death and destruction into the world," said Barney, "Old Adam has a lot to answer for – and Eve as well!"

Bert called again, "Iggy - come on!"

On the bank Iggy shook his head and stroked his hands across each other – wiping out the invitation.

"Do you believe in them?" asked Bert.

"Who? What? Oh, Adam and Eve? In a representative sense I do: *Adamah* meaning earth and *Eve* the 'mother of the living' - in Hebrew."

They treaded water.

"Something catastrophic certainly happened among early homo sapiens. I agree with C.S. Lewis, and St. Paul - and our Lord - that there is a battle, a cosmic battle going on, between good and evil; and we're caught up in it, whether we like it or not." He caught a mouthful of water, "and we have to take sides!"

"There's enough beauty left anyway!" said Bert. "Look at that dragonfly."

Both stopped swimming and floated along without a sound - only nose and eyes projecting above the water, close to a hovering dragonfly.

Barney whispered in awe, "Jesus! Isn't it beautiful!"

The gossamer wings of the dragonfly shimmered in the sunlight above its slender body - lustrous blue merging into iridescent green.

Albert whispered, "Fantastic! Only lasts for a few weeks as an adult - after anything up to five years in the nymph stage."

"A short life, but a beautiful one."

"They mate on the wing you know," said Bert.

"Begob!" said Barney. "They're better than I am: not that I'll be able to do any of that now anyway!"

"Yes. It's something to give up. I will miss that - the pleasure and the parenthood. I wouldn't have minded being a father."

"Wow!" exclaimed Barney as the dragonfly scooted away at speed. "God! Did you see how fast that moved?"

"They fly at anything up to sixty miles an hour," said Bert.

"Wonderful," said Barney. "Fancy mating at that speed! Never really looked closely at them before. Strange how you can go on not noticing things like that."

"Yeh," said Albert, "I wouldn't have minded mating at any speed." He looked slightly sad.

"Come on now mate!" said Barney. "You'll be a father in no time at all: about six years from now - and no nappies to worry about!"

In an effort to lighten Albert's mood he splashed water into his face.

"Oi!" shouted Albert, "I can't see. You'll wash my glasses off."

"Holy Mother of God! You've still got your glasses on - and I never noticed. Ye'r one of the biggest idiots I ever came across. Come on. I've had enough of this – just in case someone does come along - and we end up in court. Can you just imagine the headlines: 'Naked Monks Caught in the Act' and everybody nodding their heads over their tabloid and saying 'Oh Ho! Those monks at it again!' - and even if they bother to read beyond the headline they'll never believe that 'the act' meant just swimming! It's a cruel world - and us as innocent as babies - water babies!"

"You're putting the fear of God into me!" said Bert. "Let's go just in case it does happen!"

Barney laughed and they started to swim towards the bank.

As they arrived at the boat Barney exclaimed, "Iggy, you're really missing something!"

"He's shy," said Bert.

"I am - and I can't swim - and I'm afraid of those bunnies coming along!" Iggy seemed subdued.

The two naked figures, one bony, the other muscular, but both startlingly white against the luxuriant backdrop of green trees and blue sky, hauled themselves onto dry land and begin to dress.

"Wow! That was good," said Barney. "I told you it would work."

They began to walk along the pathway, Bert and Barney dressed only in tunics, with hair damp and unruly and faces still wet.

Just above the place where they had stood at the side of the path in the winter to allow the skating nuns to pass they saw four young nuns coming towards them, obviously postulants.

Bert clutched Barney's sleeve, "My God! We only just made it."

"Aye," said Barney, "I'm afraid we'll have to bring the togs with us next time."

The nuns came level with them, bowing slightly to the brothers, who stood aside and bowed in return.

"Good afternoon Sisters. Great day!" said Iggy.

When the sisters had gone past by a few yards one of them looked over her shoulder and called out, with a glint in her eye, "Grait dai for a skinny dip!"

They were not sure if the Australian accent was real or assumed, but there was a chuckle of laughter from the nuns as they carried on down the pathway.

Bert looked at Barney, "You don't think . . .?"

Barney raised his shoulders and spreads his hands wide, palms open and eyes wide, a silent answer - who knows?

As the groups drew apart Bert looked over his shoulder at the disappearing nuns. "It's hard to give up the idea of mating with someone as beautiful as one of them."

"Well, that's it mate. It's not for us - not even on the wing!" said Barney.

Bert laughed, "True! We've had it now. I wasn't even thinking of it in a sexual sense: just the romantic side of things – having the companionship of someone beautiful."

Iggy burst out, "For God's sake will you stop talking about it! First naked swims and now talking about sex with nuns."

Bert said mildly, "We have to think about these things Iggy! No sense hiding away from what we are giving up."

"Sorry. Not in the best of form," said Iggy.

26 Sex

The three novices lay prostrate in a meadow, basking in the hot sun. Bert's and Barney's hair were still slightly damp and askew.

Bert said, "You know what we were talking about just now?"

"Mating on the wing you mean?" Barney asked.

"Yes - well, sex generally."

"Yes, what about it?"

"I know these things are private - but do you feel embarrassed about nudity and so forth? I do."

"I do too - but I try to ignore it."

"It's an odd thing. We don't talk about it - but it can be a great problem."

Iggy sat up.

"You're telling me!" Barney agreed. "It's a strange thing though - as I was telling Kiril Kenada - that Sikh chap that came here at Easter with my brother - since I made up my mind to come here I haven't had the same trouble. I think it's partly a question of environment – partly having made up my mind that sex is verboten - and a lot of grace from the Almighty. It just doesn't cost me a thought these days." He laughed, "Far too damn tired probably!"

"But we are all quite embarrassed about our private parts," Bert mused. "Even those who claim to be liberated from such things. We have a natural reticence about going naked."

Barney chipped in, "Have you ever been on a Spanish beach in the summer?"

"Yes - but there always seems to be an element of display - bravado - in such nakedness, until you get used to it at any rate - and it's mostly birds going topless. You don't get the lads jiggling around with their danglers wobbling!"

Barney laughed heartily, "True! And even in all male society - swimming clubs and Turkish baths and so forth - at times everybody is acutely aware of their nakedness - standing around and pretending not to notice the size of each others danglers, when everybody is mad keen to see if the next lad's is bigger than theirs!"

Bert laughed in turn, "I know what you mean - trying to keep yours covered and having a little look out of the corner of your eye when you're standing at a urinal, wondering about size. Adam and Eve have an awful lot to answer for."

"Yeah," said Barney, "though I expect we wouldn't have done any better if we had been them. It's amazing the number of people who still think that their sin was sexual: that the forbidden fruit was lust... whereas it was really pride."

"It's certainly a weird situation."

"I've often thought," said Barney, "how ludicrous it is that the same apparatus that we piss with is the source of life!"

"My God but you're crude Barney!" exclaimed Iggy.

"But isn't it true? Isn't it weird?"

"It may be weird in some ways," said Albert, "– a bit comical - but it's also very beautiful! Must be marvellous for people who really love each other - to be able to come so close and give each other such pleasure: and it's a fantastic job of plumbing! Who could have combined so much in one organism - that and thinking and living and breathing as well? It's utterly astounding."

"It may be," Iggy blurted, "but I wish to hell we didn't have to talk about it so much – that there wasn't so much of it about! When you are out in the world you can't get away from people raping each other at the drop of a hat. On TV they just look at each other and fall into bed!"

"Yes," said Albert lazily, "It's a bit off-putting when you are trying to keep yourself pure and unsullied!"

"Let's face it," Barney said, "anyone these days who is trying to control his sexual urges is looked at as something of a nut! The notion of purity is just good for a laugh - mostly."

"It's not easy," said Iggy, looking at the ground.

"It's absolutely laughable the extent some people go to prove they have no sexual hang-ups," Barney exclaimed. "One of the last TV programmes I saw before I left was a lady urging us all to use condoms! There she was, blethering away - meaning very well I know, and she suddenly produces a wooden dick from under the table, plonks it down on the desk and starts to demonstrate how to put on a condom!" Barney laughed hilariously, "and she couldn't do it! Bloody funny! She was really as embarrassed as hell, and kept talking and unconsciously stroking this wooden dick - with its little plastic hat half on! The next thing you'll see is a demonstration how to masturbate!"

"Jesus, Barney - how crude can you get!" Iggy was appalled.

"Well - isn't that what they are saying? Masturbation is good for you! Keep at it! Make yourself happy! Wankers of the world unite!"

"I suppose they are. But you shouldn't put it so crudely!"

"... Or strongly," said Barney. "In my view a wanker is a wanker is a wanker, even if it's a natural thing – the hand being so close to the object, so to speak!"

He began to relax. "Sorry Iggy. I get carried away at times. It's just that I had such a hard time coming to terms with myself. I have every sympathy with people who are still struggling - not that I'm finished yet by a long chalk. It's very difficult in this day and age."

He paused, "Do you know - there's somebody in this priory whom I particularly admire: Brother Ed. There he is - one of the natural eunuchs our Lord mentioned - or a hermaphrodite - and he could have made much of it, made it an excuse for self-indulgence - as if only so called gays had difficulties about sex - but he didn't. He looked at himself, sized up his situation, and ... took up his cross. A marvellous man! Better than a million big dangler men who think that liberated and true manhood is proved by indiscriminate fornication."

"I agree with you Barney. Now - will you get off your soapbox and give our ears a rest!" Iggy had had enough.

"Right! Enough said. I blame you for that outburst Brother Bert!"

"Me?"

"You started it! You're the nigger in the woodpile!"

"Negro! – or black!" exclaimed Iggy.

"Negro. Sorry. Next you'll be saying I'm a racist pig – just because of a slip of the tongue. I'll have you know that when I was in South Africa ...."

"Barney - shut it!"

"I get the message. You don't want any more Irish eloquence!" Barney closed his eyes and for a few moments there was silence as all basked in the sun.

Eventually Bert, lying between the other two, rolled over and found that his head was close to a cowpat. He half turned and looked with professional interest at clouds of flies and small insects hovering over the pancake dropping.

By now on his stomach he looked more closely. "Did you know that there have been over 900,000 insects recorded to date?"

"Nine hundred thousand!" Still lying on his back, Barney sounded impressed.

"Yes, and entomologists discover about 10,000 new species every year."

Barney got up on an elbow, "You must be joking! Ten thousand every year! You would think that they would have recorded the lot by now."

"No. It is estimated that there may be up to 10 million insects not yet recorded."

Barney sat up, "I don't believe it!"

"Fact! They are fascinating creatures. Some can make noises that can be heard up to a mile away, though they don't have voice boxes - some have as many as five or six eyes - see better than you or me. Fantastic athletes as well! If you could jump as far as a flea - relative to your size - you would be able to jump 700 feet, about 200 metres."

Barney looked with great interest at the flies buzzing around the cowpat.

"These are all common varieties. Order of diptera: two wings. Those midges beat their wings about 1,000 times a second. There's a blowfly – bluebottle, dangerous creatures."

Iggy rolled over closer, "What's that?"

"Which one?" asked Bert.

Iggy pointed, "There, that one."

"Where?" Bert moved his head closer to the cowpat, pushed his glasses onto his forehead and squinted.

"There, that one," said Iggy, and he placed a hand on the back of Bert's head and pushed his nose and face into the cowpat.

Barney looked appalled.

"Shit!" said Bert withdrawing his dung covered face.

"Exactly!" said Iggy. "Pontificating crap!" And he took off at a run as Albert rose to his feet.

The chase that followed was energetic but short, for Iggy was handicapped by shifting avoirdupois and Albert was fired up with indignation. Barney, now convulsed with laughter, followed at an observer's pace, noting the clever little sidesteps that Iggy took, but eventually the fat friar collapsed in a heap, exhausted, laughing and breathing heavily.

Bert landed on the top of him, and not sure what to do rubbed Iggy's face into the earth and then scraped a fingerful of cow dung off his face and smeared it along the fat novice's ears and cheeks, before rolling away to sit on the grassy bank, beginning to laugh despite himself, and starting to wipe his face clean with tufts of grass.

"You're a sod Iggy!" he said, looking owlishly at Iggy as he cleaned his glasses.

"I know. Couldn't resist it. Evil impulse. Sorry," gasped Iggy, still lying on the ground.

Barney flopped down, chuckling, and as order began to be restored the three rested upon the grassy bank for a moment, lazing in the sun.

"Well," said Barney, "I suppose that after all that good clean fun we'd better get back. Duty calls."

"Pity we can't get away for more than a couple of hours at a time," said Bert.

"Aye, it's tough," said the Irishman.

"Too tough for me," said Iggy, quietly.

"Eh?" Barney was startled.

"Too tough for me," Iggy repeated, and he looked into the distance and then down at the ground.

"I've got to leave."

"Jesus! Iggy!" Albert exclaimed, "You serious?"

Iggy nodded. "Had a word with Fr. Nick this morning. Sorry lads. Sorry to leave you. Just can't stick it any more."

"I *thought* something was getting at you!" Barney was trying to adjust to the news. "I'm really sorry to hear this Iggy. I know it's hard, giving up everything, but I thought we were all through - after that hard winter."

"Maybe if I were older ... I might be able to take it. I want to - but there's so much else to do, and I think I have an itchy mind. Beautiful way of life, but I have to get out and about and do things - maybe get married or something."

Barney and Bert continued to look stunned.

There was a moment's silence. "We'll miss you Iggy." Albert was deeply moved.

Barney nodded agreement, silenced for once.

"Even if I am a sod!" Iggy was sad but braving it out.

"Sorry," Bert murmured.

Iggy rose to his feet. "Look, I had to tell you, and now that I have I think I had better go. I've arranged to catch the evening train. I'll say cheerio to you now."

Bert and Barney also rose and both shook hands with the chubby friar, their faces solemn.

Iggy was close to tears. "Right - be seeing you lads," and he turned abruptly and started to walk away.

Bert and Barney stood for a moment and then sank back onto the grass.

"I never expected that. It's a bit of a blow." Barney was very quiet.

"Me too," said Albert, "I really thought all three of us were through the worst."

In the distance Iggy turned and waved farewell. Barney was back on his feet and waving, "Keep doing that venia Iggy!"

Iggy waved again and turned away to break into a run.

As Barney sank back to ground Albert said, "Only you and I now mate!"

He put a piece of long grass into his mouth and lay back.

27 An Old Hen?

The magnum silencium bell tolled and Barney put down his pen. He closed the foolscap pad he had been working on and got up from his small desk to switch off the cell light.

There was still enough light from the waxing moon to see across the room as he knelt briefly at the side of the bed and crossed himself, before saying a silent prayer. He was wearing only the tunic of the Order, his cappa and scapular flung across the back of the chair.

He lay down on the bed and looked wide-eyed at the wall opposite, where he could see the diamond shaped shadows cast by the leaded windows and the shadowy movement of foliage and tree branches, projected and enlarged by the light of the moon. The shapes combined in a restful and pleasing pattern.

His eyes began to close and when he opened them a few moments later it seemed that the shadow composition on the wall was in process of changing.

The diamond shapes remained firm and the shapes of the branches still moved languidly, but added to them a small white shape appeared to grow in size and clarity, translucent, so that Barney could still see the patterns on the wall. He was mildly puzzled.

As he watched the figure stopped growing in size. It was a friar in the white Dominican habit. He vaguely realised that he knew who it was, but the features were obscure.

Was it Father Martin, the priest who had spoken to him so sharply on that freezing morning when he was trying to serve Mass? He could not be sure. It was like him, but not him. He was reminded of someone. Come to think of it, it looked a bit like himself, but older. It couldn't be him!

Whoever it is the man was stern and worried, looked like he had lost something, left something behind.

Barney watched dispassionately.

The figure moved and swirled, dissolved and changed, receded and came back as something else. Then, as the image became sharp and clear, Barney found himself looking at a large hen or cockerel, like a Picasso drawing in full colour, alive and pecking.

The hen raised its head as if disturbed and turned to look directly at Barney, as if aware of him.

It stared for a second, beady eyes watchful and alert, and opened its beak.

Then, with a single, sharp 'bawk' it abruptly vanished.

Barney blinked and sat up. He looked puzzled but not alarmed.

On the wall opposite there was nothing but the patterns and shadows of the window and the moving branches.

Slowly he sank back on the pillow and his eyes closed.

28 Visions

"Fr Nick advised me to come and have a word with you Father." Barney had just come into the prior's study, noticing that the desk was almost cleared, that all papers were in neat piles.

The prior himself was cleanly shaven and very much in charge of himself. There was no sign of eczema on his face.

"Yes Brother. What can I do to help?"

Barney was diffident, "I wanted to ask you Father. Do you believe in visions?"

The prior was relaxed and friendly, "What a question! You may as well ask the pope does he believe in celibacy!"

Then, becoming aware that Barney was quite serious he said, "Well, if you want a yes or no answer: yes. But I would have to qualify that. Yes, I believe in visions. We live in a very mysterious world - though a lot of people think it is all cut and dried, and only believe in what they can see with their eyes and feel with their hands, things that they regard as normal - measure."

"I believe it is more mysterious than this. There are things we don't know, because we are limited creatures; and as I believe we are surrounded by God, live in Him, in a mystery that we do not understand, I believe that he can communicate with us in various ways: through visions and heightened perceptions, or heavenly messengers: as he did with Mary when she was told that she would bear a son; and with Joseph – when he was about to break it off with her when he discovered she was pregnant - and needed a bit of persuading that she had not gone the way of all flesh."

The prior's face lit with humour at the thought.

"Yes. I believe in those visions. I believe that some of the saints have had visions. I believe that innumerable believers have been comforted by the Holy Spirit – in times of great trial and sorrow, but ordinarily we don't need visions. We need simple faith - and reason."

Then, abruptly, "Let me ask you a question. Do you believe that Our Lady appeared to Bernadette at Lourdes?"

"Yes. I think that was genuine. I feel that it was, but one has to be careful."

"Exactly! One must be very careful. One must normally go by reason: faith and reason. If God should choose to enlighten someone through the power of the Holy Spirit he can certainly do so. But we must be careful, for we have Our Lord's word for it that the spirit of evil goes about looking for a home - the spirit of lies, seeking to lead us into delusion. We have to be aware of that possibility."

"Modern people laugh at the notion of the devil. They are uncomfortable, embarrassed about it - scoff at it.

I don't know why! When one looks at the evil that exists: take Hitler and the Nazis for example, could a mere human dream up all the evil they were responsible for? "

"Such mindless perversion of the idea of purity of species!" The prior shuddered. "Or take a rapist or child murderer, where does that evil come from? Simply from the poor deluded rapist or murderer? Not on your life: that poor unfortunate creature - Hitler if you like – has allowed himself to be deluded. He has no positive motivation, only a twisted travesty of reason. You could call it madness: but that itself is an evil, an absence of good."

"The afflicted madman, the killer – Hitler - has no refuge from evil, in honest love and care for people. He cares only for his own ideas, for himself. He is not open to truth. Hasn't got the self discipline or desire to see truth. He has no protection from evil - which I believe to be a highly intelligent, malevolent force, a real being - a fallen angel in Christian terminology - who can invade the mind that is empty of faith and brotherly love – and twist and torment, bloat ideas and concepts that in themselves may be good into an exaggerated, contorted mess. We who follow Christ should be in no doubt about the spirit of evil."

"And so we must take care that we are not deluded, firstly by putting our trust in Jesus, praying to him and with him and in him, and then by seeking advice from a religious adviser, preferably one whom one trusts - which you are now doing," he smiled, "and paying me a little bit of a compliment. Am I making any sense to you?"

"Yes. What you say fits in exactly with my own thoughts ... about good and evil, and about a ... an experience I had a few days ago, which I'm trying to sort out. May I tell you about it, briefly?"

"Certainly. That's what I'm here for."

"It's a bit embarrassing, because I don't much like visions, or anything to do with them. I really like to know where I am. I don't much like mysteries - would like them to be explained – resolved."

"However, I woke up the other night, or indeed I may never have gone to sleep, and I saw this vision of myself, or it may have been Father Ma.... one of the priests, who is a bit ..." he searched for a kind word, "...fussy."

He looked to Fr. Prior for understanding and the prior nodded.

"It was quite clear, quite ordinary, almost like watching him – or myself - in real life, although I knew he wasn't in the room. Then he, or the figure, appeared to dissolve and changed into an old hen, or a cockerel, or something like that; and then disappeared."

"That's it! I wasn't afraid, or alarmed - quite calm in fact. Just went off to sleep again, felt quite peaceful. But the next morning – now even, it was as real and fresh to me as when it occurred, as real as I am sitting talking to you."

The prior nodded and asked, "Does it mean anything to you, this dream or vision?"

"Yes. I think it does."

"The reason I ask is that dreams, if it was a dream, only really mean something to the person concerned. Freud and Jung have a lot to say about this, especially Jung, who has come as close as possible to the Christian vision of things without being a believer."

"He would say that dreams do have a message, especially if one is under pressure of any sort, and perhaps does not realise a certain truth, or is even trying to avoid a truth - which I am sure is not so in your case. I'm sure you want the truth, but you might not be aware of certain aspects of the truth about you. So, it could be a dream - à la modern psychological theory - carrying a message, or it could be a real little vision just meant for you, through the power of the holy spirit." The prior smiled.

"If it has any significance you will know about it."

"I tell you what," he rose purposefully from his chair, "I know you like a smoke now and again. Disgusting habit, but occasionally it helps. Take a packet of cigarettes."

He strode over to the waste bin just inside the door and took out a packet of Capstan and his stormproof lighter and handed them to Barney.

"I haven't any use for these any more. Managed to kick the habit some time ago."

Barney smiled and murmured, "I know."

The Prior only half heard him, or paid no attention.

"I think you should just go and sit down and relax. Smoke a cigarette or two and see what you come up with, and come and have a word with me or Fr. Nick whenever you have thought things out - alright?"

"Thanks Father. After two cigarettes a day for the past eleven months I will enjoy a few extras."

"That's it then. See you if you need me."

Barney moved towards the door and opened it.

Just as he went through it the prior called out "Brother!"

Barney paused and turned.

"Just one thing! If the Holy Spirit is involved in your little vision you will know about it. Where he is there is peace and joy – no confusion. Alright?"

Barney nodded and smiled. The prior did likewise.

As he closed the door and made for the stairwell Barney was pleasantly aware that the prior's whole attitude seemed to have changed. He was brisk, affable and assured, even formidable in a kindly way.

For the first time Barney saw quite clearly why Father Luke had been elected prior.

29 Vigil

Barney sat comfortably in the bentwood armchair of his cell in the growing darkness of a late summer twilight.

Outside a swarm of bats flitted against the darkening sky and the magnum silencium bell sounded throughout the priory.

Lights began to be switched off, and in the gloom Barney used the prior's lighter to light a cigarette. In the brief flowering flame Barney's face was revealed, reposed and calm.

He sat in a sprawled, leisurely fashion, completely at ease in the bentwood armchair, occasionally drawing on the cigarette, the minute glow outlining his nose and cheeks.

The August moon rose, illuminating the interior of the room and the outside world. Through the window of his cell Barney could clearly see the full leafed trees against the beauty of the night.

In the quiet he could hear the hoot of an owl.

In the priory grounds Fr. Valentine's cat stalked the undergrowth, a dark shadow in the moonlight, eyes shining.

There was a stirring of foliage as a dim shape, a squirrel or a bird, moved in the branches of a tree.

Barney lit another cigarette and puffed calmly, enjoying the passage of the smoke into his lungs and the slow trickle as it escaped through mouth and nostrils.

Time passed and the moon slowly changed its position, altering the landscape.

In the forest outside a large bird launched itself into the air, and unseen by human eyes an otter slipped into the waters of the lake.

The dawn chorus began to sound.

Barney sat impassively, at peace with the world.

A faint hint of the sun lightened the sky.

There was a sound from outside Barney's door, and then a knock, followed by the sound of Bert's voice:

"Benedicamus domino!"

"Deo gratias," Barney replied, quietly stubbing out a cigarette. There were four cigarette ends in a soap dish.

He could hear Bert moving to Fr. Nick's door and the salutation repeated; Fr. Nick replying.

Barney moved to the washstand and sluiced his face, put on his scapular and cowl and ran a comb through his hair.

He opened the door and joined Bro. Albert in the corridor, already lined up in what once was the novices' procession to Matins.

They greeted each other with silent nods and a half smile.

Fr. Nick came out and Bert began the processional psalm as they moved out of the novitiate.

The novitiate door banged shut behind them and they moved down to the cloister, a tiny procession praising the Lord of creation and giving thanks for the day.

The choir stalls appeared to be almost deserted, and at the end of the rich and beautiful words of the psalms the curtain separating the brothers from the body of the church was drawn back by one of the lay brothers and the friars scattered throughout the church as usual for private prayer and meditation; each friar huddled and cowled in his private, isolated world in the dawn light.

30 Decision

Bro. Barney knocked on Fr. Nick's door and the novice master sang out, "Benedicite! Come!"

Barney opened the door and went in. He stood on the threshold.

Fr. Nick was seated at his desk.

"I've been sitting up all night, smoking some of Fr. Luke's Capstan."

"Horrible things. Why didn't you ask me and I would have given you some tipped?"

"I didn't really need them. I have come to a decision. I will have to go."

"I'm really sorry to hear that Barney. Come in and sit down."

"It's become pretty clear to me," said Barney, taking a seat. "I don't like it, but I have got to face facts. If I stayed I think I would become an old hen of a man - striving after a false perfection. I want to stay, but I can't. It wouldn't be wise."

Fr Nick offered him a cigarette.

Barney waved away the offer and continued, "I would become less than human – a bit dried up, not really a rounded human being, and I think that's what God wants above all, that we become full, rounded human beings - perfectly human and caring – before he can make us saints. Do you follow me?"

"Perfectly," said Nick. "There's always the danger in monastic life of becoming a dried up old stick. There's no doubt that when our Lord says 'you must become perfect as your heavenly father is perfect' he means that we must become perfectly human, as unselfishly loving as we can, and then we will be lifted up and made perfect like He is now – our humanity enlarged so that we can share his divinity. We certainly can't become perfect without acknowledging our humanity."

"So that is why I think I have to go," Barney agreed. "I think I have been trying for a false perfection - been a bit obsessive. I have to think it out and live it a bit before I understand it fully."

"We will miss you. You are certain about this?"

"No doubts - unfortunately. Despite the hardness, and the fact that I have been pushing after an exaggerated, false kind of perfection, I really enjoy the life. There is a great peace in giving up all things - and great fun, a great spirit."

"You'll find it hard adjusting to the outside world again."

"I know. But needs must when the devil drives – rather," smiling, "when the Spirit leads - I hope! And when I was leaving the Company that I was working for the MD sent a message that a job would be waiting for me if I ever changed my mind."

"Good," said Nick, "at least you won't starve. When do you want to go?"

"Straight away I think. No sense in hanging about. I want to see Fr. Prior and one or two others to say goodbye. Then I'll pack."

"Right," said Nick, "I'll arrange for Bro. Edward to leave you to the station for the afternoon train."

"For what it's worth, I think you have probably made the right decision, in-so-far as one can be certain about these things."

Fr. Nick sat forward in his chair and leant across the desk, seeming to search for ideas, and the words to express them.

"Forgive me if this appears critical Barney. You have seemed at times to be forcing yourself to do everything absolutely perfectly - and that kind of perfection is, as you say, a bit obsessional. It's not the perfection that Our Lord wants. He wants kindness and faith above all - true love for humanity, including one's own."

"Obsession is a subtle thing to combat. Only a relaxed and childlike trust will do it – no matter what walk of life you are in. You are halfway there now I think."

The concentration on Fr. Nick's face eased and he sat back in his chair. "It's hard to face up to truths like that. It goes against the grain when you are determined on a course of action. It requires strength of mind and humility – real honesty. Hard to get to the truth."

Fr. Nick moved and they both rose to their feet.

"We'll miss you very much," said Nick, and they shook hands warmly.

31 Albert

The door to the novitiate recreation room opened and Barney came in, dressed in his grey suit.

Brother Bert dropped the book he was reading. He looked astounded, his eyes and mouth open.

"Jesus!" he breathed. It was a prayerful rather than a thoughtless exclamation. "You're not going!?"

"Sorry! Have to."

"Mother of God," said Albert. He looked aghast, sorrowful.

"Jesus!" he repeated, and then, "I'll miss you."

"Me too! I mean I'll miss being here. But I have got to go. Got a kind of message from on high."

Bert recovered and gave a slight smile, his eyes moving heavenwards, "Oh - from the big boss!"

"Aye," said Barney, his Irish accent becoming more noticeable, "Clearin' out all the rubbish!"

Bert was annoyed, "Come on Barney! That *is* rubbish!"

"Yes – of course, but I think he would prefer me elsewhere, for my own good. Damned bloody nuisance - just when I had made up my mind that this is the place for me. But there you are. Man proposes: God disposes - if you don't mind the cliché."

Bert shook his head, "I thought . . . ah well, you know what I thought."

"So did I m'oul son. Ask Fr. Nick about it, will you. He'll explain better than I can at the moment. Tell him I said it was O.K. Basically I have suddenly realised that I would become a bit of a dried up old prune if I stayed... a bit of an old hen. You wouldn't want that m'oul mate!"

Bert decided to cheer himself up, "Nah! You're bad enough when you're a raw new prune. God knows what you'd be like wizened."

Barney smiled, "Aye, horrible. Well, I'd better go. If I hang around I'll get a fit of the dumps. I'll see you around. Okay?"

Bert got up from chair he was been sitting on and they shook hands.

"Cheerio Barney. Take care of yourself."

"Same to you Bert. Right, I better be off."

Barney stepped outside the door and shut it, unintentionally hard, with a bang. He looked annoyed with himself and for a moment thought about opening the door to apologise. Then he made up his mind and walked away.

On the other side of the door Bert sat alone. He gazed down at the floor for a long time, his shoulders bowed.

"Dear God," he said, and then lifted his book, squared his shoulders, and carried on reading.

32 A Tear for The World

The old community station wagon sped along the narrow, winding roads, leaving the spire of the priory church behind and snaking through the countryside, sun glinting from glass and rusting chrome remnants.

Brother Edward had not said much since they left the priory. It was obvious that he had been deeply affected by Barney's decision to leave. There had been an awkward moment or two when he had arrived in the novitiate to help lift Barney's trunk down the stairs and into the estate car.

"Really sorry Barney," was all he had said, and all Barney could do was to put a bright face upon things, pretend that all things were under control and that this was an everyday occurrence.

It was not, of course. Underneath his breezy manner Barney too was deeply disturbed. He knew, or thought he knew, that he was doing the right thing - agreed totally with Fr. Nick's acceptance of the rationality behind the decision.

But reason was at odds with a deep desire of the heart to continue to live in the priory, enjoying a disciplined daily structure that aided thinking and study in tranquillity, and, not least of all, provided the constant pleasure of giving praise to the Creator in the beautiful words of the psalms, in unison with the brothers, in a language that he was beginning to appreciate had a brevity and a terse beauty.

However, reason, as a way of understanding truth, had to be followed, even if it went against the feelings of the heart, and he found it difficult to express exactly what he was going through, so although he felt that Bro. Edward instinctively understood something of his dilemma, he could not express his thinking fully, so that in the car their conversation was limited, with Brother Edward, not his usual ebullient self, chatting about the malfunctioning vehicle more than anything else, and when they drove into the Station yard it was obvious that both were glad that the short journey was over.

They got out of the station wagon and carried the trunk to the platform, where they stood around for a few minutes until the train arrived.

With relief they lifted the trunk into the guard's van at the rear of the train and Barney opened the door of the adjoining compartment to throw in a satchel, containing a few books.

"We're going to miss you Barney," said the big friar.

"Me too," said Barney, "I'll miss this place like hell – well, like heaven."

They shook hands firmly, each gripping the other's elbow with the other hand, and then they spontaneously gave each other a hug. There was no need to say anything more.

Barney got into the carriage and shut the door, and as the train started to move he let down the window and gave a goodbye salute to Bro. Edward, who lifted a hand and smiled before he turned away and began to walk towards the car park. Barney saw him shake his head briefly, a gesture of mixed regret and disbelief.

The train gathered speed and Barney remained leaning out of the window, watching from an increasing distance as the black and white clad figure strode vigorously towards the priory station wagon.

Barney shut the window and collapsed into his seat. There was no one else in the carriage, so he was able to put his feet up on the bench opposite, relaxing and only aware in a peripheral way of the bright sunshine outside and the beauty of the countryside.

He was partly stunned by the events and the emotions of the past few hours. The pain of separation was to some extent anesthetised by immense tiredness, created by a year of focused activity, a minute by minute concentration that had never been relaxed, not for one second during each working day, except when he slept.

"Definite obsession," he muttered, feeling a great emptiness, a lassitude that contrasted with the keyed up determination he felt when he arrived at the same station twelve months before.

He was surprised to find that he was actually shaking, with emotion and tiredness, an entirely unusual experience. He had become accustomed to being in control, of directing his energies with purpose, except on that one occasion when he had almost passed out when trying to serve Fr. Martin's Mass.

Now the reaction to his massive twelve-month effort was setting in – a way of life that he had come to love, and that had ended in nothing.

As the train rumbled through the countryside a kaleidoscope of memories slipped through his mind, appeared and disappeared in no set order - the devil in the chamber pot, the seraphic expression on Iggy's face as he slid along the novitiate corridor, the falling blanket of snow seen through the window of the Chapter room, the hushed beauty of the line of nuns as they passed in evening darkness, the aching exhaustion of shovelling coke, the howling gale of the walk over Minchinhampton Common, the stupendous, heartfelt singing of the Easter Gloria, the beauty of the dragonfly among the lily pads, the cat playing with the dead fieldmouse.

He felt his heart almost break at the thought of those moments, now lost forever; never to be repeated;

never to be possible in the ordinary life to which he must return.

Life in the priory had been magic, he realised; lived with an intensity and clarity of purpose that was impossible in ordinary workaday life. He would have to reduce his sights, live at a pace that was far removed from the total dedication of monastic life, the silence, the concentrated thought and prayer, the fellowship of morning, noon and evening worship in the words of the psalms.

It would be hard to adjust to a world of people crammed into city flats, working at jobs that were basically just to earn a living, quite possibly providing little satisfaction, constantly threatened by the need to pay rent or mortgage, coping with the shifting pattern of industrial and commercial economy, experiencing frustration in personal relationships at work and at home – if such relationships existed, and if not, dealing with loneliness and isolation.

Life in a big city was a make-do, artificial existence, without the easy familiarity of home, where the heart was, where family and friends interacted joyfully.

Work was essential – even if it was the worst four letter word in the English language that ended with a K, a curse but a necessity, and when the only reason for being in a particular location is employment there is little other reason for being there, without family and long-term friends.

He was not looking forward to rejoining modern society in this context, where people flocked to offices in crowded trains and buses, traffic fumes stank, cars hooted and road rage gripped people on slow moving motorways, neighbour fought with neighbour, lovers betrayed each other, unruly children fought among themselves and with their parents, Saturday nights were full of drunk people escaping from stunted lives - and sane people hoped that at some time before death they might escape to a peaceful place in the country.

"What a world!" Barney thought. "One in which the greater number of people have no clear idea that we are loved beyond measure by a God who has created us and destines us for a life beautiful beyond measure, provided we seek truth and learn to love."

"Well, I suppose I have experienced another possibility, another way of life," he sighed, "even if it is not for me."

He felt unusual sadness as the train began to enter the city, sadness and concern for the people who lived in the rows of houses along the outer suburbs - good quality dwellings, but achieved by what work sacrifices and scrambles for better-paid jobs, ambitious career moves to meet the worries of crippling mortgages. What a trap, unless for a period one had good neighbours and family life – or at least a life that one could cope with, until children grew up and moved away, or began to make mistakes and cause deep worry, hurt and anxiety

"An imperfect world," he reflected, "and I don't know where I fit in."

As the sun began to fade the train slowed, passing by small streets that ran at right angles to the rail track, separated only by brick walls and high wire fencing. They were soulless, unbeautiful places.

At the end of one bare, grey street he saw a newspaper borne aimlessly by a desultory wind, drifting round an empty street corner, in front of a fish and chip shop, shuttered and deserted.

The street was treeless, mean, devoid of life.

A single tear rolled down Barney's cheek, a tear for the world.

33 Angel Again

Poor Joseph – poor Barnabas.
He has learnt a lesson, that one can aim too high, that ego and pride can distort, that obsessions can twist a person into a shape that he should not be.

At least Joe had the commonsense to realise, with a gentle hint from me and the Holy Spirit – for we work in unison, Wisdom and myself, fully in accord. I am always his servant.

I write from time ahead, and I should add, perhaps, that for forty years Joe did not mention the fact that Wisdom whispered to him that He would bring him into Himself and burn him free of all things.

He now realises that it was almost certainly true, and is prepared to live with any opprobrium or praise that may result, for he also knows that while the words were whispered in his soul they are meant for all men of goodwill, at all times and in all ages, and should be shared with them.

Criticism and disbelief are to be expected, and praise is only due to Yahweh, who acts according to His judgement.

Joe only received two further direct gifts by Wisdom, insights beyond the normal.

The first was when, after ten years of dark and unrewarded faith, going through a bad personal relationship, he was praying in his local church.

For a fraction of a second he saw above the altar, in the spirit, a Cardinal of the church gazing at him, for a split second, being given an awareness of Joe's determined faith in the darkness of unknowing. Joe recognised that the Cardinal was undergoing a crisis of faith.

The second was as Joe strolled through the cemetery at Ardglass, in solitary meditative prayer. As he paused over the resting place of a deceased parish priest God gave him a sharp vision of the fact that the priest was in purgatory. I saw Joe jump and recoil, exclaiming, "I don't want to know that!"

But he did know, in both cases, and the knowledge was given so that he would realise that all men are subject to God's judgement, that priests are not necessarily saints.

Joe, in common with many people, shares an instinctive reverence for those who are ordained by God.

They exaggerate the state of priesthood, are reluctant to criticise in a normal way, and must learn that ultra reverence for the ordained can amount to exaggerated human respect – a grievous fault, as taught by the church. It is a debilitating attitude that detracts from truth.

This, for the moment, is my final word – except that I should say that Joe's reservations about aspects of Dominican life were rectified by the Vatican Council that was called by Great Pope John XXIII in the year that Joe became a novice.

Altars were turned round so that the people of God could gather round the Table of the Lord. Mass in Latin became a thing of the past – except for those whose religion is dictated by nostalgia and cannot bring themselves to understand that the celebration of Eucharist should be in words that people understand.

A further desirable change, pointed to by the prior, is that men and women are no longer required to change their names in religion. The newly thinking church recognises that the greatest name given is the one at the moment of baptism, when people are given a share in the divine life of Jesus.

To the regret of some in the Dominican Order the venia was abolished as a means of seeking pardon, and obligatory weekly confession was also done away with. In addition, all of the brothers, whether ordained or lay, were enjoined to share their daily recreation periods, a development that would have pleased Joe. It seemed that he had been in accord with the developing mind of the church on these matters.

My amanuensis - the nominal writer of this tale – is aware of the help that we have given, for he is a soulful man, but he does not fully realise how much guidance has been necessary, and occasionally he has missed points of inspiration, for he is a most fallible creature, as with all of the sons of men.

Even those who were with Jesus in his days on earth, and wrote accounts of his life, were not aware of the full measure of inspiration, the nature of inspiration.

Those who refer to the books of the bible as the inspired word of God do not appreciate that inspiration does not interfere with the identity or personality of the writer. The words that they use are theirs, expressing their own thoughts. Inspiration by Wisdom is a subtle movement of the spirit, supplementing and strengthening thoughts, giving force and meaning to words - similar to the muse that your poets experience, the state of heightened awareness and creativity that enhances the words of those who struggle to achieve understanding and express meaning – very similar in fact, for on occasion it is Wisdom who inspires at all levels.

You should not discount this, not believe that divine inspiration is restricted to the words of the prophets and the apostles.

Wisdom is not dead. He is alive and active, weaving his way into your thoughts, and we, his messengers, are always with Him, seeking to help those who seek truth, for true inspiration is only open to people who seek to live by the truth, who look for truth.

Those who make loud and wordy public proclamation declaiming against the ills of the world, seeing no good in it, almost certainly seek personal glorification, and in doing so frequently mislead weak-minded brethren. Beware! These are sons of the liar, assisting the devil to spread panic and disorder, hatred and anger, confusion, to the devil's delight.

Joe has taken a considerable step in the right direction. He has avoided dedicating himself to a way of life that would have reduced the reality of himself to a shadow of what he must become: a rounded, complete man, open to reality, not imprisoned by an abstract, idealised idea of perfection.

His initial ambitions were false; notions that would have led to the creation of a cipher, a depersonalised, cheapened, unreal image: an animated lie in fact.

The personal path to integration and wholeness of being is fraught with danger, for even what is seen to be good may be less than good. It is only when someone truly repents and really denies himself or herself undisciplined pleasure, takes up the cross of self denial, that one achieves holiness and true joy, empties himself or herself of vanity and selfishness, seeks to take a lower place, ignores the urge to seek fame and glory.

But for someone like Joe, who is now prepared to walk and talk humbly, not seek advancement or preference, not seek fame, who prays to remain in the spirit of the living Lord, this person will never be far from the help that he needs.

'Pray that you do not enter into temptation – be put to the test,' says He who is the Lord of life. It would be a foolish person who ignored the advice.

Forgive the extravagance and inadequacy of these words. The nominal writer, my amanuensis, does not at all times listen to me, does not properly reflect my thoughts. I continually hope that he will cooperate with my gentle touch.

I have little more to say about Joe. He is in a state no different from that of any of his brothers and sisters. He must earn his living by the sweat of his brow, realise the value of ordinary work, no matter how menial and apparently unimportant. Joseph is a good hearted, simple soul. He has much to learn about evil, about his own limitations, about stability.

He has suffered, as all men do, and will suffer further. It may be that I will be given the opportunity to record his current and future stumbling progress, for he is at least open to me.

But stay a while. I have an important thing to say.

You will remember I wished to clarify the relationship that we angels have with our creator.

I wrote, through your author, "I would ask you to note with special care our relationship with Yahweh - the exact quality of it: that we are not part of him, that we are distinct."

By nature we are greater than you. But you should not be envious, for in some amazing respects your abilities are more varied than ours and the ultimate purpose of your creation is infinitely greater.

You, for example, can generate new life. We, as angels, have no such privilege. The Lord God has seen fit to save this great gift for you: a wondrous privilege – though greatly misused and abused, as all men know, often regarded as a mere animal appetite, divorced from the loving creation of new life, and because of this disorder and lack of perception often surrounded by confusion and guilt.

The Word incarnate became truly a man, as you are men and women, living in a dangerous, destructive world, amazing in its goodness but subject to ills that were brought about by your race in the garden of the world.

That act of disobedience that separated you from God was the fault of all mankind. It was wrought by a group of men who represented all people in time.

Repentance to repair the break was due from you, from mankind, but you men were incapable of this, even though it was due in justice.

So, to repair the breach, to make atonement – to bring about at-one-ment between God and man – God the

Word chose to enter the world he created, and bring about this atonement in person.

Only He had the power to make amends. As true God and true man, he was able to rectify the great original fault, subjecting himself in an extreme fashion to the ills of death and suffering that afflict his brothers and sisters.

Because he was and is a man he was able to satisfy the demands of justice. Because he was and is God he had the power to wipe out the fault of the first Adam: 'Father, forgive them, for they do not know what they do.' This was directed not only to the soldiers who crucified him, but to Pilate, the chief priests of Judea and to all who have ever done wrong.

You are forgiven – and as this Jesus shared your humanity you are to share his divinity. By his gift you are brought into his divine life, wondrously sharing in the love that he has for his eternal father.

This is a gift way beyond that given to we who are angels. We move in the spirit, acknowledging the greatness of God. You, because you are brothers and sisters of Jesus, share in His divine life, the inner life of God; lifted far beyond our angelic state.

The smallest child of man, baptised into this new life that Jesus gives, is higher in the heavenly realm than the greatest of the angels. The lowest, repentant sinner - murderer, thief or adulterer though he may have been - is lifted higher than the angels, provided he or she has the humility to repent.

It behoves you well to think of these things, to know that while you are now imperfect you are not to judge yourself or others, not to be inflated by pride in any thing that you do – for pride is the central sin that all suffer from, whether we are fallen angel or a man with exaggerated and distorted vision.

It can be a hard thing to acknowledge the truth – and yet the easiest of all.

Remember what happened to the greatest angel of light and to those who choose to follow him, adopting pride in place of reality, choosing destructive power in place of creative purpose, exchanging hope for despair, returning hatred for love, never to be released from an eternal choice - freely made, never to be undone.

Your proper place is above and beyond the place of angels, united in the Person of Jesus, worshipping and adoring the Father through the power and love of the Holy Spirit, living eternally in Their Love, resurrected with the Christ to repopulate the vast universe that even now is being made new – the new garden of Eden.

Perhaps you are afraid to think of this.

It would be a pity, a failure, to recognise who and what you are to become, through the kind gift of your creator.

Addendum

Thinking?

Cogito ergo sum?

Addendum Content

	Page
Trust Thinking?	191
Sex, Love, Marriage, Divorce, Nullity & A Caring Church?	195
- including Letter to Benedict XVI	206
Afterthought	223
Troglodyte?	225
The God Search	231
Incarnation	233
Mary, Mother of Jesus	237
Authority	251
Questions About Authority & Parish Priests	261
Predestination?	275
The Face of Jesus?	285
Spirit	289
The Trinity	293
Evil	299
Life & Death	307
Heaven, Hell & Purgatory	315
Prayer	319
End Notes	326

Trust Thinking?

"**Cogito ergo sum**" – 'I think, therefore I am,' wrote René Descartes, the 17th Century philosopher and mathematician.

It is a daft statement, as any normal person over the age of seven can immediately tell, though a seven year old might need help to appreciate that the valid statement would be 'Sum ergo cogito' – 'I am, therefore I think'.

But Descartes' famous dictum seems to have robbed subsequent philosophers of common sense and basic trust in the way that we gain and develop knowledge.

Descartes distrusted the senses and tried to isolate reason in an effort to investigate the possibility of knowing whether or not there is a creator.

His approach seems to have plunged philosophers into a whirlwind of introspection in which doubt about our power of knowing is the chief ingredient, despite the fact that he later clarified his thinking, stating that he accepted as an *ipso facta* necessity that in order to think we must first of all exist.

A sensible person will have no doubt about the matter. We human beings, alone of all creatures on earth, possess an impressive rational power, and we possess it not because we can think about it but just because this is the type of creature we are.

We ask questions about our existence, and I would suggest that if we can ask a reasonable question it is likely that we can arrive at a reasonable answer, perhaps not immediately, but in due course as our investigation proceeds, provided we seek truth diligently.

We must question the correctness of our discoveries, of course, ensure that we are functioning in a rational manner, but fundamentally we should trust that reason has the power to properly guide, help us to come to a verifiable conclusion – as much in philosophy and theology as in the physical sciences.

We may not know exactly how a scientific phenomenon works, but it would be a foolish and irrational person who would deny that electricity generates light and atomic fusion power. The evidence is there. The end products of hypothetical speculation and reasoned investigation are quite evident.

Similarly, if we trust reason, if we ask the right questions, we can arrive at an understanding of the nature of creation itself. I will not stipulate how we are to do this, or what the answers may be, but I am perfectly certain that natural reason is capable of pointing to a truthful conclusion.

Whether or not we understand it, whether we accept the answer we find, is another matter.

Decartes ultimately came to the conclusion that it is a necessary consequence of existence as a rational being that God does exist. I agree with his conclusion, and share his concern that too ready a trust in information acquired through any of the senses can mislead. We can be deluded, but with healthy awareness of this possibility, and with a normal faith in our rational ability, plus a certain amount of courage in speculation, I have little doubt that we can arrive at sure conclusions, even if they seem to indicate possibilities that appear to be almost unbelievable, too big or too grand to hope for.

A hundred years ago men would have laughed at the idea of going to the moon. When it happened it was described as a giant leap forward for mankind. Now it is seen as a comparatively small step towards further space exploration.

It was a fantastic idea at the time, and still is, but not remotely as grand and as other ideas we can conceive.

I leave you to ask your own questions.

Mine are asked in this book, and at least by implication answered, to my satisfaction.

A few related questions and considerations arise.

Some follow on these last few pages. I would consider it an honour if you will join me in my thinking, even though it is certainly inadequate and obviously incomplete.

Thank you for the hospitality of your mind.

Sex, Love, Marriage, Divorce, Nullity and a Caring Church?

I n 75 years of going to Mass, daily for 50 of those years, I have never, ever, heard a Catholic priest speak in praise of sex - though up to the age of seven or eight I would not have had much of a clue what they might be talking about!

Extraordinary, isn't it? There we sit, either men or women, identified by our sex, created by the sexual action of our parents, and the word is never mentioned.

Extraordinary!

God, the creator of all, gives us this great gift of being able, in love, to create other people, new citizens for his kingdom, and we rarely mention it. Extraordinary!

We leave it up to prurient press and media, novels and films, to graphically depict sexual activity, of all kinds, but in church it is accepted that we are only there to praise God for his gift of life and never mention how it is given.

It is assumed that we know all about it, that we have stumbled our way through to a basic knowledge of procreation, but little education is offered, and it is certainly not explained or put in perspective in church congregations, during normal Sunday meetings of the faithful.

It is apparently agreed that it is not suitable, not polite, to mention sex in mixed company, in the presence of children. We all got here by sex. Everyone knows it, including the children – at a suitable level of understanding, if they are brought up properly – but a convention of delicacy dictates that we do not examine the matter further; that we close our minds to further education and understanding. There is little or no discussion about the matter, despite the fact that discussion is *the* major way that we learn and come to understand, regardless of what is the subject.

It is left to children and young people to discuss it among themselves, to come to conclusions without open discussion and caring, informed guidance, so that sexual norms of an increasingly paganised society take over, resulting, at this point in time, in widespread acceptance by a complete generation or two that casual, recreational sex is the norm - completely acceptable - and living together is an open-ended agreement, as opposed to a total, resolute commitment of love for the other person, in sickness and in health, throughout difficult times and the aging process that leads to death.

This is where the church has got it right of course, but fails to hammer home the message as part of real, in-depth, sexual education.

Admittedly, in recent years, classes in Catholic schools have tried to deal with all aspects of a relationship, but there is a tardy and somewhat embarrassed approach to the perennial problem of sex and there is no open discussion.*

Sexual relations are often regarded as a totally private matter, sometimes as an animal activity that should not be mentioned or discussed in polite society. It is easier to consider an airy-fairy emotional and romantic love, or even heavenly love, not so easy to deal with the earthly expression of love between male and female. In fact, in the minds of some, there tends to be a reluctance to consider sexual coition, almost a distaste for the subject, an unspoken inference that sex is *not* about love, that it is merely an animal activity that tends to belittle

---

* Of course, celibate priests are not supposed to know anything about sex - in the practical order - making open discussion almost impossible, in the face of a farrago of po-faced presumptions. Pity! It could be instructive, even fun – if people were honest. It is the duty of priests, despite their reluctance, assisted by lay members of pastoral councils, perhaps even led by lay people, to take the initiative. The benefits of open, healthy discussion could be immense.

men and women, detract from our worth and value. There is a failure to publicly recognise it as a beautiful, pleasurable gift from God.

It appears that ever since Adam and Eve came to the realisation that they were naked, and covered themselves in shame, all humankind share in their embarrassment.

What a pity, that those whom God saw to be good, along with the rest of his creation, find themselves closing their minds to this goodness, and the church, the body that represents Christ on this earth, through its ministers, closes its collective mind on the subject, instead of openly praising our sexual capacity and leading people to an understanding of how wonderful it is to be human, how wonderful are our bodies – despite the lack of proportion and beauty in some, including mine.

The failure to realise and express the fundamental worth and value of the human body, including our sexuality, has from time to time created devastating, destructive heresy, where the body has been considered to be evil.

Failure to emphasise the goodness of human procreation is an evil in itself, and proper education has been continually missed throughout the past two thousand years, simply because we men find it difficult to control our sexual thoughts and actions, fail to live up to the norms of behaviour that are desirable – chaste and loving sex within marriage.

From earliest times Christian leaders within the church have struggled to deal with the extraordinary gift of sex, the ability to generate life. Because sex is so pleasurable, normally first experienced by men through the almost uncontrollable urge to masturbate, people fail to look clearly at problems that arise.

Always the ideal has been presented, especially by Saint Paul, that celibacy is the highest aim. 'Better to marry than to burn' is what he recommends.

In my youth I thought he meant 'better to marry than to burn in hell'. It would have been a useful thing to have known that he meant 'better to marry than burn with sexual desire' - if you cannot devote yourself to a life of celibacy; but no one in the church thought to explain this to me, for discussion about sex was regarded as unseemly, and still is. Something to be avoided.

The Lord Jesus Christ, arbiter of all things, gives us instruction on the matter, but his servants do not follow up with an explanation of his words.

He says, speaking about celibacy as an alternative to marriage, that:

> *"It is not everyone who can accept what I have said, but only to those whom it is granted. There are eunuchs born in that way from their mother's womb, there are eunuchs made so by men and there are eunuchs who have made themselves that way for the sake of the kingdom of heaven. Let anyone accept this who can."* - Matt. 19 10-12

Is he saying that sex is dirty and unworthy? Of course not; he is simply commenting, in the context of discussion and teaching about divorce, upon the difficulty of remaining faithful in marriage.

Now, what am I trying to say?

I am trying to point out that to come to an understanding of our human situation we must squarely face issues that we tend to avoid.

For many hundreds of years there was a Canon Law that prohibited the ordination to the priesthood of men who were born outside marriage. It was a most unjust law.

It was, in fact, aimed at priests of the 4th century, who were supposed to be celibate, but in practice were not, regularly keeping women in their community and availing themselves of sexual pleasure, without marriage, and in the event of generating a son they would later use power and patronage to establish such an offspring in a priestly benefice. The practice was so widespread that church leaders created the law referred to.

So from earliest times church leaders have struggled to control sexuality, their own and others, and eventually, over a period of 700 years or so, urged by princely rulers and aiming for the highest good, even if it meant ignoring the words of Jesus, succeeded in establishing, pretty well universally, that all priests will be celibate.

I say ignoring Christ because this is what they did, and continue to do, by making an obligatory link between priesthood and celibacy. It is, to my mind, a disaster. It is understandable, given St. Paul's strong advocacy, given the fact that the first pope, St. Peter, according to tradition, left his wife in order to serve Jesus – I hope, I am sure, making provision for her and any children they may have had, and there is no reason why they should not have had a family. Scripture says nothing about it, and despite the fact that all within the church agree that a man should not desert his wife Peter did so, without any hint of disapproval.

The early church had no preoccupation with sex, no exaggerated esteem for celibacy.

It was advisable that a Bishop should ideally have had only one wife. As Paul wrote to Timothy

> *"A bishop then must be blameless, the husband of one wife, vigilant, sober, of good behaviour, given to hospitality, apt to teach. . . . Let the deacons be the husbands of one wife, ruling their children and their own houses well."* 1 Timothy 3:2, 12

But subsequent church leaders ignored St. Paul's advice and did not consider the truth that Jesus himself pointed to, that *"not everyone can [be celibate], only those to whom it is granted"* and imposed an arbitrary requirement that all who desire to serve as priests *must* be celibate - with the highest motive, but imposing something not advocated by the apostle Paul and clearly stated by the saviour of mankind that it is He alone who can give the gift of celibacy - to those who are willing to accept it.

The argument put forward by church leaders is that they, as successors to Peter and the Apostles, have the power given by Jesus to rule and control the church:

> "... You are Peter and on this rock I will build my Church. And the gates of the underworld can never hold out against it. I will give you the keys of the kingdom of heaven: whatever you bind on earth shall be considered bound in heaven; whatever you loose on earth shall be considered loosed in heaven." – (Matt. 16, 18 – 20)

I accept this totally. Peter and his successors do have this authority. Jesus identifies Himself fully and completely with the Church, His Body in the world. Witness His question to Paul, "... why are you persecuting me?" Acts 9:4 – a total identification of Himself with His people; "I am Jesus and you are persecuting me." – not 'My people' or 'My Church' but 'Me'.

But even if the successors of the Apostles interpret this identification as including the power to give the gift of celibacy – a step too far I think - I do not think it is wisely exercised. To seek to impose a mandatory celibacy upon those who desire to serve as priests goes beyond the authority given, I believe, seeking to impose group celibacy by profession rather than allow the gift to be given individually by He who is the Lord of Life. As Jesus said, "It is not everyone who can accept what I have said, but only those to whom it is granted." (Matthew 19:11)

Would it not be better to accept the wonder and beauty of devoted marital life, as was accepted without question in the early church, saying to all, whether married or single: you may serve God as priests, looking after the brothers and sisters of Jesus, and if He gives you the call to celibacy you are wonderfully blest, but if He does not give to you this special calling you may still serve him at the Table of the Lord and in the care of your brothers and sisters?

I believe that we should reverence reality, not impose where imposition is not required, not lay an unnecessary burden.

There are many fine married men, capable of holding down well-paid and important jobs in society, who would willingly sacrifice income and position to serve the Lord Jesus in this way, but the church prohibits their freedom to choose, imposes an artificial barrier, all because of an exaggerated respect for celibacy. I say exaggerated, for this is what it is – elevating it to something that it is not, failing to understand that it is a special gift, and seeking to establish it as a norm, which it is not, as is made clear by He who is the Lord of all.

It would be a healthy church that permitted freedom in this respect. It would be a more human church, a more caring, actively involved body of people. It would be a holier and more wholesome church, which would be more effective in carrying out the mandate to teach and baptise, to welcome into the body of the church those who have great need of the food of eternal life that is within it.

It's all very well to have a monolithic organisation that all – or many – admire, but there are aspects of the church as it presently exists that are distinctly repellent, including a mindless veneration of clergy – an elevation of the Pope to almost the stature of deity – certainly a deity substitute in the minds of many people - and most obnoxious of all, the creation of a rule-bound clergy and people – them and us, militating against brotherhood - in a system that tends to stifle the utterance of the Spirit and quell the freedom offered by Jesus to learn to love Him.

An exaggerated point of view you think?

Possibly, but I believe it contains elements of truth. There is a personal isolation that exists in the church, a lack of warm community awareness, and to a certain extent a failure to effectively recognise the reality that we are brothers and sisters to each other, united in the Body of Christ, locally and universally, in his humanity as well as in his divinity. Reorganisation is vital, and it is slow to come, despite the efforts of Great Pope John XXIII to open the people of God to a fresh awareness if what is required.

The fire that Jesus came to cast over the earth is dimmed and diminished by lack of trust and love for Him and for each other, a failure to live as human beings, organise structures that aid human development and perception of the divine – rather than a stifling, impersonal reverence for rules and regulations.

I don't know the answer to all of the problems that exist, except in ways that are automatically rejected by those who traditionally exercise authority within the church.

I advocate freedom to marry and become priests... an act of trust in the innate goodness of people, male and female.

I advocate the acceptance of women as priests. Shock! Horror! We are not allowed to even *think* of such a thing. There is a crazy attempt to forbid any discussion.

What a shame that our pope and many bishops should so close their minds.

One half of the population of the church is cut off from certain types of active service within the church because of gender - the fact of their sex. It's abysmally sexist, and all because a few old men retain an atavistic attitude inherited from cavemen ancestors.

"Oh," they say. "Our Lord came to earth and appointed twelve *men* to carry on with His work of redemption.. He could have appointed women but he did not."

Such a view fails to take into account the norms of society that existed when the Word became incarnate, the approach that God adopted to entering His universe, quietly, in the womb of a little girl in the Middle East, not in a blaze of glory or with trumpet blast, seeking to immediately alter society.

"Ah," say the combined traditional clergy, "That was the great triumph of women, that Jesus chose to give himself to the world via a woman. This is their highest moment. This is what they are for, to give life to the world, in this case Divine life! What more can they want?"

They want to be treated as human beings with a value equal to that of men. But they are not. They legitimately require absolute equality, for they *are* equal, whether atavistic, muscle-minded, troglodyte men recognise it or not – within or outside the church. I would love to tone down these words, but I dare not. The point must be made strongly, just as Jesus did when he categorized the Jewish priests of his day as "a brood of vipers!"

I would not dare to make such a criticism of today's priests. There is great goodness among the men who devote their lives to the service of the living God, but as with all priestly classes in all religions, there is a tendency to impose a regulatory thought pattern, a shared outlook that can militate against fresh, personal realisation of the truth, create a deadening effect.

So I say, with respect, there is a danger within the Catholic Church that the self-perpetuating oligarchy of elderly men who rule it will deaden the message, fail to communicate the wonder of Jesus, block the well-springs of reality, without intending to do so - suffocate the spread of truth.

As time goes on those who currently rule the church will, of course, be replaced, and the power of the Holy Spirit will sweep through the people of God, I believe, enabling new leaders to come to a fresh realisation, achieve a liberating clarity of mind - along with a guilty recognition of the truth - that women and men *are* equal: equally fallible and irrational at times, but also equally capable of thinking, bearing witness to and teaching the truth that we are set free by Jesus our living Lord, and entirely capable of offering praise to God through celebration of the Eucharist.

We do this already of course, as members of a congregation, but there is no earthly reason why the main celebrant should not be a woman. Mary offers her son to the world. There is no reason why other women should not be enabled to do the same.

There will always be men who equate authority with power. They have inherited power through a selection process dominated by men, and as a group based upon gender they will struggle to retain the power they have been given, excluding fellow human beings because of gender, just as they currently exclude married men from sharing in the burdens of the priesthood.

It will change, I believe, as men begin to think outside the preconceived norms of today; and a hundred years from now, or even less, because the process of change is accelerating, from the time, a hundred years ago, where women were regarded as distinctly inferior, not even permitted to vote in any democracy that I know of. Now they supply Prime Ministers and leadership in all walks of life.

The Church that Jesus established will probably be the last organisation to recognise the value, worth and abilities of women, just as it took a long time for a traditional, unreflective, power driven clerical organisation to recognise the reality that the earth revolves around the sun.

Human reason and experience will always struggle with those who rely exclusively upon revealed truth, who do not realise or fully accept that all are on a voyage of discovery, and that reason and experience are the only way whereby truth may be understood, even with respect to revelation; that without reason and experience we would not have begun to recognise the true nature of Christ or gain wondrous insight into the Trinitarian nature of God – just as we have begun to accept that democracy, with all its faults, offers the only practical way to organise society; and scientific knowledge, with all *its* faults, is inevitable and mostly beneficial, provided it is conducted with respect for life.

There is no actual *reason* why women cannot do the majority of jobs that were once the preserve of men. All there is against it is prejudice, and this is *un*reasonable, and unjust.

Those who refuse to use reason, neglect this great gift, court disaster. Persistent refusal to live by reason and love can lead to insanity, regardless of outward appearances; and in the Christian context the rejection of truth that reason reveals may lead to the ultimate disaster of rejecting He who is truth. One would hope for mercy, but what can Almighty God do in the face of intransigent rejection of truth? Not much. We find ourselves where we are by a continued sequence of choices, freely made.

It's time to wake up!

I have further criticisms to voice, very reluctantly, about the direction the church is taking at this moment, and this directly involves our present pope.

I would take them up directly with Benedict, for I am not here involved in criticism from the outside.

I am Benedict XVI's brother, just as I am Christ's brother, through His great gift, and it is in a brotherly way that I confront Benedict, and to a certain extent Jesus, for, of course, I do not know Him fully, always seek to understand what may be in His mind.

Contention is the last thing on my mind. Life is too short to argue about passing things. But there are concerns that one cannot shrink from.

Then it is an absolute duty to state one's beliefs clearly and strongly, with due respect for those who hold an opposing opinion.

I have no doubt whatsoever that Benedict XVI loves God and His people, that he serves our redeemer in every way that it is possible for him to do, but I cannot help being critical, and at this point I make my criticism directly to him, should he ever happen to read these words.

I am not one to say something in the third person.

I like to be direct, and would be, face to face, person to person, with Benedict XVI, were it not for the fact that I am merely one little man among 1.2 billion Catholics.

So,

Dear Benedict, - my brother, despite the kind and loving man that I take you to be, I must say that I think you are a man caught in a straitjacket of historical imperatives – surprising in a person with such a broad view of history and such a love for Jesus.

Anyone who has read your first encyclical *"Deus Caritas Est"* - "God Is Love" - will immediately understand that in you we have a man who thinks clearly and presents the truth of Christianity in a thoughtful, restrained manner.

Emotional ranting is not for you.

I would recommend *Deus Caritas Est*[*] to anyone with the slightest interest in the meaning of true love. It is sharp, clear, a compelling analysis of the human condition and how people should behave with respect to love, human and divine, *eros* and *agape*.

You obviously respect the liberty that we have from God to think and either accept or reject the analysis you give, and I am particularly pleased that you emphasise the need of all religions to respect human life and liberty, not seek to impose by force of any kind, and in addition, state that we who believe in Jesus should not proselytize but simply live our lives with care for each other, relying mainly on our prayers and way of life to impress our neighbour with the worth and value of our

---

[*] Easily downloaded in many languages from the Vatican website, or *Googled* to bring up a few hundred references. Ruth Gledhill, of the LONDON TIMES writes, "I started reading Deus Caritas Est expecting to be disappointed.... How wonderful it is to be proven wrong... he indulges in some of the most beautiful and passionate writing I have ever seen in papal prose ... the Pope was former head of the Congregation of the Doctrine of the Faith, the body once known as the Inquisition. But this encyclical is not the work of an inquisitor. It is the work of a lover — a true lover of God."

beliefs – prepared to state beliefs strongly, with straightforward courtesy, but with respect for those who hold conflicting views.
As you say,
> 'Those who practise charity in the Church's name will never seek to impose the Church's faith upon others. They realize that a pure and generous love is the best witness to the God in whom we believe and by whom we are driven to love. A Christian knows when it is time to speak of God and when it is better to say nothing and to let love alone speak.'

Given this, I am surprised that you seem to be a prisoner of tradition, even though, along with all Catholics, I appreciate that much tradition is valuable and should not be ignored.

Let me give an example or two of where I believe your adherence to tradition shows a surprising lack of perception, a practical failure to accept what is happening in the world and in the church. They are comparatively trivial in themselves, but they set a tone.

Had I been Cardinal Michael O'Shea – well, *anything* is possible! – and then elected pope, I would have retained my baptismal name, given by my mother and recognised by Jesus as the name given at the moment I received His eternal life through water and the gift of the Holy Spirit.

My mother would have been pleased to call me Michael I, as Jesus would, I think, knowing that I reverence baptism.

As a matter of fact a friend of mine says I would have made a very *good* Pope, but he may have changed his mind when he is released from the Downshire Mental Hospital. Who can tell?

In the world of reality however, you - ushered into divine life by baptism and given the name Joseph - chose to change your name to Benedict.

Why? Because you reverenced Benedict XV and the great St. Benedict. Good. Why not? If you felt like it.

Jesus, when he changed Simon Bar Jonah's name to Peter had a vital purpose, to underline the fact that Peter was to be the Rock upon which the visible church is founded. Many subsequent popes took this as setting a precedent, that their name should also be changed, a tradition that started with the Hebrew Abram to Abraham, but subsequent to Vatican II the men and women who traditionally followed a similar practice when they joined religious orders, taking a new name to indicate a new phase in their lives, were required by the Bishops of the world to retain their baptismal name, or given the option to do so.

The old practice traditionally expressed the fact that one was called to a higher purpose; but Vatican II had the effect of reminding us that there can be no higher purpose than living fully the life of Christ, given at baptism.

I would have thought then, that you, brought into divine life and given the name Joseph, would have chosen to recognise this new understanding, and been content to be known as Joseph I.

You have not. You chose to follow a lesser tradition. I repeat, the only name change that had real meaning was in the case of the first pope, where the person who made the change was God incarnate, for the reason we understand.

I would have expected you, working at the centre of the church and realising the essential nature of the conclave of bishops called by John XXIII, would have implemented the mind of the church fathers in every way possible.

The point I make is small, and relatively unimportant, but it indicates a mind-set, a lack of lateral thinking and alertness to the changes that have taken place in the universal church.

Then, when I consider that almost your first public act as pope was to reach out to the schismatic group of bishops and priests that had left the church, led by the renegade Archbishop, Marcel LeFevre, when he rejected the findings of Vatican II, ostensibly about the use of Latin but possibly really disturbed about ecumenism, I wondered why this should have priority.

It is, of course, an excellent thing to heal schism and division within the church, but at what price?

I now discover, in 2008, that similar minded groups throughout the world are to be encouraged to revert to saying the Mass in Latin, or given total freedom to celebrate the Eucharist in Latin. In *Latin*? A language that no person speaks naturally and that probably only 0.01% of the world population understands, to a limited degree!

Is the clock to be put back? Is the tradition of the Latin Mass to be reintroduced and imposed upon the faithful despite the recommendation of the Bishops of Vatican II regarding the change to the vernacular?

It would appear so. As I write I hear about a friend, a prayerful Catholic, who went to London at the weekend and found herself attending three Masses, all in Latin, by virtue of the fact that she attended Mass in three different churches over the weekend, including Westminster Cathedral, to find to her astonishment that in each church the Mass was being celebrated in a language that she did not understand.

It's an extraordinary *volte face*, and it seems set to become a regular occurrence throughout the world.

I am very much in favour of freedom to celebrate the Eucharist in any language that is relevant, but Latin is just not relevant, not to the people of the world who struggle to communicate, understand and express the nature of our faith.

I regret to say that I have other complaints.

I was astounded a few years ago to read – in January 2000 - that you, as Cardinal Ratzinger, Prefect of the Congregation of Doctrine of Faith, had instructed an American priest, Fr. Robert Nugent, and a nun, Sr.

Jeanine Grammick, to stop talking to homosexual and lesbian people and their worried relatives – cease trying to bring comfort to fathers and mothers who thought that their deviant sons and daughters would automatically go to hell.

Fr. Nugent and Sr. Grammick had been working with such people for more than twenty years. You, as Cardinal Ratzinger, put a stop to it.

I was quite angry at the time and wrote the following to an Irish journal. *(Ceide, Vol.3 No 2 Dec/Jan 2000)* There is one word I used in the letter that may cause annoyance, but let it stand:

> *[Dear Editor],*
> *Lucky Fr. Robert Nugent and Sr. Jeanine Grammick that they are not under house arrest (following in the footsteps of Copernicus etc.) or physically tortured to alter their mindset of loving concern towards homosexual and lesbian people.*
>
> *It really is sickening that obtuse members of such a Congregation in my church (just as much mine as theirs) should appear to lack the courage and love that is required by those who seek to follow the example of Jesus.*
>
> *I suspect that if Doctrine of Faith Congregation members had witnessed the prostitute Mary Magdalene wipe the feet of Jesus they would have joined those who muttered behind their hands about the unsuitability of such a relationship. But now that this ex-prostitute has been safely dead for a couple of thousand years – and provides no threat to seemliness and church bureaucracy – the occasion can be viewed as a one-off demonstration of Christ's mercy towards sinners – which should never be attempted by mere human followers of Christ.*
>
> *Good, practicing Christians of today would not wish, if they were normal and orthodox, to have anything to do with such people.*

> 'Leave them alone and they'll come home, wagging their tales behind them!' would appear to be the attitude of this Scared Congregation towards the sexually unorthodox – a 'pink-bows-and-bonnet' approach rather than the urgent plea by the Good Shepherd to seek and find the sheep (our brothers and sisters) who appear to be lost in the mists and storms of life and sexuality.
>
> Does not God still love the sinner? Are we not allowed to express our love? The prohibition of pastoral work by Messrs Nugent & Grammick among homosexual and lesbian people is positively against the two most important commandments of God [love God and neighbour]. It is a lunacy in Christ's Church and totally abhorrent."

I really was angry, and still am, and I regret the use of the word obtuse – for I know that you are anything but.

It amounts to obtuseness however, a blindness in my opinion, that you and your team should have thought to put a stop to such pastoral work, on the grounds that Messrs. Nugent and Grammick were guilty of failing to maintain the teaching of the church that homosexuality is intrinsically sinful – an accusation that both deny, despite years of investigation by the Congregation.

These are not the only events that give rise to the suspicion that all is not well with the direction the church is moving under your leadership.

The prohibition against your former colleague Fr. Hans Küng, forbidding him to teach theology at the University of Tübingen, dealing mainly with clarification of the doctrine of papal infallibility I understand, remains in force, despite your meeting with him in his retirement, during which, it appears, you and he decided to ignore past difficulties; and then there is Lavina Byrne, the former nun, proscribed for promoting the case for ordination of women to the priesthood. She has every right to remain unhappy with your prohibition of her book,

"*Woman at the Altar*" and with your effort to stop all discussion of the matter.

I am astounded too that you highlight the offer of Indulgences in this day and age, after the appalling misuse of the power in the Middle Ages, still resonating in the minds of people, associated with Martin Luther's rebellion.

I suspect that the vast majority of Catholics do not fully understand this Church practice: that you and other bishops have the power to remit temporal punishment due to sin, the guilt of which has been forgiven. It is an arcane doctrine and should be relegated to the theological vaults, even though it may bring relief to souls in this world and the next. It is surely injudicious to invoke a power that is so misunderstood – a public relations disaster that recalls a mediaeval disaster to the minds of many. It is not what I personally wish to see highlighted in my church at this time, even if your use of the power may be theologically correct.

What is wrong with everyone accepting the due and appropriate consequences of our sins?

Please let us have no more theological dodgery.

A further disquiet that I feel, very acutely, is concerned with your instruction to diocese throughout the world that nullity of marriage should only be granted where there is *absolute* proof of invalidity.

Truth is the word you used, but this, as I now know personally, has been taken in a legal sense, where witnesses *must* be available to attest to a particular set of circumstances.

I had the distressing situation of a marital separation long before you were elected pope. Civil divorce was almost immediate, but I had to wait seven years before cumbersome church procedures produced a declaration of nullity. Seven years! As one parish priest in Belgium commented at that time, "You can tell immediately that this marriage is invalid. It should only take about six months to come to a definite, secure conclusion!"

Seven years is a large chunk of life, and had I been younger, and contemplating marriage, it could have destroyed my spirit.

It is a natural thing to seek loving companionship, and had I been a young, or a different man, it is likely that I would have been tempted to establish a union without church blessing. It appears that thousands do, jolted into a *de jure* state of sin by cold ecclesiastical logic, inefficiently administered.

Current judicial procedures, undertaken by overworked staff trying to pick up the pieces of unhappy relationships, are ponderous in the extreme, starting off, in my case, with my parish priest, a meticulous, kindly man, typing out all relevant details. It took a total of seven hours. I did not mind this. I admired the dedication of the PP, though even he asked, "Michael, why do you want to go through with this?" My reply was that I simply wanted the record set straight; that I wanted to be free – face the truth.

The real delay began to be experienced at diocesan level, where it appeared that urgency was the last thing on anyone's mind. There appeared to be a very leisurely approach, partly because - I got the strong impression - the priests in charge were exasperated by the failure of people to better organise their lives, and, as one lay person said over the phone, "We can't have people think that Nullity is divorce by the back door."

As a consequence of my unhappy experience I would recommend that those at the centre of the church consider more workable alternatives, possibly a decentralisation within each diocese, with initial investigations carried out and recommendations made by a group of three or four priests – or educated laymen - from adjoining parishes. It is not so difficult to understand and apply canon law, certainly not beyond the competence of dedicated and educated priests, or appropriately educated laymen.

As a truly caring body the concern of the church should surely be centered on the welfare of members of the Body of Christ, not with fastidious, protracted compliance with exaggerated legal standards, investigated by overburdened Diocesan staff.

Regardless of any such possible reorganisation I have a further major concern that I must lay at your doorstep.

I know that you urged Nullity Courts to deal expeditiously with problems that people face, and you stated that nullity should only be granted in the light of truth.

I have no quarrel with this. Truth is absolutely essential.

But in my direct experience, with two nullity courts, one in the UK and one in Germany I find that your directive is interpreted as meaning absolute, independent witnessed proof in a given situation.

There seems to be no possibility of considering the truth or otherwise of a nullity plea that cannot meet an exacting process of stringent legality, barren law without reference to the love that Jesus has shown.

Consider the following case.

A young woman, a compatriot of yours, met a man when he was 18. She was 21. Both were Catholic, and three years later they were married, in a Catholic Church in north Germany. During the next seventeen years they generated six children and the lady became pregnant with a seventh child.

From her point of view the marriage was good. She had worked to help support their children but with so many she had to stay at home and look after them, while their father worked away from home in Germany. The separation was not ideal and they planned to combine home and place of work as quickly as possible.

One weekend the husband, having spent a few days at home, returned to work. The next day he telephoned and told her that he was not returning to her and their children.

She was devastated. She had no idea what was going on in his mind. There had been no argument or discord. She arranged for her children to be cared for and flew to Germany to confront him. He was adamant. He was not returning. He could give no explanation other than they had grown apart. She was desolate, heartbroken, betrayed by a man who seemed not to have understood the permanent nature of marriage.

Following a period with her mother, devastated by this event, she decided that she had to return to the United Kingdom, believing that she and her children would have better life opportunities in that country rather than the region of Germany where she had been born.

She arrived at Heathrow, shocked and unhappy, heavily pregnant, and with six children aged between 2 and 16.

She had no blood relatives in the UK, and little money, but she managed to find a place to live, and as soon as the baby was born – and I mean within days - she found a job as a hotel receptionist; and for the next twelve years devoted her life to housing, feeding and educating her children, with little or no help from her husband, whom she divorced under civil law. He disappeared from the scene.

Constantly working and with the help of educational grants and student loans she managed to send five girls to University, four of whom have now graduated.

It was only at the age of fifty four, in 2007, that she began to have time for herself, and as she had met a man three years before and found that she had grown to love him, she decided that she would like to marry. He was a devout Catholic, a daily communicant, retired and living on a modest pension, and as she had always gone to Mass and had brought up her children in the Catholic faith she had to begin to seek a Nullity decree in order to marry; but Church authorities refused to even consider her plea - because of instructions you issued.

Arguing on her behalf I put forward the case that the father of her children had demonstrated by his actions that he was incapable of contracting a valid marriage, that even before the marriage took place he was not a fit person, suffering the impediments laid out in Canon 1095: exhibiting

> '*A grave lack of discretionary judgement concerning the essential matrimonial rights and obligations to be mutually given and exchanged*'

- and –

> '*Because of causes of a psychological nature ...unable to assume the essential obligations of marriage*'

He certainly proved in practice, by his actions, that he was unable to assume these essential obligations. His behaviour betrayed a deep-seated inability to live up to the obligations he had verbally undertaken during the marriage ceremony – unless one refuses to face the plain facts of psychology and excuses his behaviour on account of some imaginary, unexplained 'notion' that came out of the blue.

It is more likely and more reasonable that his actions can be explained by an enduring psychological and moral defect, a personality disorder, but because of the strict interpretation put on your instruction regarding nullity, requiring witnessed proof - impossible in this case - a fine and honourable woman is treated with a lack of loving and truthful care, consigned to the matrimonial scrapheap by bureaucratic church laws that do not exhibit the communal care that is essential, as you say in *Deus Caritas Est*.

I quote:

> "*Love of neighbour, grounded in the love of God, is first and foremost a responsibility for each individual member of the faithful, but it is also a responsibility for the entire ecclesial community at every level: from the local community to the particular Church and to the Church universal in*

its entirety. As a community, the Church must practice love."

In the case outlined above, and probably in many others, it is apparent that this essential loving care is absent.
The love that Jesus has for us is not made evident. The church is failing in this part of its mission.[*]

In 1969, as plain Fr. Joseph Ratzinger, you stated your belief that the church would possibly be reduced in size and that
> *"As a small community, she will demand much more from the initiative of each of her members and she will certainly also acknowledge new forms of ministry and will raise up to the priesthood proven Christians who have other jobs. In many smaller communities, respectively in social groups with some affinity, the normal care of souls will take place in this way ....*
> *It will make her poor and a Church of the little people .... All this will require time. The process will be slow and painful ....*
> (Five lectures you gave in 1969 at radio stations in Bavaria & Hessen.)

I am not too sure about your prediction regarding size, but I am certain that the church is and ought to be about *the little people, and that care for its members is*

---

[*] In the case cited immediate action may be taken by reference to the Nullity Court in the Diocese of Erfurt. As I prepared some documents my name is associated with the case, so it can be easily identified. The last communication this lady had from the Offizial there is dated 19 March 2008. Regard this as special pleading if you wish. I would equally plead urgency in other cases if I knew of them. To turn away from such people is to close one's heart to suffering humanity. Would Jesus apply church Law so rigorously?

best and most effectively shown in smaller communities, in social groups with some affinity.

I also agree that the church, with shrinking numbers of vocations will *demand much more from the initiative of each of her members, and will certainly also acknowledge new forms of ministry, raising up to the priesthood proven Christians who have other jobs.*

Perhaps even those who are married?

I am a devoted, struggling Christian; your brother and servant, and as a man in the same age group I look forward to meeting you in heaven within comparatively few years; brought there by the power of the Holy Spirit, sent forth by the Father and His Son.

In the meantime I hope and pray that you will instruct ecclesial jurists to exercise more loving care for those who are betrayed by those who have little understanding of love, are incapable of expressing it, and fail to live by it.

As you say,

....if in my life I fail completely to heed others, solely out of a desire to be "devout" and to perform my "religious duties", then my relationship with God will also grow arid.

It becomes merely "proper", and loveless.

Only my readiness to encounter my neighbour and to show him love makes me sensitive to God as well. Only if I serve my neighbour can my eyes be opened to what God does for me and how much he loves me.

I must register one further, most important criticism, and make a suggestion that may seem outrageous, though it is not.

When you were head of the Doctrine and Faith Congregation you wrote, on May 18 2001, to all bishops of the world, instructing them to report to you serious crimes *(De delictis gravioribus)* such as the offence of a cleric, a bishop, priest or deacon, who commits a sexual sin with someone less than 18 years of age. Rules of secrecy were laid down *(secretum pontificium)* about such reports, and it was made clear that violation of pontifical secrecy, if deliberate, is a grave sin – with excommunication a possibility.

It is not clear why you did this, for local bishops still had responsibility for dealing with such crimes, mostly ineffectually and secretly, until independent news reports and government investigation forced revelations.

Only in 2010 did you write to the people of Ireland to express your sorrow over the vile treatment of young boys and girls by some priests and religious; events that call out to Heaven for vengeance

You did not refer to your own part in creating the secret Vatican reporting system that tended to diminish local Bishops' sense of responsibility and militate against effective pastoral action. You rightly castigate them – but some may feel hurt and unhappy that you have not confessed to any personal involvement or accountability.

It is evident that the children and people of Ireland have been betrayed by systemic negligence and confused procedures, combined with exaggerated reverence for the See of Peter and fear of the Vatican disciplinary machine – created and maintained by you for almost 30 years.

Until you have admitted involvement in establishing a failed system of control apologies are incomplete, ineffective, and permanently damaging.

The hurt to the body of Christ remains until sorrow is expressed in a way that reflects the responsibility of all who share in the apostolic succession.

Peter has a special place, but he was not and is not an absolute monarch, and his fellow bishops need to have the means and the courage to oppose unnecessary or ill-conceived rules, as Paul did to Peter in the nascent church regarding Peter's erroneous belief that those who wished to become Christians must be circumcised.

You would not now make such a mistake, but today's world is complicated and it is a simple fact that one man, even with local advice, is not capable of effectively dealing at all times with worldwide problems.

In his day Peter would have had almost daily contact and discussion with his fellow apostles, at least initially, but as there are now over 5,000 Catholic bishops it is impossible for all who inherit the apostolic mandate to take part in full, regular meetings.

I suggest that a small but representative group of bishops should be created, possibly not more than six from each continent, *elected* from among their own number at four or five year intervals - easily done these days by email or postal ballot.

Such a body, open to refreshing change after five years of service, would be able to partake in regular open-ended meetings with Peter's successor; enabling informed discussion of all matters of church teaching and practice – to agendas presented by local bishops and by the Pope, and in agreement with him able to take vital practical decisions, all in the light of established church teachings of course.

Such a proposal may at first appear startling and bizarre. But is it?

The physical centre of church government would be unchanged, but you and your successors would be alerted to vital and changing needs of the universal church, on a truly universal basis – with Vatican staff (the necessary ecclesiastical and State civil servants) reminded that they are there to serve and implement decisions made by those who participate at the highest level in the apostolic teaching authority given by Jesus - the bishops of the Catholic Church.

It is impossible to replicate the close and immediate human exchanges that occurred in Peter's day, but it is surely desirable that remote and isolated church government should be replaced by a body that reflects the worldwide dedication of individual bishops to carry out the wishes of Jesus: a church that is truly Catholic.

If we love God Incarnate we should be prepared to reorganise our church – His Church - in ways that reflect his humanity as well as His divinity, make it evident that we are a loving, united body of people bearing witness to Him.

I make these points as lovingly, as kindly as possible; obedient to the truth that I know, in the brotherhood of our loving and forgiving saviour, Jesus, Lord of all.

Michael O'Shea

Afterthought ...

> *"If anyone says, 'I love God,' and hates his brother, he is a liar; for he who does not love his brother whom he has seen, cannot love God whom he has not seen"*
> (1 Jn 4:20)

As I came out of Mass one Sunday with my youngest son he said to me, "If you don't mind I think I will not go back to Mass. I get the impression that I am being talked at rather than talked to."

I had to accept his position. He was aged 14.

Throughout history those who lead the church have found it easier to announce rules, search for heresy and seek to condemn and suppress rather than engage in dialogue and discussion.

The attitude tends to be perpetuated in ordinary, everyday situations within the church, at all levels. There is a failure to explain, a failure to trust in the ability of people to understand. There is no dialogue and discussion. It's all one-way traffic.

Quite often the attitude of clergy is, 'This is the teaching of the Church! Take it or leave it!' There is a grievous failure to patiently, lovingly educate - probably because priests themselves have little idea how to present the great mysteries of the Incarnation, the Trinity, the Resurrection, the Immaculate Conception, the taking of Mary into Heaven, the Real Presence of Christ at the Eucharistic Celebration, the reality of sin and the unending love and forgiveness that Jesus has for each one of us - and there is never a word of praise for God's wonderful life-giving gift of sex – merely dire warnings against lust.

Homilies also tend to avoid explanation of scriptural readings – despite the injunction of the fathers of the Church in Vatican II. Preachers will laud the Pope and the great saints (whose holiness we can never hope to emulate) - praise the impressive size of the church and the charitable work it does in foreign lands, but fail to educate and explain the wondrous dealings that God has with us in the Person of Jesus, in the ever present love of the Holy Spirit.

It is a great pity, a great neglect.

Failure to teach, to explain, to strive for realisation and understanding, is one sure way to fail to love one's brother.

Can we then say in truth that we love God?

Trglodyte?

Sigmund Freud thought of sex as mankind's main driving force. Alfred Adler believed it to be a desire for power.

Had our cave-dwelling ancestors of 150,000 years ago thought about it they would have had little doubt that it was a combination of both, plus the need for food and personal safety in a dangerous world.

Then, about 2,000 years ago, Jesus confirmed the Judaic teaching that love of God and neighbour is the most basic and powerful need - and for the next two millennia leaders of the Catholic Church strove to establish mandatory celibate service as the highest expression of this love – promoting it as a desirable norm, despite the fact that the norm established by the Creator is the creation of life through the sexual union of male and female.

This heady mix of power and sex, the basic need for love, plus an imposed celibacy (as distinct from the God-given gift) has contributed much to widespread sexual abuse by Catholic priests, and in the light of this, and horrific outrages against children in Catholic Church institutions, I suggest that leaders of my Church should realise the limits of their Christ given authority, reject imperial attitudes acquired through history, and become more realistically and compassionately loving.

In the cavern of the mind,
entombed in dark bone dome
- afraid of love and reason, blind to light,
men dwell - forever troglodyte
- especially in Rome.

Am I unfair to men, especially to the men in Rome who rule the Catholic Church?

I think not.

For centuries men have regarded women as inferior in all things but child bearing.

It is irrational, and it is an insult to women and to the loving God who creates all people in His image and likeness. *"Even women?"* do I hear you ask? Then you *are* a troglodytic, misogynist male!

The men who fail to recognise the value and worth of women - in the church or outside it - reflect a caveman mentality, a throwback to cave dwelling ancestors of 150,000 years ago where women were regarded as objects of sexual pleasure, useful for gathering kindle and tending a cooking pot, and necessary for the care of the infants that emerged as a result of sex. Well, you know how it is classified even today - *women's work!*

It would appear that in those days, as far as men were concerned, children were only really valued if they were male. Female infants were regarded as extraneous baggage, unless they grew into attractive physical specimens, in which case they might be worth fighting over, in order to establish ownership of a desirable property.

Things have not changed much in the minds of many, despite the fact that within the past hundred years or so women have begun to be recognised as human beings with character, wit and ability, as a result of education, emerging democracy and continual campaign for gender equality.

Residually in the minds of many males, however, is the assumption that men are the real power, the only people born to command, to rule – and in the minds of those who have embraced Christianity the highest aim now presented is to become permanently celibate, the greatest manly challenge for the sake of Christ - even if it is in opposition to His reminder that all are not capable of existing without sex, that voluntary celibacy is the direct gift of God:

"It is not everyone who can accept what I have said, but only to those whom it is granted." (Matt.19)

Despite this Catholic church leaders – all male of course - have gone on to enforce celibacy as a condition of being ordained priest, so that females during the past few hundred years have had to overcome the additional hurdle of being viewed as sexual temptresses, possible occasions of sin - to those of normal sexual orientation of course: Church leaders prefer to ignore the probability of creating a pressure keg of homosexuality and paedophilia.

What dreadful treatment of one half of humankind! All because of failure to recognise the wonder and beauty of the normal, God created male-female relationship and a gross attempt to impose celibacy as the norm, rather weirdly refusing to listen to Jesus, and ignoring St. Paul – a strong advocate of celibacy - when he advises the people of his time that

"A bishop .... must be blameless, the husband of one wife, vigilant, sober, of good behaviour, given to hospitality, apt to teach. . . . Let the deacons be the husbands of one wife, ruling their children and their own houses well."
1 Timothy 3:2, 12

So it all boils down to this:
Sex and power (or gender and authority).
Gender? Males regard themselves as superior.
Authority and Power? Men have it and will not give it up without a fight, even in civil life – or *ever*, in the Catholic Church! Catholics are forbidden by papal decree to even *think* of it!

An unbelievable arrogance!

It is this heady mix of power and sex - harking back to thoughtless, troglodyte days, when physical power and domination was the hallmark of leadership and survival– that has contributed to horrific outrages of systematic violence, sexual abuse and rape of children in Catholic Church Institutions – as exposed in Ireland, Australia, Britain, America, Germany and the Netherlands.

Two reports by the Irish Government's 'Commission to Inquire into Child Abuse' - both undeniably truthful – detail an abomination that lasted for decades under Catholic Church leadership.

If we believe what Jesus says it is certain that such offences will be punished.

"Obstacles are sure to come," he says, *"but alas for the one who provides them! It would be better for him to be thrown into the sea with a millstone put around his neck than he should lead astray a single one of these little ones. Watch yourselves!"* – Luke 17.1-3

"Alas for the one who <u>*provides*</u> them!" So punishment is not reserved for those who perpetrated abuse but also awaits those who created and maintained the institutions that enabled it, and servile government ministers that failed to put a stop to it.

We may be sickened by the whole thing, wish to bury acknowledgement of abominable actions and how they have come about, retreat to a comfort zone of an imagined 'faith'. We may be reluctant to accept that while there is great good in the church it is the arrogant attitude of Catholic Church leaders, in conjunction with a silent, seemingly subservient lay membership, that has caused such abominations - for arrogance is what it is - in Rome and elsewhere within the worldwide episcopate – a world view of power inherited from the early days of Imperial Rome (from Emperors Constantine and Theodosius throughout the 4th Century) and maintained through centuries of Catholic mediaeval grandeur and power, distorting the teaching authority given by Christ and subverting it from a deeply loving spiritual and saving force to a worldly imperialism.

There's not much of the imperial power remaining, except in the 110 acre Vatican City State and in the system that promotes Vatican Bishops and Cardinals, and local bishops.

Such appointments seem to involve an abdication of personal thought, or at least a subjugation of judgement to the overall requirement of obedience to Vatican administration, always aware that a step out of line will bring retribution.

It's a distortion of the authority given by Christ, changing it from a loving, educational mission of salvation, affecting mind, heart and belief, into a powerful, vigilantly prohibitive organisation with a tendency to destroy creative discussion and discovery. Control is the aim. The exterior social and political standing of the Church becomes a top priority. Loving pastoral care assumes a lesser degree of importance, as illustrated by recent occurrences - and free discussion of certain subjects is actually forbidden, as I have already observed; in much the same way that prohibition of teaching as a fact the Copernican theory that the earth circled round the sun resulted in permanent house arrest until death for the scientist Galileo Galilei in 1633.

It is a power that has become so disruptive that it tends to create anxiety among priests and bishops that they may possibly espouse an attitude contrary to a perceived church norm. It's a sad reflection upon the freedom promised by Jesus to those who seek truth and wish to discuss their understanding of it.

Some fellow Catholics will suspect me of heresy because I criticise the thoughts and actions of popes and bishops, as though criticism is a sin, and - woe upon woe - I am probably also regarded by many traditional believers as a disobedient rebel – though distinctly unimportant and certainly not worthy of note: an attitude commonly adopted by those who refuse to examine the validity of an argument, failing to follow the advice of Thomas Aquinas: to consider what is said rather than the person who says it.

In fact, as I have said before, I am a Catholic, a daily participant in the Mass for more than 50 years, and I have found much that is good in the church - dedicated, loving care by many, many priests – sometimes an astounding holiness.

I love the church, truly Christ's Body, and in obedience to the request of Jesus I share in the Eucharistic feast that he established at the Last Supper, believing that as I consume His Body and Blood, in an act of faith, He consumes me in Love, brings me into His eternal reality. I do not understand it fully of course. No one still in the body does. But Jesus assures us that it is His everlasting invitation to eternal life.

Because of this I go to Mass in the company of my brothers and sisters, and no doubt this belief about the Eucharist is central to the motivation of the great majority of priests, though their dedication and education is contaminated by the power needs and structures of the church, all of which desperately need to be discussed and revised by church members, especially among those who receive Christ's mandate to teach and enlighten and turn it into a ruling and controlling power.

A revision of present concepts and intentions, moving towards a renewal of the real apostolic mandate – plus a decent humility and repentance - is essential to the welfare of the church.

I have attempted to outline the reality of some attitudes and problems in this section of my book.

It's worth reading, I believe, especially by priests and prelates, for the ideas that I present are not simply my own. I know this by talking to many people. How else are prelates within my church to understand what is going on in the minds of fellow Christians?

Is this not important to them?

However inadequately expressed my thoughts confront problems that have a permanent urgency within the Catholic Church - and because of recent events must be of great concern to society in general.

Those who believe in the divinity of Christ will pray that Wisdom, the spirit of truth, will be our guide – in sublime love and light - helping men to move beyond that which is troglodyte.

The God Search

I am born. I come into the world with no baggage, no opinions, no knowledge, except for those unknown, unreflective experiences of floating in my mother's womb.

I spend my first weeks sleeping, eating, defecating and urinating, crying out for food or because I have painful experiences of wind clogging my alimentary canal.

I am lovingly attended, winded, fed and cleaned by my parents. My parents do everything for me willingly and lovingly, despite nappy smells and milky burps, provided they are good parents.

I take it all for granted. I am such an adorable little creature. I am magic, and I live in a magical world, gradually beginning to focus on the world around me, recognise the faces of those who feed and care for me.

It is a beautiful world, except for pain from growing teeth and then cuts and bruises.

Boy! What a world! I begin to learn about it.

It's natural, I suppose, that I inherit attitudes and beliefs from my parents as I grow and awareness develops.

"Why?" I ask. "Why this? Why that?" Driving my parents wild.

They begin to use words like God, and I gradually get to know that there is an unexplained Being who is Lord and Master of Creation, All-Powerful and Loving.

I don't know much about Him. I just accept that He is. It seems reasonable.

If I am born into a Catholic family I might eventually discover that God is a Spirit and that He is known, mysteriously, as the Trinity.

It takes a long time to even begin to understand.

Jesus is a great help. He speaks like someone who knows.

Later I have to learn for myself, ask adult questions and work out the answers, verify my knowledge.

The gospels and letters of the New Testament tells of things that happened the early days of what became known as Christianity.

Verification of the reality of these events was regarded, until recently, as independently verified by the Jewish born Roman historian Josephus Flavius, but there is now grave doubt about the reference he made to Jesus.

It appears that this may have been inserted at a later date by the 4th century bishop Eusebius, intent upon reinforcing claims about the divinity of Jesus and the nature of the church.

Whatever about this, followers of a person called Jesus Christ increased in numbers in Rome following the death of Jesus, proclaiming that he had been raised from the dead.

This new religion was seen as a threat to the established Roman order, as mentioned by the Roman writers Tacitus and Pliny the Younger, born in the closing stages of the first century.

Subsequent persecution of Christians confirm the perceived threat. Christians were a fact, giving witness to a man named Jesus Christ and their belief that he was God Incarnate. It is untenable to hold that such growing numbers of people believed something about a person who had never existed, and despite a few differences in accounts by different New Testament authors all reasonable historians accept that the gospels and writings of the New Testament verify the existence of Jesus Christ. The internal, textual evidence is too strong to be ignored.

They are historical records of a reality.

In the meditations that follow I accept totally not only the existence of Jesus but the marvellous things that flow from it. I believe him to be Lord and creator of the universe, become man for our sake.

The Incarnation

He Who created the universe did not think it beneath His dignity to enter the world - in the womb of a little Jewish girl ....

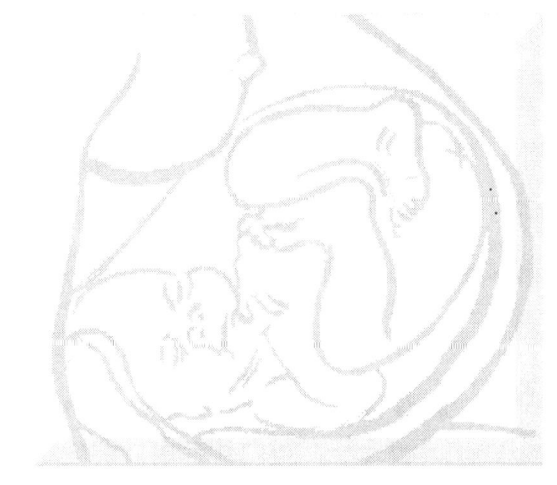

> *"My soul proclaims the greatness of the Lord and my spirit exults in God my saviour; because he has looked upon his lowly handmaid. Yes, from this day forward all generations will call me blessed ...."* Lk1.46

As his brothers and sisters we share in his humanity - and we are invited to share in His Divinity ....

Jesus is one Divine Person possessing two natures: the nature of being truly human - drawn from the body of Mary - and the nature of being fully and truly God, possessed as of right.

It is not surprising that this is a mystery!

Only God knows Himself perfectly. Our human way of knowing is restricted - by virtue of our created human nature - strange that we can often forget that we *are* created!

Jesus is the Word in the Mind of God, according to the disciple John. He is the perfect image and knowledge that God has of Himself.

It is this Word Who has come among us, fully sharing our human nature and offering to share with us, give us, full participation in His own Divine Nature.

He touches us through the love of the Holy Spirit, normally associated with baptism, and draws us into the glory of his Divine nature.

When we are first touched by the Spirit of God we may think we have gone mad, for this way of knowing is beyond our nature, beyond our natural way of knowing.

As created human beings our ways of knowing are limited.

Development can be painful, even in the natural order, for we are not fully aware of the spiritual aspect of our being, not aware of the power and strength of spirit, human or divine, of the possibilities involved.

We should not, of course, scorn the earthy side of our nature. The fact that Jesus now shares in our humanity, is truly become flesh, for our sake, redeems and uplifts human nature, emphasises the value of ordinary life.

Through the gift of faith we are temples of the Holy Spirit, even in this life. Here and now we share in Christ's Divinity, enabling us to live with unselfish love.

We should not be surprised by moments of realisation of just how imperfect we are - how grubby, earthy and selfish we are by contrast with the intensity and purity of God's love. Such awareness is an introduction to the reality of God. We can be filled with fear, with awe; and it is something we must learn to live with. It is an introduction to real faith. We can feel guilt and sorrow - which is necessary for health.

But we should not be surprised, also, if we occasionally find ourselves uplifted to a joy and peace beyond our understanding, caught up in the laughter and love of God.

In the celebration of the incarnation and Birth of Christ we can be touched by a spirit of love that goes far beyond our nature.

May we be brought, by God's power, into the greatness, glory and love of His nature.

This prayer will be answered insofar as we leave ourselves open to Him in faith, and strive to lead our lives in that faith.

God is truly with us, in the Person of Christ, through the power of the Holy Spirit, truly our brother. He is especially close to us when we feel, and acknowledge, that we are not worthy of such a relationship. At this point we become worthy, and capable of growing in worth and value, becoming more like Jesus, in whose image we are made.

Mary, Mother of Jesus

To many people it appears that Christians, especially Catholics, worship the Virgin Mary as some kind of Goddess.

THE ATHEIST HUMANIST looks upon Christian devotion to the Virgin Mary as the superstitious cult worship of an idealised female form, a sanitised pagan Goddess under new guise: Christianised, but entirely imaginary and just not relevant to real life.

Such serious minded people regard with scorn and disbelief the Catholic teaching that a young Jewess became the Virgin Mother of God. Of course, in their view the notion of a Divine Creator is also an illusion, a distraction from reality only to be believed by weak minded and deluded people who are in need of help.

AGNOSTICS, less assured, tend to look upon this particular Christian doctrine as a quaint and rather charming eccentricity - an irrational tribute to the beauty of femininity, "....but why all this fuss about virginity? How can one believe, my dears, in such a thing as a virgin birth?"[*]

OTHER OPINIONS tend to echo the view that Jesus and everything in relation to him are of minor importance: e.g. the Koran mentions Jesus as a minor prophet, which, from an Islamic point of view would reduce the worth and

---

[*] COMMENT: [from Catechism of Catholic Church p.112] "Faith in the virginal conception of Jesus met with the lively opposition, mockery or incomprehension of non-believers, Jews and pagans alike" [S .Justin: Dialogue, 708 709], so it could hardly have been motivated by pagan mythology or some adaptation to the ideas of the age. The meaning of this event is accessible only to faith.

value of the mother of Jesus as a woman – though, in fairness and as a bit of an exception, Mary is lauded in the Koran, much more than her son.

Buddhism, presumably, would welcome Jesus and his mother into the great All of Being - accept all, believe all - a poetic mysticism in which people and things loose their particular and specific identity - their real value.

A SUBSTANTIAL NUMBER OF CHRISTIANS themselves appear to view Mary merely as an icon. She may have been a real person once upon a time, but she is now deified and unreal. She bears the title of the Mother of God - but as a real person she is so far elevated from ordinary human existence that she is only to be worshipped, from a distance - slightly more approachable than Jesus, but not much.

Such people find it vulgar and unthinkable that the Virgin Mother endured such earthly indignities as the breaking of her waters and the cutting of the umbilical cord that joined her to a blood-spattered male baby. Notions such as these would destroy her purity, her virginity - threaten Her godlike status!

All of these attitudes are travesties of the reality.

THE REALITY

Consider the situation.

Mary was a young Jewish girl, probably aged fifteen or sixteen, when she learnt she was to be a mother. Young women in the Eastern Mediterranean, even today, are physically mature, ready for marriage, at an early age.

According to first century Jewish practices Mary was actually married to Joseph, who - it is not unreasonable to speculate - was a modestly well established village tradesman, a carpenter, economically ready for marriage - on this basis probably aged somewhere in the range of late twenties to early thirties.

In accordance with the Jewish custom of the time there was a waiting period of six months or so before the marriage was consummated. We would call this relationship 'an Engagement'.

In his account of the life of Christ Luke, the doctor turned writer, describes how Jesus was conceived:

> *In the sixth month the angel Gabriel was sent by God to a town in Galilee called Nazareth, to a virgin betrothed to a man named Joseph, of the House of David; and the virgin's name was Mary.*
> *He went in and said to her, 'Rejoice, so highly favoured! The Lord is with you.'*
> *She was deeply disturbed by these words and asked herself what this greeting could mean, but the angel said to her, 'Mary, do not be afraid; you have won God's favour. Listen! You are to conceive and bear a son, and you must name him Jesus. He will be great and will be called Son of the Most High. The Lord God will give him the throne of his ancestor David; he will rule over the House of Jacob for ever and his reign will have no end.'*
> *Mary said to the angel, 'But how can this come about, since I am a virgin?'* [Literally 'I have not known a man']
> *'The Holy Spirit will come upon you' the angel answered 'and the power of the Most High will cover you with its shadow. And so the child will be holy and will be called Son of God. Know this too: your kinswoman Elizabeth has, in her old age, herself conceived a son, and she whom people called barren is now in her sixth month, for nothing is impossible to God.'*
> *'I am the handmaid of the Lord,' said Mary 'let what you have said be done to me.' And the angel left her.* (Lk.1:26-38)

If you don't believe in angels this will appear to be so much hogwash. The choice is yours - but before you dismiss the story as irrelevant consider the natural process of conception and birth.

Imagine a creature from another planet listening to a description of how human beings are generated.

'A man has a fleshy thing that hangs between his legs, which he normally uses to drain off excess body water. At moments of high excitement this fleshy thing becomes erect, and he then lies on top of a woman and puts it into an orifice between the woman's legs and with intense pleasure squirts a bit of juice into her - and she becomes pregnant. That's how human beings are made!'

"Come off it!" I can imagine the extra-terrestrial exclaim. "What an unbelievable story!"

Unbelievable - but upon inspection and observation ET will be forced to agree that in outline this is exactly what happens, even should he fail to appreciate the deep love and friendship that, ideally, accompanies such an act.

The generation of life is a wondrous, marvellous thing, a mystery - and no matter how explained in terms of ovum and sperm, people who have generated new, small, human beings instinctively realise that there is something much greater than mere biology at work - no matter how wonderful *this* is.

There is an awed awareness of the physical and mental characteristics of each individual child, and a puzzling, dawning realisation that unaided we could not have generated such an astonishing creature.

Imagine for a moment that God really does exist

(I firmly believe it, but I do not take your faith for granted).

As the author of life an all-powerful deity can dispense, theoretically, with any part of the normal and natural processes that He has instigated. Even the genetic scientist can artificially inseminate an ovum - and God, the arbiter of all things, will not alter His life-creating action simply because men, some say foolishly, have managed to isolate egg and sperm and combine them in a laboratory.

I'm not certain that God approves of such procedures - except possibly when they are reverentially and lovingly directed towards the creation of life by and for infertile couples, but I am certain that He does not approve of the destruction of fertilised ova that are considered 'disposable'.

There is no doubt, however, that He himself can generate life directly and immediately, without human ovum and sperm - should He wish to do so and should it be appropriate - not offending against the norms that He has established.

Followers of Jesus, flourishing in full faith, believe that it has been appropriate and will only ever be appropriate in one case: the conception of Jesus - for Jesus has only one Father, not another man, but God the Father, the originator of all life.

We believe that God Himself directly fertilised an ovum in the body of a young Jewish woman. Wonder of wonders, God, the author of all life, has, on one unrepeatable occasion, enclosed himself in the womb of a female member of the human race, becoming a real and living brother to all mankind. *"Gestant puellae viscera,"* cries out Thomas Aquinas in awe and reverence: "Growing in the belly of a young girl".

In the womb of a young virgin, anticipated and prepared for through aeons of time, the Word of God becomes an embryo, by the direct act of His Father.

There was no need for human seed. Such an intermediary would have been mere playacting.

God was and is the Father of Jesus - not in the same sense that He is creator and generator of all mankind but in the sense that Jesus is a Son equal in nature to His Father, equally God, in the mystery of the Trinitarian nature of God.....

Hence the church confesses that Mary is truly 'Mother of God' *(Theotokos)* - as defined by the fathers of the Church at the Council of Ephesus in the year 431, and, in the Council of the Lateran in 649, that Jesus was 'conceived by the Holy Spirit without human seed'.

True God, but also true man!

I have no difficulty in believing that God, the author of all life, should show his love for all mankind, all creation, in this way. It is, naturally, difficult to understand *how* He did it, but not so hard to know why.

As St. Paul says in his letter to the Hebrews:

> *'It was essential that he should in this way become completely like his brothers so that he could be a compassionate and trustworthy high priest of God's religion, able to atone for human sins. That is, because he has himself been through temptation he is able to help others who are tempted.'*
> (HEB2:17/18)

So what does all of this amount to?

From the Christian point of view there is a specific understanding that Mary is truly the Mother of a Divine Person.

The fact makes her remarkable. God has chosen her, this young woman from the eastern Mediterranean. Was He wrong? Should He have chosen someone else, possibly someone more worthy? Scarcely! Who is the best judge?

The subject of His choice is worthy of great veneration:

As Mary herself said:

> *'My soul proclaims the greatness of the Lord and my spirit exults in God my saviour; because he has looked upon his lowly handmaid. Yes, from this day forward all generations will call me blessed, for the Almighty has done great things for me. Holy is his name, and his mercy reaches from age to age for those who fear him'.*
> (Lk.1.46-50)

But what did her son have to say about it?

'Now as he was speaking, a woman in the crowd raised her voice and said,

'Happy the womb that bore you and the breasts you sucked!'
But he replied, 'Still happier are those who hear the word of God and keep it!' (LK11:27)

He was still speaking to the crowds when his mother and his brothers* appeared; they were standing outside and were anxious to have a word with him. But to the man who told him this Jesus replied,
'Who is my mother? Who are my brothers?' And stretching out his hand towards his disciples he said, 'Here are my mother and my brothers. Anyone who does the will of my Father in heaven, he is my brother and sister and mother.' (Mt.12:46)

Does this reduce the importance of Mary?
Certainly not!
Jesus is saying that he loves every single human being with the same intensity as he loves his mother, and will do for each of us what he has done for her - provided we strive to do His will i.e. love God and our neighbour honestly and truly, with full mind and heart.
St. Augustine of Hippo (in 397 AD) underlines the point I try to make:
"Mary is more blessed because she embraces faith in Christ than because she conceives the flesh of Christ".
She is blessed, of course, in conceiving the Word incarnate in her womb, but it is her faith that has made it possible.

---

* In Hebrew and Aramaic (and many other languages), 'brothers' is the word used for cousins or even more distant relations of the same generation. There is no sustainable tradition or record of Jesus having a blood brother by the same mother. It is entirely in keeping with the tradition and teaching of the church that Mary gave birth to one son, generated by the eternal Father. – See SPECULATION, below.

Christ promised that He would lead all to the truth, that the gates of hell would not prevail against the holy body of His people (MT 16:18), which would always teach the truth. The truth revealed by Christ through His Church, about His Mother, is that she has been taken, body and soul into heaven*, given an immediate share in her son's resurrection. We too, of course, will share in this bodily resurrection in due course, provided we live good lives.

Mary is the first fruit of many.

SPECULATION

There is no doubt in my mind that from the moment John the beloved disciple accepted the dying Christ's request to look after his mother she was held in great veneration.

Was she not the mother of Jesus, this remarkable man who had come among them? How else could it be?

I love to ponder upon some basic facts.

First, Mary was and remained a virgin. The belief has existed in such strength and depth for such a long time that it would be impossible to deny it.

St. Augustine, in a 4th century sermon, says of Mary:

> "She remained a virgin in giving birth to him, a virgin in carrying him, a virgin in nursing him at her breast, always a virgin"

And so, as the Catholic catechism puts it, the liturgy of the church celebrates Mary as 'Aeiparthenos', the 'ever-virgin'.

In the practical order of things there would have been no reason why she and her husband should not have come together and expressed their love for each other sexually.

But in the light of her stupendous mission, her almighty privilege, I can well imagine that she and Joseph

---

* *The Doctrine of the Assumption (Latin: assumere, to take up)*

received such great grace and love from on high - were in a state of awe and continued, questioning contemplation as to who Jesus might be, were so greatly empowered by God, that they realised how fitting it would be if they did not express their love sexually.

Which is more important, after all, sex or love? There is for all human beings, "a time for embracing, a time to refrain from embracing". (Ecclesiastes 3:5)

With Mary and Joseph the time was merely extended, with their full-hearted co-operation, in loving faith.

Unbelievers will scoff, and individual Christians will have doubts, but the teaching of the Church, the belief of the disciples, carried down the ages, is based upon solid foundations.

Following her son's death and resurrection we know that Mary and others met together constantly in prayer and thanksgiving, dwelling upon and discussing the momentous events that had taken place.

The life, death and resurrection of Jesus was a reality. They had seen and talked to him, eaten meals with him a few days after they had taken his dead body down from the cross! They knew he had died, but they also knew that he was alive once more! Amazing! What joyful discussions must have taken place! What questions there were to be asked, what details of his life had to be assimilated and understood!

Would Mary not have recounted to her friends, to those who shared in these extraordinary events, the details of her life, how she and Joseph had lived, what their relationship had been? Of course she would - especially to John, and she was as knowledgeable about sex as any woman, even from an early age (Quote: *"... How can this be since I know not man?"*).

During the years following her anguish at the brutal murder of her son and the amazement and joy of his resurrection - when she would have grown into a mature woman in her early fifties - would she not have said with equal candour to John and the others, "Joseph and I lived together, but we did not know each other as do other husbands and wives."?

To the disciples, as to believers today, she would not have had to offer any explanation other than the fact that her son was a special man, with a special Father; that Joseph and she had often speculated about the amazing circumstances surrounding his conception and birth.

Jesus was and is the focus of their thoughts.

They were only slowly becoming aware of all the implications, starting out on the long road to the realisation of the truth that their son is, amazingly, the only begotten Son of God the Father, sharing in His divine nature, but also, as her son, sharing fully in Mary's human nature - our human nature.

THE LIVING & DYING OF MARY & JOSEPH

To many of us it is an irritation that we do not have exact, recorded information of all events in the life of Mary, and her husband. Poor Joseph scarcely gets a look-in at all, overshadowed by his wife. But even the information given about her is sketchy, and to the modern mind inadequate.

Had the birth of Jesus taken place today some lively person with a camcorder, functioning in the unremarkable village of Bethlehem, might have recorded a moment or two of the event, and later on possibly fed it to the media - perhaps as a tailpiece at the end of the Ten O'Clock News - when the nature of the birth came to be realised.

Of course this is exactly what occurred at the time, within the limits of the media of the day, with only a few written scraps to assuage our thirst for first-hand information; and we must accept that this always will be so.

Fortunately, while there are few details about Our Lady, the main facts concerning her son are quite clear, for those whose minds are open to truth.

The accounts of the life, death and resurrection of Jesus are clear.

But what about Joseph, and Mary?

In my young day Joseph was viewed as a rather elderly gentleman who could never have had any vestige of a loving, sexual desire for his intended wife. As an old fellow he could be presented as being past it!

His existence was then, and still is to some, I believe, an embarrassment and a difficulty of faith - for those who are aware of sexual urges and the difficulty we experience in controlling such powerful, natural inclinations.

In some societies in the immediate past there have been people who felt uncomfortable in even thinking about sex. Within the Catholic Church there has been a distortion and misunderstanding of the recommendation by Jesus to make oneself a eunuch for the sake of the Kingdom. There is a widespread failure to recognise that Jesus also said, *"It is not everyone who can accept what I have said, but only those to whom it is granted."* (Mat.19.11).

Out of this failure to perceive the rounded, complete truth of Christ's word on this matter there has arisen a petrified, statutory concept that would threaten to elevate celibacy to the highest norm and reduce sexuality to a second-class activity - almost a threatening aberration - diminishing the worth and value of the great, God-given pleasure of expressing intimate love; an act that unites a man and a woman with God, as He and they create new life.

Most of us, aware of our own sexuality, will have some difficulty in the concept of a man and wife living together in shared celibacy.

Many will fail to appreciate the power of God to grant absolute sexual continence - for we don't have it! - and a very large number also fail to understand the complete and perfect faith, the absolute self-giving love of Joseph and Mary.

We can imagine such a fusion of divine and human love, but we do not, as yet, possess it. We are not yet saints.

In addition, some delicate and sensitive minded believers (particularly in the European and Anglo Saxon world and those communities throughout the world whose heritage is derived from these sources) cannot imagine that the physical aspect of ordinary day-to-day marital relationships would apply in the case of Mary and her husband - that Mary might, would certainly, for example, see Joseph having a pee (on many occasions) - and many would not wish to imagine Our Lady, Mother of Christ, crouching over a typical Eastern one-holer! (I swear I just heard Our Lady laugh!)

Okay! The vision may strike some as inelegant, and my mention of it inappropriate, but I really can imagine Our Lady smile at the thought, appreciating fully that urination and defecation, despite a lack of elegance on occasion, are vital components in the marvel of creation - and also a help in deflating human conceit.

We must not hide from such physical reality. If we do so we may fail to appreciate the full wonder and mystery of life, the reality of body and soul that is involved in being human.

Such a failure will detract from our awareness of Mary and her husband as real people, living in a real place at a real point of time, and - even more important - may endanger our grasp of the astounding reality of the incarnation of God in the Person of Jesus - a loving brother to all men, sharing every aspect of our life.

Should we have such difficulties of faith and perception - allied to trouble in controlling our own sexual urges - we may feel uneasy about Joseph's close and loving relationship with his wife. The notion of the Virgin Mary having a fit, healthy husband with normal sexual desires can be awkward to some - an embarrassment! Better to kill off Joseph - present him as an old man with no sexual impulses or expectations. It's easier that way! But it is not real.

EXPECTATIONS & REALITY

It is likely that Joseph was perhaps as much as fifteen years older than his bride, and quite a normal man, judging from his reaction to the news of his fiancée's pregnancy. A kindly man, who did not wish Mary to be stoned to death by neighbours - in that extreme era the usual community punishment for adultery - Joseph must have been heart struck at the thought of her unfaithfulness. He must have felt great desolation and pain at the death of his plan to marry this beautiful young village girl.

Can you imagine the moment when Mary told him that she was pregnant? Joseph had great need of the words of the Angel Gabriel to enable him to accept the divine nature of the event. What torture of spirit and mind he must have been going through.

Up to the point of Mary's astounding conception of Jesus their expectation of a normal marriage was mutual. Even allowing for a certain amount of marriage arrangement in that place and at that time there can be little doubt that Mary would not have agreed to marry just anyone. She undoubtedly knew Joseph very well, and both liked and loved him, intended him to be her husband in the normal human way.

Their betrothal created problems, first the amazing and unanticipated pregnancy and then a question of how they were to live together as husband and wife - slowly beginning to understand that theirs was to be, to say the least, an unusual and demanding marital relationship.

Alas, we do not know the details of their relationship - though perhaps we can imagine some of it, with due respect for their privacy - in the light of the understanding and teaching of the church from earliest times that Mary remained a virgin.

It is strange that we do not know at what moment in their marriage Joseph died. We simply know nothing; which is rather weird, another lack that we must accept.

Even more mysterious, given Mary's special friendship with the writer of John's marvellous gospel, we must accept that we do not know when *she* died.

There have even been some, throughout the ages, who have believed that she did not die, that she was taken up to heaven before this event could took place.

The theory is based upon the absolute teaching of the Church that Mary was conceived in her mother's - Anna's - womb without the stain of original sin[*] and that, because of this, she would not have been subject to death - a central consequence of the sin of Adam & Eve.

The theological rationality of this escapes me, for Christ was sinless and he faced death.

I believe that at the very moment of her death, having lived the remainder of her life in the fullness of faith, with an ever-deepening, prayerful realisation of her son's identity as God incarnate, she was taken up to heaven, body and soul - at the very instant of her death.

Any loving son, if he had the power, would do whatever he could for his mother. Jesus has the power of love and life, and perfect judgment. So what if he has brought his mother into the fullness of the resurrection!

Our time will come.

---

[*] *The Immaculate Conception: defined as an article of faith in 1854.*

Authority

Despite the imperfections of all individual Catholics - including popes, prelates and priests - it is this body of believers that fully and authoritatively maintains the truth about Christ.

The mandate to the Apostles and their successors can not be clearer:

"Go teach all nations, baptising in the name of the father and the son... and I shall be with you until the end of the world."

"He who listens to you listens to me...whose sins you shall forgive are forgiven, whose sins you shall retain are retained." John 20:22-23

Mighty power indeed, if you believe, as I do, that Christ is God incarnate. It is no wonder that believers throughout two millennia have hesitated to oppose those who quoted such authority, even when priests and bishops began to think it their duty to organise every aspect of everyday life.

No wonder also that a number of those who wielded such power failed to realise their own limitations, and the limitations of the authority given them, and slipped into the imperious mode of the 'rulers of this world'.

Such church leaders (and sycophantic followers) must be forgiven of course, but even now there is, I believe, a hankering among some in the Church for a return of such power, to a certainty of faith and obedience to perceived norms of Christianity. It would make such a tidy world, easier to manage.

There is a failure among those who generally regard themselves as orthodox (i.e. *right*) in that they appear to be unable to recognise the limitations of the commission given by Jesus. Some appear to believe that Christ - true God and true man and indeed possessing "all authority in Heaven and earth" - has passed on this absolute authority to His Church.

Sinful, wayward humanity, such people believe, mistakenly reject this untrammelled, limitless authority - which the Bishops, as successors of the Apostles, share fully with Christ, through his gift.

I am a believer, a daily Mass goer who accepts the authority of the Bishops as successors of the Apostles. I do not, however, accept that bishops and priests have total authority over me, or anyone else for that matter. Such an attitude beggars belief!

The real authority the church has is to feed humanity with the truth about creation and redemption - point to Christ's saving power, the need to live for good and reject evil, the power of Jesus over death, and the sublime fulfilment of the bodily resurrection of every individual to eternal life.

The central magisterium of the church on earth cannot have power to legislate and rule over and direct every aspect of individual life.

The teaching authority within the church is finally vested in the church magisterium (which I understand to be all of the bishops in conclave - nothing more or nothing less). These are the successors of the apostles, to whom Christ said, "He who hears you hears me". Everything that is taught by this body I accept as truly authoritative.

FREEDOM

But we must take care, and individual members of the magisterium must take care. The teaching office is not something separate from the body of the church.

The magisterium is not a special elite with insight, placed on high, with an unruly, illiterate mob below.

No. They have been told by the Lord God incarnate that they, individually and collectively, are to be servants of the people.

Even should individuals be in error they must be treated gently. Churchmen are not to sit in judgement and have been specifically instructed not to attempt to root out the weeds from the productive crop "...because when you weed out the darnel you might pull up the wheat with it." (Mt.13:29)

Isn't it a curious and dreadful thing that some who wish above all to be servants of Jesus could forget this injunction? The horrors of the mediaeval Inquisitions would never have taken place if those in authority had heard what Jesus said, listened to Him and obeyed Him.

Hopefully the proud and thoughtless spirit of dogmatic certainty and intolerance that instigated such pogroms will never be repeated, but there are no guarantees that ecclesiastical power will never again be abused. Vigilance is necessary - especially in the minds and hearts of priests and bishops.

God has given individuals the gift of freedom, and even where beliefs are mistaken this great gift must be respected. Error must be refuted, truth clearly stated and consistently argued, but browbeating force and coercion is anathema.

My God-given freedom to think, to search after truth, to grow in understanding, to freely love my Creator, could be so obstructed (despite beneficent intention) that the tendency would be to negate the purpose of God's creation with respect to me.

I am not an empty vessel to be filled by sets of propositions by which I am to be saved. I am a person made in the likeness of God, in that I have a capacity to know and love, and it is in learning to know Jesus that I am saved from death. My capacities are only capable of being enlightened and enlarged through loving faith in the man who is also God.

Forceful imposition is quite contrary to love, for love is essentially a free gift of self. Should a man think that he understands perfectly and require people to see things in an identical manner he runs the risk of living in grave error, and thereby diminishing himself.

We are not to be remade in the image and likeness of any pope, prelate or priest. We are to be directly remade by Christ Himself, in His own living likeness.

The Christian's main job is to indicate that this is so, and how it may come about. His job is not to rule or control or demand total conformity with the norms that he perceives. As the first pope wrote, *"Never be a dictator over any group that is put in your charge...."* (1 Peter 5.3)

It is the job of a responsible and knowledgeable believer - be he bishop, priest, layman or woman - to reassure his fellows that God, perfectly expressed in Christ, loves each one of us with undying and powerful love, demonstrated by him while sharing our life on earth.

The individual who would seek to impose conformity with a prescriptive and exhaustive list of moral and theological notions runs the risk of being mistaken, as well as ineffective. Even in Ireland, where I live, and where an old fashioned concept of Church Authority is still uncomfortably and residually present, priests and bishops are beginning to return to the fundamental necessity of calling for a personal love and understanding of the person of Jesus, rather than insist that priority be given to an exact and detailed interpretation of Church and Canon Law.

The revised attitude is healthy. It is the only way that people stand a chance of being refreshed by the living truth, God Incarnate.

A holy and loving priest speaking the truth he understands in a personal way has much greater effect than a dutiful, impersonal ecclesiastical civil servant who is perhaps fearful of distorting an abstract compendium of truth, and is unaccustomed to revealing his own personal faith and understanding.

Personally I am much impressed when I hear someone admit that his understanding is limited, and then attempt to lead me to knowledge of what he does and does not understand. It stimulates thought, clarifies the limits of human knowledge and deepens my faith and understanding, my awareness of brotherhood.

I should add here that I have a great respect for the highly motivated men who have given up much to follow Christ. Faults all priests have, as every Catholic knows, but their intention and devotion is clearly seen in every parish throughout the world - certainly in every part I have visited.

Together with the people of God we are the light of the world, a city seated on a mountain top, reminding people of the existence of God, of the person of Christ.

Don't misunderstand me! I do not think that all Catholics are great. Quite the contrary. It is amazing that, despite our inadequacies and idiocies the light of Christ shines through. It is God's doing that we are one visible body, directly traceable to Him.

I would simply implore priests to more readily reveal their personal love for and understanding of Christ - to the same extent as they express their obedience to the magisterium of "The Church", and recognise that it is out of the continuing faith of the people that they are called to the special service of the priesthood.

OBEDIENCE

For organisational purposes church leaders tend to emphasise obedience to the local Ordinary (the diocesan bishop) as equivalent to obedience to Christ himself.

"He was obedient, obedient unto death" is the preferred quote.

It is necessary to have obedience, but not to the extent that ecclesiastical zombies are produced.

The man who abandons all personal thought, and the prayer that flows from it, makes a poor servant of Christ.

In fact, had anyone been independent enough and courageous enough to speak out against inquisitorial activities in the Middle Ages he would have been doing a great service to Christ and the Church. No doubt he would have been castigated, judged by his superiors to be lacking in obedience - perhaps accused of heresy and suffered imprisonment, and possibly a brutal death - conceived in hell and executed by those who believed themselves to be Christ's servants. But such a man would have been obedient to the truth of Christ and his merciful love.

Blind obedience is a ridiculous thing. It is not what Christ practised. He clearly understood what he was doing when he was obedient to the truth, to his destiny, to his unseen Father.

It is the same Father that Christ wishes us to know, in Him and through Him, by the power of the Holy Spirit. Anything less than this will not do. We have to recognise Jesus in the beggar as well as the bishop, in people rather than precepts.

A TRUE GUIDE

Nevertheless, the Bishops in Conclave are indeed the successors of the Apostles, and if this body, in union with the successor of the Apostle Peter, defines something to be true and necessary for salvation we can be certain that it is so.

I have made much of the dangers of empty-headed obedience to church authority. I would fail the truth, run the risk of doing great disservice, if I failed to point out the genuine authority the church possesses and the great benefit of the magisterium.

Jesus himself has guaranteed that He will be with His church until the end of time

> *"... make disciples of all the nations; baptise them in the name of the Father and of the Son and of the Holy Spirit, and teach them to observe all the commands I gave you. And know that I am with you always; yes, to the end of time."* (MT 28:20)

By the blessing and with the authority of Jesus the Christ, the Church will teach the truth without fail. From this comes the doctrine of Papal Infallibility: that Peter (formerly Simon) in union with the rest of the Church, will never fail to teach the truth about Christ.

> *"...I have prayed for you, Simon, that your faith may not fail, and once you have recovered, you in your turn must strengthen your brothers."*
> (Lk. 22:32)

Individual bishops, including successive bishops of Rome, are as prone to error as anyone else. As individuals we are liable to make mistakes, be unsure of certain aspects of Christian teaching.

Reference to the teachings of the Church as expressed and defined through the magisterium of the Church during the past two thousand years is a clear aid to understanding the great truths about the nature of Christ, the inner being of God, and all aspects of His dealings with us.

> *'Anyone who listens to you listens to me; anyone who rejects you rejects me, and those who reject me reject the one who sent me.'* (Lk. 10:16)

DAY TO DAY MINISTRY

As a consequence it would be quite ridiculous for me, or any other Christian, to ignore the presence of those who have given up their lives to serve Jesus, and are authorised by Him to teach in His name.

Almost without exception I have discovered the priests I have consulted to be ready to help in whatever way possible. The trouble is, as I have mentioned above, that occasionally there is a tendency to follow a party line, to fear revealing any possible personal confusion or inadequacy, or lack of clarity in Church teaching.

Such men, such priests, must, I believe, be prepared to reveal their doubts as well as their certainties

- the fact that they too are human and frail - if they are to give an adequate lead to fellow members of the Body of Christ. They certainly must do so to themselves if they are to come to know the reality of the person of Christ, in Spirit and in truth, not merely repeat Church dogma in the hope that that this will lead to salvation. Personal love of God and neighbour is vital.

> *"Anyone who says that he loves God and does not love his neighbour is a liar, for he who does not love his brother whom he has seen cannot love God whom he has not seen."* 1 John 4:20

It is vital that all believers to be converted heart and mind towards loving and understanding the living person of Christ in a deep and personal way, and to be ready to reveal this understanding - and its limits - clearly and unequivocally. Mere lip service and quotation of abstract authority is not enough.

When priests use such referential terms as "the Church" there is a temptation to think only of the magisterium of the Church.

The magisterium, i.e. the Bishops in conclave, is only one section of the Church, and cannot be separated from the Body of Christ, those already in Heaven as well as those struggling for virtue.

Jesus is my God and saviour. I owe faith, obedience and service to Him. Peter is my guide and my mentor - as long as his name is not Borgia!

Membership of Christ's body is a great privilege, a great gift. The demand is that I always look for truth, be ready, even, in brotherly love "to withstand Peter to his face", should it be necessary.

I am not another Paul. I have no special mandate from Jesus. I simply know that, in common with all who have learned to believe, been given the full gift of faith, I will be taken by Him into Himself, through the power of the Holy Spirit, and be burned free by His love. I depend entirely upon Him, fed by His Body and Blood in the Eucharist, through the ministration of his priests.

This does not mean that I have to close my mind to the fact that a few priests are idiots, all are limited, some are ecclesiastical zombies, and in common with all humanity, every single one of us, all are prone to sin and error.

In the deep darkness of the faith that He has given to believers - a darkness that is sometimes full of light and joy - may the living Lord Jesus lead us into the Way, the Truth and the Life that is fully summed up only in Him.

May He and His Father send forth their Holy Spirit, the burning fire of love, the whisper in our conscience, to enlighten our minds and lead us out of the blinding and debilitating effects of sin.

How my Great-Grandmother Went to Heaven and My Grandmother Went to Bradford - leaving me with
Questions About Authority & Parish Priests

Margaret Ann Magee, the only one of my great-grandmothers I know anything about, died on June 21st 1882.

She left behind, in the family home - a small bar and hotel in the village of Ardglass, Co. Down - her husband John and two daughters: Margaret Theresa (20) and 12-year old Agnes (my Grandmother). Three older daughters had married and left home, one to live locally.

A week after Margaret Ann's death the Parish Priest came into the house and told John that he had thought the matter over. He had come to the conclusion that it was not right for a young girl to be brought up above a bar. He had arranged for Agnes to be taken into a convent in Bradford.

A week later Agnes was shipped off.

So, within a fortnight of her mother's death a grieving twelve year old was removed from her father, her sisters and cousins, her friends and neighbours, her home and her country - all by the decision of the Parish priest.

NOT TODAY

A few years ago I related this small item of family history to our parish priest.

His reaction was similar to mine. "It would never happen today!"

"You're dead right it wouldn't! " I agreed. "If you attempted to do that today you would be told what to do with yourself!"

Now I must record that - 126 years after one of his predecessors banished my Grandmother to Bradford, no doubt with the high aim of saving her from the influences and attentions of the disreputable and drunken Catholic Irishmen, and a few non-sectarian Prods, who hung out at the Old Commercial Hotel in those days - the priests of the parish Dunsford & Ardglass have mostly been helpful to me during the fifty years that have passed since I stumbled back into the Church - a returned prodigal picking pig meal out of my teeth and hungry for real food.

I have a great respect for most of these priests. Each one is an outpost for all those who seek contact with the unseen God, dedicating themselves to a sometimes lonely and much criticised way of life (some individual criticisms soundly based, for are they not merely imperfect men like the rest of us.)

However, among them, in England and Ireland, I have met with much heart-warming kindness and, on occasion, a great and wonderful holiness, enabling God's grandeur to shine through.

Despite this there is little doubt in my mind that today, as in 1882 and throughout time, there are priests who are unclear about the actual authority they possess, diluting and contaminating it with notions of earthly authority imbibed from the social norms of each age.

REAL POWERS

Consider the actual powers of a priest.

On a day-to-day basis he is the practical mediator between the sinner and God. When he baptises he imparts a sharing in God's inner life. Equally he forgives sins with the authority of Christ. Through his words and intentions bread and wine become the body and blood of Christ. He holds in his hands the living bread of eternal life, Christ

himself: body, blood, soul and divinity, without whom there is no salvation. The words of Christ make it clear,
"Unless you eat of my flesh and drink of my blood you will not have life within you." *

The priest is therefore the local embodiment of that authority given by Christ to Peter and the disciples, to provide the means of achieving eternal life: ultimately a sharing in Christ's resurrection.

Who would not be in awe of such powers? Who, among believers, would dare to challenge or dispute such authority, even if, at times, those who wield it can quite obviously be as sinful and erratic as the rest of us?

EXAGGERATED AUTHORITARIANISM

Because of social attitudes in Ireland, even today, it is a brave man or woman - among school governors, for example - who will challenge the decision, or even the firmly expressed opinion, of a Parish Priest; mostly out of courtesy but also with a hint of superstitious fear, reasonable in the light of distorted notions regarding the power structure of the Church, but entirely unreasonable and at odds with the love of Christ, which casts out fear.

In this typical case it is usually the parish priest's viewpoint, in his automatically held position of Chairman of the Board of Governors, which decides the issue - a modern situation in which the Authoritative nature of the Church overflows into areas where genuine consensus would almost certainly produce more realistic and beneficial management decisions - and don't tell me that consensus is the norm! The priest's word is mighty

---

* People who are genuinely unable to receive His Body and Blood in the sacrament of the Eucharistic will certainly be brought into His divine life by virtue of the love they have for the truth that they know. But there is an onus on everyone to love God and neighbour in practical ways, to seek Him with full mind and heart, to search for the truth and act accordingly - and this can be costly and inconvenient, but with God's help not impossible.

weighty, listened to with great deference, and quite often forms the basis of decisions in areas where he has no special knowledge.

This is only one small example of the residual traces of the exaggerated authoritarianism and unreal reverence that exists in the church, and has existed through the centuries, attitudes based upon an oversimplified and ultimately false view that full church authority is vested solely and exclusively in the persons of bishops, and then delegated by them to priests.

Such a view infers an unspoken concept that, when it comes right down to it, the opinions and attitudes of the general mass of the people are of little account. The faithful are there to be fed the truth: not to discover it, not to contribute to it, for they do not share in the Authority of the Church.

WRONG

Such attitudes have been labelled erroneous by the Bishops of the Second Vatican Council, which acknowledged that God's guiding Spirit resides in and operates throughout the whole church, the complete body of people.

I quote from Vatican II:

> *The laity's "powers of knowledge, competence, position, give them the means, or rather, the duty at times of making known their opinions on matters which envisage the good of the church..... With the help of the laity's experience, pastors are able to make clearer and more appropriate judgments in spiritual and temporal matters alike...."*
> - DOGMATIC CONSTITUTION ON THE CHURCH (De Ecclesia) 21 November 1964

and again:

> *"Lay people, because they share the priestly, prophetic and royal work of Christ, have active parts of their own to play in the Church's life and action. Their activity within the communities of the Church is so essential that failing it even the Apos-*

tolic work of the Pastors will often lack its full effect..."
- DECREE ON THE APOSTOLATE OF THE LAITY *(De Apostolatu Laicorum)* 18 November 1965

Despite this there still appears to be an assumption that a great gulf of responsibility, knowledge and authority exists between priests and "ordinary" Christians.

Traditional seminary education has tended to produce priests who have, perhaps unconsciously, been conditioned to view themselves as an elite, better educated type of Christian (which may or may not be so), an upper strata whose job it is to sit in judgement on the rest, moral policemen with the power to guide the less informed and habitually sinful.

This perception is almost certainly reinforced by wearisome experience of people's sinfulness and apparent stupidity - deepening and hardening the realisation that people are naturally recidivist - while the priestly self-image, certainly in Ireland, is reinforced by the ultra-respectful attitude of the faithful, amounting at times to uncritical adulation, increasing the ever present danger of priestly hubris and sabotaging at root the vital and joyful awareness of shared and equal brotherhood in Christ.

A BROTHERHOOD OF SINNERS

God has no favourites. He loves all with equal intensity. The same cannot be said of men and women, and in the case of some men who are priests (and may have forgotten that they are primarily men) their contribution to the building-up of faith among their brothers and sisters has sometimes been to put such faith to the test - mostly, in my youth, by calling upon congregations to endure burbling 45-minute sermons each Sunday, often interlarded with strict admonitions about the duty to support one's Pastors more generously.

My faith, and the faith of various congregations I have belonged to, has also withstood the knowledge that a venerable and much loved Canon's passing addiction to whiskey is - was - a slight and foolish fault, and that a curate's well-documented romance with a female parishioner (wife of another parishioner) was understandable, in the light of loneliness for love.

I take no pleasure in recalling the fact that in one London parish where I lived, over forty years ago, I was even able to absorb, without detriment to my faith, some of the crazed hurt caused by a local priest's paedophilic attentions to a mother's altar-boy son - a lad who died mysteriously at the age of fifteen, leaving his mother demented and understandably bitter about priests, despite her obvious goodness and love for those around her.

Gluttony, alcoholic abuse, excessive love of money and power, lack of chastity - common among the sin-inclined people of God, lay or priestly, are not new in the church.

A compounding sin, born out of the desire to set high standards among the faithful, has been the willing acceptance of the notion that priests not only have to be perfect but are perfect, because they are priests; a public attitude promoted also by automobile manufacturers with respect to the latest glossy car, and accepted by both sets of consumer in that spirit of hope that flies in the face of reality.

Cars and priests may be mostly serviceable, though requiring regular maintenance, especially after a few years on the road. But both can suffer breakdown, and the easy and thoughtless acceptance that they are perfect is a lie: in the case of priests an attitude not worthy of a Church devoted to the truth.

St. Paul's attitude of profound and hope-filled confidence in Christ, and lack of trust in his own human powers, is the only possible attitude. The spirit is willing but the flesh is weak.

Sanctity by appointment is a delusion, and the result of easy acceptance of such an illusion is that when grievous fault becomes apparent among the clergy, equally unreal and unnecessary pain, anger, shame and disappointment are felt.

What to do about it? Perfectly clear in the case of a gleamingly unsatisfactory car. Return it to the maker.

Much more difficult in the case of an erring priest, who needs help rather than total condemnation, no matter how heinous his crime. Who would be a bishop or religious superior in such cases, torn between compassion for the sinner and duty to the faithful?

The traditional solution would appear to have been monastic seclusion for a period, followed by transfer to other duties or other parishes - always open to the accusation that the priest who sins is protected from the full consequences of his actions. More recently psychological treatment has been used in the quest for rehabilitation, and where actions have offended against just laws of the land imprisonment has resulted.

As church leaders have recently stated, there can be no hiding place in the church for priests who have grievously offended against society. It would be entirely wrong for priests to be excluded from the consequences of abominable actions simply because of their vocation and position. Clearly such an attitude would bring the entire Church into disrepute.

I would hope that this attitude would be extended by the Church to include priests who have offended against chastity and, say, fathered a child. Men such as these should be given personal responsibility for contributing to an offspring's welfare, in every way possible, according to the reality that they face.

Certainly offenders should not be palmed off upon another unsuspecting local church as perfect examples of Christian living.

If I generate a child out of wedlock I am responsible for it, whether I have taken a vow of chastity or not. I cannot expect a Bishop to shoulder my responsibility - treat me gently and privately of course, but not hide me away and prevent me from shouldering my responsibilities like a man.

I am a man first and a priest second - if I have the privilege of that great vocation - and if I cannot be a good man I certainly cannot be a good priest.

I was deeply heartened a few years ago with respect to this situation when a parish priest in County Antrim told the congregation at each Sunday Mass that he had fathered a son and had maintained this offspring for eighteen years or so, using his own money, not that of the church.

His confession, if that's what it was, and his apology, was greeted with spontaneous applause by the congregation. I was also heartened that he had made this declaration with the knowledge of the bishop. There had been no question of his removal.

But in other, less worthy cases, the Old Testament designation *"you are a priest forever according to the law of Melchisidech"* cannot mean that there is never a case for depriving a man of the priestly office. The priest undertakes to do a job, for Christ, for his neighbour. If he cannot do his job properly he should be sacked, as with any job - made redundant, compulsorily retired, excluded from the brotherhood of the clergy: if unrepentant regretfully regarded as a pagan and a heretic.

If authority means anything in the Church this is one disciplinary power that a bishop certainly does possess (with due safeguards regarding right of appeal). And if the collective authority of bishops means anything they should similarly be able to dispose of one of their own number - if he has not the grace to resign, as in the case of one former Bishop of Kerry.

Am I being too hard? Not at all, I think. It's a matter of reason and common sense and truth. It is self-evident that a man must be confronted about the truth of himself and the consequences of his actions if he is to be given the chance to repent and be saved. This is the ultimate kindness: not to be confused with the ruthless logic of those medieval prelates who 'kindly' burnt heretics at the stake with the same objective.

There is a considerable difference between torturing a man in order to change his mind (and burning him alive if he will not do so), and putting the same man on the job market because he has proved to be unsuitable and unreliable.

RESPONSIBILITY

All have the responsibility of doing their job as effectively as possible, and the priest has the daunting task of leading people into holiness, introducing them to Christ, helping them to develop in faith and love.

He can only do so if he personally is imbued with these qualities: totally committed in faith. Sometimes such faith and love and hopeful trust, in God and neighbour, seems to be lacking, or at least lukewarm. On occasion our priests seem to lack the power and conviction that can only come from personal knowledge of our Creator and his beloved son. Some can, at times, I regret to say, give the impression of obedient rote men - obedient to Church rules and regulations, afraid to show warmth and passion, fearful of allowing personal faith and love for the living Lord take hold of them, to inspire their lives and the minds and hearts of their congregations. Cerebral, distilled notions appear to take the place of wholesome, heartfelt love.

I put this proposition with some diffidence. I am very much aware of the many devoted priests whose lives are given in constant service to their brothers and sisters. But I would not be expressing an honest impression if I failed to state that at times the public face of religion can be boring!

Boring! The life, death and resurrection of Jesus Christ reduced to boring, repetitive formula and a restatement of abstract moral rules combined with Church organisational procedures! What an indictment of our church! What a scandal! That my sons, and many young people - as well as those not so young - can find public expression of faith in Christ flat, colourless and unconvincing!

Such perceptions cannot be dismissed as the fault of a sinful and unenlightened people. This is too easy an escape. The plain fact is that much that is presented as religion *is* boring, because of the attitude and lack of ability of those who conduct our services.

Even the magnificent re-presentation of Christ's sacrifice through the Eucharist can sometimes appear lacklustre - a real and abiding scandal, where it occurs.

The people of God gather to hear the word of God in preparation for the Eucharistic celebration and they hear words without compelling explanation or enlightenment - or so it can appear, because the nice, angry, weary, irritated, bored or despairing man who conducts the service may not have prepared himself in his heart, his mind and his soul.

I merely point out that because Christ operates through people the perceived quality of the Eucharistic offering can vary according to the qualities of the man making the offering. A truly holy priest, utterly devoted to loving God and his neighbour, and relaxed about it, brings a physical and spiritual quality to the offering which appears absent when the same sacrifice is offered, or perhaps just recited, by a disillusioned priest who views the Mass as just another one of his daily chores.

The essence remains the same, of course, but whereas one man enables Christ to shine through, the other tends to stifle the loving utterance of the Spirit.

Am I making too much of this? Different men, different priests, arrive at differing stages of holiness and fullness of belief and love at different times. I cannot, am not, would never wish to be, judge of when this should be. My concern is that all priests should be striving for holiness, and it is quite evident from recent events that all are not doing so.

Recent examples of scandalous, horrendous behaviour by priests have horrified and saddened all decent believers.

It is reasonable to suppose, with great regret, that more such horrors remain hidden from the sight of men.

How are we to know who have fallen and who have not? The answer is, of course, that we cannot. We can only hope that it is not many. But what we can be certain about is that "all" (without exception) "have sinned and fallen short of perfection", that all of our priests, in common with every other human being, cannot avoid the daily struggle for virtue: against one or more of the potential sins of pride, envy, lust, sloth or lack of faith and love.

Anyone who thinks he is without sin is deluded - or in St. Paul's more forceful language, "a liar".

We may just hope and pray that the level of sinfulness is not great - that it will be gradually replaced by goodness and holiness, in all of us.

THE NEED TO BE REALISTIC

For the good of the Church we should be more realistic in our perceptions and expectations. We should not enclose our priests in a straitjacket of false presumptions about perfection, and they should not allow such false assumptions to be made. We are all sinners, all tempted in various ways, all merely imperfect men, and if this truth is finally and fully accepted and acted upon, the church in our diocese, in our country, will have taken a massive step towards health.

Perhaps, under the gentle, guiding hand of God, this is the real message of recent disturbing disclosures:

> *"Live in the world of reality. Scandals will come, because you are a defective people, but you are still My people. Confess your sins to one another, and to Me, and live in hope and genuine brotherly love. Serve one another in truth and humility. I am with you all days, even to the end of the world."*

It does not take much creative thought to imagine Our Lord slightly rephrase His original words.

REAL AUTHORITY

As part of an attempt to achieve a realistic, truthful awareness of the Church in all its aspects there must come a revision of our concept of authority within the church. What type of authority? Where does it begin? Where does it end? How is it to be wielded?

Bishops and priests do not possess their apostolic authority in a vacuum. The entire people of God participate in Christ's mission of salvation, and we need to obliterate any notion that priests and people are separate entities.

A divisive "them and us" attitude prevents God's people from working together as brothers and sisters, equal in the eyes of the Lord, equal in His community, equally responsible for doing the different jobs that we do.

We must not be influenced by false notions of Church Authority.

What the church's authority is *not* has been clearly laid out by our Lord.

Church rulers are not to rule like those who have authority in this world. They are to be servants, as Christ was and is a servant to us; seeking only to heal and make whole, to cure ills of soul and body by prayer, kindness, compassion and practical love.

Jesus does indeed have all power in heaven and earth, but He has not handed on all His powers to mankind: power to teach the truth, yes; to convey a sharing of His inner life through baptism and the forgiveness of sin, yes; to feed the people with His Body and Blood, yes. These are all powers he has handed on.

Equally, while Peter and his successors have direct authority to "bind and to loose", i.e. to make rules and regulations, such rules must be primarily to lift non-essential burdens from humanity, as in the case of Peter alone and Peter in conjunction with the apostles lifting the Jewish requirements regarding 'unclean' food and circumcision.

Christ is concerned that burdens be lifted from the faithful, not imposed upon them.

It is quite evident that Christ did not give the Church authority to attempt to root out heretics and torture them into submission, as priests and bishops attempted to do in the 12th and 15th centuries. Equally He did not give authority to a 19th century parish priest in Dunsford and Ardglass to remove my grandmother to Bradford.

Such notions of church authority are patently absurd at best and at worst directly and cruelly in opposition to Christ's mandate.

It is an escape from reality to classify such aberrations as things of the past. The dangers are ever present.

Christ is present in each of our parishes, in the minds and hearts of his faithful, and he expects his kind and forgiving friendship to be continued: towards the sexually vagrant, the poor and the dirty, the diseased, the money-lovers: the lowest in society - as well as those afflicted by physical and mental illness.

It is through us that he now seeks to convince each person how deeply we are loved and valued, with a love that goes beyond the confined, common sense, measured out, watered down version that we often present - and it is the job of the priest, above all, to become one Person with Christ, to make His kindness and love truly present.

If he is not doing this he is not doing the job he has undertaken.

Fortunately most priests do quietly proceed with this difficult but not impossible task, one of the greatest difficulties being to escape from the role-playing expected by society, to avoid becoming depersonalised icons of religion.

Whether by nature or by traditional seminary education, or by fitting into public expectations, many seem uneasy about allowing their real human personality to be known, as if afraid that public acknowledgement of the faulty, sinful nature we have in common would cause offence. In my experience the more a man admits the truth about himself the more likeable he becomes; the more he admits his insecurities the more people are able to identify with him.

Quite a few priests, and others, seem to think that they must present themselves in public as superhuman, faultless - in order to give good example. Others have a lunatic belief that through ordination they *are* superior to normal people.

By failing to face and present the truth about themselves, accepting their total dependence upon God for the goodness they possess, they increase the danger of clogging up the wellsprings of humanity, and make it difficult for Christ to communicate the reality of His love through them.

ONE GUIDE AND HOPE

As with all other Christians I have only one guide and one hope: the man Christ Jesus, who is Lord and Saviour, and it is only through meeting him, sacramentally and in the person of other people, and, especially, through the writings of the evangelists, that I can begin to appreciate the type of man he is now and was in history.

Jesus is the measure of the man whom I must become. Note well: the *man* I must become. If I cannot become a good man, a kindly human being, reflecting the humanity of Christ, what hope have I of reflecting His divinity?

And if this applies to me, without any office in the Church, how much more does it apply to those who share more explicitly and fully in Christ's redemptive priesthood? Only if we acknowledge the humanity we share with Christ can we be made perfect - perfectly human that is - to the point where we are ready to share fully in His divinity –but perfectly human first.

The time to be truthfully and truly human is surely with us?

"Better late than never!" I can hear my Grandmother say.

Predestination?

I simply don't believe in it!
The notion that Someone Somewhere has decided in advance what I shall do and where I shall go - in this world and eternity - is simply not believable.

I am too much aware of the fact that I have free will.

You don't believe that we *have* free will?

So you believe something like: "God knows all things. He creates people, and knows from the outset who will go to heaven and who will go to hell."?

O.K. - He does know, for He is omniscient, but does this mean that He specifically creates and identifies some people whom He destines for Hell, and selects those who He decides are to go to Heaven?

The notion is ridiculous! God loves all equally - wills each one of us to share in His Divine life, for this is the gift that is offered to us by Jesus. As man Jesus participates in our human nature so that he can raise us to a participation in his divinity.

A problem only arises if we believe that God will cruelly create people who have no chance of going to Heaven. This is to falsify the nature of God and fail to understand the nature of human freedom.

FREE TO CHOOSE?

Some say that by virtue of our environment - the 'accident' of our birth, our physiological and psychological defects - we are not capable of making a free choice. There are too many extraneous influences affecting us. We are not really free.

To my mind we are free, in the essentials that matter.

The circumstances of my birth and makeup will certainly affect my choices, but in essence I have a freedom that cannot be taken away from me.

Such freedom is related to my nature as a human being. Because I am human I cannot fly. I do not have wings. I cannot swim underwater for long periods because I do not have the gills of a fish. I cannot run at 75 miles per hour because I am not a cheetah.

But I can run and swim and walk in accord with my nature as a human being, and I can think and make decisions as a human being.

Even if I suffer handicaps of mind or body that limit or threaten to destroy my functions I still possess in essence all of the attributes of a human being.

Mental or physical illnesses can be cured. Even in the midst of calamitous malfunction there is always the possibility of being restored to health and to proper human decision-making and creative action; and where grievous illness or deprivation does affect the mind we - obviously - cannot be held fully responsible for thoughts and actions, just as a baby cannot be held responsible until it develops to a degree of adulthood.

Within the limits of our education and ability and despite social or environmental pressures and influences, there is at least a minimal capacity to choose - to do or not to do, to recognise truth and act upon it, or refuse to act.

This is what we mean by free will.

We cannot be something other than men or women who exist in a certain time and place. We are surrounded by, influenced by and restricted by hereditary factors, and the social, physical and financial environment; but we are still free in essence. Even if we are in prison we are free - at least free to think, to make choices about what we believe, to react to the restrictions that are imposed: free to love or hate.

This is the basic freedom of choice as it affects salvation: to love or not to love, to endure or not to endure, to believe or withhold belief: to recognise truth or reject it.

Even in the confines of a defective body, or in the painful struggle to hold onto reason when grief and despair threaten sanity, it is possible for a man or woman to grow in stature and become more truly worthy of the name human.

Tested by suffering, enduring all things, a man or woman can become a profoundly loving human being, truly worthy of sharing in God's Divine love. It is also possible for the same man or woman to give way to despair and hatred, refuse to endure, refuse hope, refuse love, and refuse to recognise truth.

Only God can judge who lives in love and who lives in hate. We can be mistaken. God cannot.

Heaven is living in the love of God, sharing in His life, accepting His forgiveness and forgiving ourselves, accepting with rejoicing our life in the light of His love.

Hell is being caught up in this same love - incapable by our own choice of returning it. If we hang grimly onto pride in self, isolate ourselves from God's mercy and love, choose our own judgment in place of His, we are guilty of the sin that cannot be forgiven, a deliberate rejection of truth and love: the ultimate sin of pride, the living out of the original sin that separates mankind from the love of God.

The choice is truly ours.

God helps each of us in the search for love and truth. He has gone to the extremes of joining us in our humanity, in the person of Jesus, searching for us, sharing suffering and death in the greatest possible act of love. If we reject him, either formally or by implication, it is our free choice.

PREDESTINATION AS VIEWED IN HISTORY

St. Augustine, Bishop of Hippo, (4th century, North Africa) came late to belief in Christ, having engaged in superficial philologistic philosophy and self-gratifying sexual activities.

Upon realising the truth about himself in relation to the goodness of God he realised that he had been in danger of hellfire. His subsequent thinking and teaching with respect to salvation had a great effect upon Christian practice and belief.

The custom of infant baptism, for example, can be traced to him. To my mind he appears to have been under the illusion that there was something magical about baptism, of believing that even without the element of personal choice, impossible in the case of an infant, the very fact of being baptised would have saved him from falling into grave sin, saved him from hell. I have the impression that these views were formed out of fear, a reaction to the horror of realising how bereft of goodness he was - at the time of his self-realisation.

Many, including me, have gone through a similar experience - despite being baptised as an infant - and possibly the depth of sinfulness arrived at in these cases – in my case - was greater because of rejection of the great gift of eternal life given by baptism.

Whatever about this - and I do tend to believe that infant baptism is a sentimental but loving practice rather than a practical necessity - I believe that Augustine was unclear about the magnitude of the love that God has for us, that he failed to understand that God, in the Person of Jesus, will take into heaven all those who do not deliberately reject Him, baptised or unbaptised - especially unbaptised children.

Probably Augustine put too much weight upon Jesus saying, "He who believes and is baptised will be saved; he who does not believe will be condemned". (Mark 16:16)

Augustine does not appear to have allowed for what Catholic theologians later called baptism by desire: i.e. the teaching that all people of goodwill, even though they be pagan, if they look for truth and live by the truth that they know, by implication desire the baptism of Christ.

In other words: such people will be saved in exactly the same way as if they had managed to arrive at the truth of Christ while on earth.

Great saint and teacher though he was - and is - Augustine also firmly believed in predestination, holding that only those elected by God will attain salvation. No one knows who is among the elect, he taught, and therefore all should lead God-fearing, religious lives.

I accept that the latter is advisable of course - hopefully arising out of a proper awe and love and reverence for God, with full trust in His loving mercy, and it is true that only God can take us into Heaven. Only He has the power to do so, as a gift beyond nature.

But the notion that God has already decided whom He will call introduces an element that I fail to understand. I appreciate that He *knows* who will accept His call and who will reject it, knows this even before and at the moment of our creation (if we can use these terms about a Being whose knowledge is not confined by the sequence of events that exist within the bounds of Time).

It is certain that throughout all eternity He calls all men to eternal life, a sharing in His love, even when they reject it. This must be one of the horrors of Hell, knowing that one has rejected a perpetual, everlasting invitation to infinite love. We humans need to be able to change our minds. If we do not we cease to grow and learn. God, knowing everything totally and perfectly, does not need to do this.

If God loves me (as He does) and has opened the eyes of my mind to the necessity of faith, and given it to me (which He has), and if I am determined to pray and work for my salvation, depending only upon His goodness (which I do) then I have nothing to fear.

To be one of the elect it is necessary that I freely choose to love God and my neighbour. There is no compulsion about this. It does not interfere with the freedom that God has given to me. It fulfils it. The truth sets me free, gives me an even greater freedom than that which I possess by nature, elevates it to a new dimension, whereby, because I place my trust in God as revealed in Christ, and accept baptism by water and the Holy Spirit, I am taken into eternal life even now, while in the body.

I believe this on the strength of the assurances given by Jesus, who is the Lord of Life.

This is the virtue of faith, and is not to be equated with the sin of presumption: which is an attitude of mind adopted by someone who believes that by Faith alone he will go to Heaven - regardless of how he behaves!

This unhealthy and self-deceiving version of 'faith' tends to exist in the minds of those who are under the impression that everything has already been decided, and who make an act of faith in their own goodness rather than trust in the living God's mercy and love.

At the root of this attitude is the original sin of pride. Some such people do not appear to realise that all that is necessary is to admit fault and ask for pardon. Deep down they may be aware that they are unworthy, but they are perhaps so paralysed by mistaken notions of predestination and fate - and an exaggerated sense of responsibility - that they are unable to act with proper humility and a reduced, real responsibility.

They may tend to excuse sin rather than seek forgiveness. In effect they believe, mistakenly, that they can make it to heaven by their own efforts.

The true and healthy attitude is that adopted by St. Paul, whereby he accepts his sinfulness, and God's forgiveness, and gets on with the work that he must do - in his case the preaching of the Good News of Christ.

The decent and honourable man recognises that he must continue the struggle to be moral, to live responsibly in faith and hope and love, in order to win the prize of eternal life. While we are alive in the body there are always personal choices to be made. There is no such thing as resting on laurels until the race is run, and won. There is no such thing as a pre-determined, pre-destined, fatalistic end.

Again, just as I can sin by presumption, so I can sin by doubt. Wilfully doubting God's love and forgiveness can damage as much as libertarian presumption. I am free to doubt of course, but it is unwise to do so. A continuous act of faith is necessary and reasonable, despite any doubts that may arise in moments of darkness and frailty of mind.

God gives me faith and love; I freely accept it. There is no unalterable destiny about it. I am not robbed of freedom by my choice. In fact, by my choice I achieve the greatest freedom possible, to become a true son of God, brother to Jesus. There is no predestination involved. I simply accept God's will for me, which is the same for all mankind, that we should believe in Him and love Him, and our neighbour, through and in the power of Christ and their Holy Spirit of Love.

Throughout scripture the Greek word translated as "predestination" is found in very few passages, and where an element of predetermination is indicated, such as in Old Testament prophecies, there is not the slightest justification for believing that God has interfered in human decision-making in any way other than as a loving and helpful guide (though His enemies may not see it so!). He is full of love and power, and gives enlightenment as He wishes and judges to be necessary and appropriate - vital, in fact.

In the biblical accounts of His relationship with men the supreme glory and power and wisdom of God is recognised and praised.

Nowhere is there an indication that God creates some people for heaven and some for hell. The notion is, in any case, anathema, to those who believe, even in theory, in the perfect love and justice of God.

JOHN CALVIN & MARTIN LUTHER

Many Protestant sects, notably Calvinists, exaggerated and built upon Augustine's teaching regarding predestination. They completely excluded the possibility of free will as a vital ingredient in the process of salvation, appearing to believe in a God of absolute power who pays only lip-service to the freedom that He has given to men. This attitude, in conjunction with the erroneous doctrine of justification by faith alone (no elements of behaviour and choice involved), led the French/Swiss reformer John Calvin and his German counterpart Martin Luther to deny that human beings are capable of free choice. They blamed the clouding of the minds and wills of men that occurred as a consequence of the Fall of Mankind in Adam.

They have a point of course, considering the aberrations we all suffer from, but generally speaking we are not totally bereft of wit and wisdom, or freedom of choice.

Calvin went farther than Luther in elaborating a doctrine of predestination - i.e. that certain persons are preordained by God for salvation, while others are not even considered - rejected even before they are created and consigned to eternal damnation from the moment of conception. Calvin wrote: "We call predestination God's eternal decree, by which he determined within himself what he willed to become of each man. For all are not created in equal condition; rather, eternal life is foreordained for some, eternal damnation for others"
(Institutes 3. 21. 5).

He appears to have based this belief upon his observation that all men 'are not created in equal conditions' and extrapolated to the unwarrantable conclusion that this inequality of birth, apparently preordained, must be duplicated in eternity.

This form of double predestination - God deciding in advance who will go to Heaven and who will go to Hell - was condemned as heretical and untrue by the Catholic Church during the Council of Trent (1545-63). The teaching of the Catholic Church is quite clear, according to Trent and as far back as the Council of Orange in 529 A.D.:

"God predestines no one to hell. For this a wilful turning away from God (mortal sin) is necessary, and persistence in it till the end. In the Eucharistic liturgy and in the daily prayers of her faithful the Church

implores the mercy of God, who does not want any to perish, but all to come to repentance". CATECHISM OF THE CATHOLIC CHURCH (#1037).

The same source points out that
"Faith is an entirely free gift that God makes to man. We can lose this priceless gift, as St. Paul indicated to Timothy: *'Wage the good warfare, holding faith and a good conscience. By rejecting conscience, certain persons have made shipwreck of their faith."* (1Tim1: 18-19)

FATALISM

Some people confuse predeterminism with fatalism. They are not the same. A fatalist believes that all events occur according to a fixed and inevitable destiny that no one can alter. This is a dangerous concept, militating against freedom of thought and action and tending to absolve people from responsibility. Events are seen as taking place in accord with some mysterious and unavoidable decree issued by some mysterious and unknown power.

The Theist's version of fatalism is the acceptance of all events as "God's Will", and while this may help people to survive the trauma and grief of death and other disasters it is unfair and irrational to allocate to the loving God of Life a determination on His part to inflict an inflexible, capricious and hurtful destiny upon His creatures. In many cases the causes of events can be identified as purely natural and rational, scientific if you like. Where suffering and evil exist as part of such phenomena we must look for explanations of how evil can co-exist with the goodness of God. *(see Evil, p.299)*

RATIONAL & JOYFUL FAITH

Belief in a loving God, and in His abiding presence in the minds and hearts of men through the power of His Holy Spirit, should not be confused with any predeterminist or fatalistic belief.

God does not rob men and women of our human dignity. Quite the contrary. He creates us, gives us life, and offers to share his own divine life with us, leads us away from death and towards eternal life. In the Person of Jesus He shows us the way, the truth and the life in a manner that is possible only to Him.

God's Knowledge is not the same as His Will.

His will is that all should return His love, but He knows that some will reject this invitation.

In justice and love should we wish Him to withdraw the gift of freedom - extinguishing the very quality of soul that makes it possible for us to love?

Should He alter the very thing that makes us human in order to pander to those who deliberately choose to live evil lives - ultimately choices arising from pride and hatred?

Should He obliterate the possibility of accepting the gift of eternal life, through enduring faith and love, in order to cater for those who choose to live without either of these qualities?

There exists a free choice between love and hatred, between obedience to truth and rebellion against it.

It should console us that not one person goes to Hell without freely choosing to put himself or herself in this shameful, dreadful state. The choice is ours.

There is no such thing as predestination to either Heaven or Hell. We choose, by our attitudes and our actions, which place we wish to go to, which type of person we wish to be.

The Face of Jesus?

I tend to think so - but it is not an article of faith!

When I first saw this picture, some forty-five years ago, I was impressed by the strength of the man behind the poor quality image, a reverse photo of the actual image on the Shroud of Turin.

One longs to see more clearly the real man in life.

Compare this face with the vast majority of pale, pasty-faced, eyes-up-to-heaven images of Christ that disgrace our churches!

Forty-five years ago I reserved judgment - but even then I said to myself, "This face has the strength and nobility that I would expect to find in the face of Jesus."

I suspended judgment then, for how can one be sure about a thing like this? I was prepared to believe that it could be an impression of his face. Would one not expect the death of God Incarnate to be marked in some way?

Various efforts, through chemical analysis and carbon dating, have been made to analyse the physical make-up of the shroud. I am simple minded enough to trust honest scientific analysis - accepting the word, technical ability and integrity of scientists at face value (no pun intended) - so when the carbon-dating report came back a few years ago, placing the manufacture of the Shroud of Turin as probably of the 12th century, I shrugged my shoulders and accepted it as a fact.

Then I discovered that the small portion of the fabric taken as a test sample had been cut from a mediaeval repair. Now I am not so sure. One of two leading carbon-dating experts in the world was honest enough recently to admit that in the case of the remains one of the 'bog-people' he had been examining - an ancient body found preserved in an English bog - he would have to allow a dating latitude of between 500 and 800 years, because of assimilation by the corpse of sifting and changing matter from the bog waters.

In the case of the Shroud of Turin chemical analysis of the fibres showed various external contaminations, pollen and dust that could only have come from the Middle East. So, making allowance for possible contamination over the centuries, I have had to undo my primitive faith in the accuracy of carbon-dating and allow, once more, for the possibility that this piece of material could have survived for 800 years longer than the estimated mediaeval date.

I find that I am relieved of an interior conflict, for when I look upon this obscure but powerful face I experience an instinctive reverence and the onset of awe - with, upon one occasion, to my surprise, a great sorrow for my sins, an awareness of my unworthiness, and a profound regret that this man suffered death.

I tend to believe, therefore, that when I gaze upon this image I look upon the face of Christ, captured in death - and my awe increases.

At the moment of my own death, when I am brought into full realisation of the truth, I half expect to recognise this face as the face of the man we know as Jesus Christ -   mysteriously and marvellously alive, fully known, in the light of my changed awareness, as the Man who is also God - magnificent and glorious beyond human expectation.

I am prepared to discover that I am mistaken - knowing that in eternity, caught up by the power and glory that is God, and sharing in His knowledge, I will have no difficulty in recognising the man who is in fact true Man and true God.

Is the face that is mysteriously burned into the fabric of this shroud the face of God Incarnate?

I have to say that I believe it is. When I look upon this face my natural inclination is to exclaim, "My Lord and my God..."

Spirit

To many the word 'spirit' seems to indicate something wraithlike and insubstantial - not real or lasting when compared with the solid matter that we can touch and smell and break apart to examine in detail.

The word is derived from the Latin *spiritus*, 'a breath' and *spirare*, 'to breathe' and these root meanings are loaded into our imaginations in a way that would indicate impermanence and lack of reality.

We need to guard against purely imaginary concepts and concentrate on reason. Imagination is a useful, creative tool, but it must be subordinate to reason and truth if we are to avoid living our lives in a state of imaginary delusion.

Observation and reason indicates that it is the material order that is subject to continual change and alteration. It is real, and valuable, but impermanent.

A spirit does not change its essential nature. It is permanent and everlasting.

In addition to meanings such as:

> *a ghost... a frame of mind... an emotion... an enthusiasm ... a disembodied soul etc...*
> (CHAMBERS DICTIONARY)

there are deeper, more thought provoking meanings, viz:

> *... a vital principle... the principle of thought ... the soul - the animating principle of life.*

The material of the physical world is constantly changing, is always capable of being broken into its constituent parts, is dust, or atoms: electrons and neutrons. The spirit, or animating life force of a man or woman cannot become anything other than a spirit.

Its main activity, thinking - knowing and loving - and its subsidiary potential of animating matter, is a permanent and enduring reality. The spirit gives form and meaning to the physical universe.

I am a spirit, animating the material of my body, which is constantly growing and changing. My thoughts and perceptions may also change, the way I think and what I regard to be true, or important, but my soul, because it possesses a central, indestructible unity of being, cannot change into something else. I can grow and become stronger in love and understanding - or become mean and selfish - but in my essential being I will never go out of existence.

The animating, knowing and loving spirit of a man or woman, though invisible, is more permanent than the material of the body, or of the universe.

It is in our spiritual nature that we resemble God. He knows and loves all that there is, past, present and future. We know only in part. He is more permanent and enduring than the universe He creates. He is a Spirit, to be worshipped in spirit and in truth, and because He is a Spirit it is possible for us to become united with Him in a permanent act of loving union - eternal and joyful, for He is love without end, knowledge and love without end - and in His love we truly learn to know and love each other.

Because it is not material a 'spirit' can be described as having no width, or depth or height; no touch, taste, colour, sound or smell. A good description of 'nothing'? Not at all. It is God who creates the physical world as a magnificent but pale shadow of His internal reality. From His nature is derived all the colour and beauty of the physical universe. It is created to last. It reflects God's permanence; but the reality is that the vast Universe is dependent upon the ceator for its existence, not the other way round. It is He, almighty in His power who gives shape and form to this Universe, and all the creatures in it, including ourselves, made in His image and likeness.

It is God, Who is spirit, who gives us shape and form, creating us as human beings with an innate capacity to know and love, the same *animus* - or spirit, or soul - that at the moment of conception enlivens cells in the womb which grow and develop into a living human being.

It is that same soul - the centre of being and knowing of each person - who, hopefully ennobled by brave and loving choices, continues in love as the body falls away at the moment of death.

It is the same soul, knowing and loving, who will once more enliven a physical body at the everlasting moment of the resurrection, through the power of Christ.

What this will be like we do not presently know; but it is the reason for our existence, and in due course we will find out.

The Trinity

What a marvellous concept! Well, much more than a concept, for this information is from a most reliable source - God Himself, revealing his innermost nature.

We are to spend all eternity in the presence of God, the Holy Trinity, so it is a good idea to try to get to know where we are going, before the event that we call death.

The Trinity is a mystery, the greatest mystery of the universe, but as a friend of mine always said, "A mystery is something that we know *something* about - not *nothing*!" And it is our job as Christians to try to understand what we know and what we do not know.

First we should acknowledge that we would know very little about the reality of God if our Brother, Our Lord Jesus Christ - God incarnate - had not revealed it.

He is the source of all knowledge.

Think with me.

God IS - He was not created. He is the source of the universe. He made it, created something where there was nothing, and continues to create and recreate, for He did not simply create a universe and leave it to accidental evolution. No - He is active behind everything that moves and lives and has being, always creating and guiding, to a plan that He alone knows fully. This, of course, leads to large questions about the imperfections of this same universe - how can a good and all-powerful God permit such aberrations? But that's another matter. *(see Evil, p.299)*

In the meantime, sticking to the subject, what about Him? What about the nature of God Himself?

He is not dependent upon the universe. The universe is dependent upon Him, upon His continuous creativity, and He has a plan for this universe, revealed in the incarnation, death and resurrection of His Son Jesus Christ - leading to the resurrection of all mankind and the renewal of this same universe.

We can not, of course, know at this time the full details of this recreated universe and our part in it. We are limited men and can only know in broad outline. We will not know the reality until it is achieved.

But we can know in outline what the plan is, for it has been revealed by Christ... Only from him can we receive sure and certain knowledge, knowledge that only God knows of right.

In essence this knowledge is that we are known and loved by God our creator, and that we will be brought fully into His love if we allow Him to enlighten us and show us the way.

God is a Spirit Who must be known in spirit and in truth, Jesus tells us.

A Spirit you may say! There is nothing very substantial about a spirit! You can't touch a spirit, or see a spirit. A spirit has no dimensions, no depth, no colour! The word spirit could well be a description of nothing!

Wrong!

A spirit is the most substantial thing that there is. Things that are material, that have width and length and depth, can change. A tree grows from a little seed. It can be cut down and made into furniture or floorboards, or burnt and reduced to black ash.

Mountains, created by earthquake or the vast movement of matter at the dawn of the universe, are continually changing, eroded by water, wind and ice.

Our human bodies grow from seeds in the womb to become adult men and women - and when the spirit that animates our body leaves these same bodies they rot and decay - turn into dust, cease to be animated.

It is this animating spirit of life that distinguishes men and woman from dust, from inanimate matter, from other life forms. (See *Spirit* for further thoughts. P.289)

It is our intellectual, spiritual ability to know and love that makes us unique among other living creatures. This is our chief likeness to God. We can know and love, like God but not equal to Him - for we know only in part and our capacity for love is restricted by the limits of our created nature.

God's knowledge and love, on the other hand, is without restriction. He knows and loves all things perfectly, including Himself. This is the first clue to beginning to understand in outline the mystery of the Trinity. God is love, the pure essence of love that will eventually burn away the dross of pride and selfishness that afflicts each one of us. He is the pure essence of love - but loving what? Loving whom? you may ask - apart from loving us and the universe He creates and recreates.

Loving Himself is the answer!

Is this not mere selfishness? We may be tempted to ask.

We tend to think of self-love as something unworthy, because we tend to love ourselves in a disordered, selfish way. Our job in this life, through loving God and our neighbour, is to learn to love ourselves properly. To learn to love properly is our main task.

Consider the question of knowing oneself. God knows Himself perfectly. We know ourselves in a very limited, changing way. We change and grow and our idea of ourselves alters accordingly. Our knowledge and perceptions change. We know ourselves in bits and pieces. Only God, who is outside us - as well as within us - knows us fully, is aware of our true identity.

But however good an idea one might have of oneself there is one sure thing - the idea that each one of us has of himself cannot love us back! Not so with God. God's idea of Himself is perfect, lacks nothing that the Mind that fathered it possesses - is Himself God. God the Father has an Idea of Himself, a Word in His Mind, a Word that is truly God, truly a Person.

This Word in the mind of God is the Word that John the beloved disciple refers to when he wrote:

"In the beginning was the Word and the Word was with God, and the Word was God, and the Word became flesh and lived among us."
This is our first reflection upon the nature of God, the mystery of God.

"I and the Father are One," Jesus says, and, *"He who sees me sees the Father."* And He promises that when He returns to Heaven after the resurrection He and His Father will send the Holy Spirit to bring back to mind everything that He has said.

The mystery deepens when we think of the Holy Spirit, for this Spirit lacks nothing that is possessed by the Father and the Son, is not a mere messenger. He is totally identified with the Father and the Son, IS the Love that flows between them, shares fully in the Godhead, is truly a Person. So there are three Persons Who possess the nature of being God. A vast mystery, something that we can just about begin to know in this life, in a small way.

There is nothing irrational about three Divine Persons possessing the nature of being God - just as there is nothing irrational about you, and your neighbour, and I, being three persons who possess the nature of being human. It is a fact.

The Father, Son and Holy Spirit are three Persons, distinct from each other, but possessing a complete unity of being. There is only one God, consisting of three distinct Persons, sharing in the nature of being God, just as you and your neighbour and I are three distinct persons sharing in the nature of being human.

But whereas the three Persons of the Trinity act in total unity, knowing and loving perfectly, you and I and our neighbour know imperfectly. We are limited in many ways, and it is a healthy thing to admit our imperfections, that we do not know things perfectly. This created life is mysterious; never mind the life of God.

We cannot in this life fully understand His nature, His innermost being. It is the greatest mystery of all. But it is a mystery that we can begin to understand.

Provided we believe in the Person of Christ and accept with positive love and faith that He is Our Lord and Saviour, that He is God incarnate, true man and true God, He and His Father and the Holy Spirit will gradually burn us free of selfishness and bring us to the point where we will know and love as we are known and loved. *"Now we know as through a glass, darkly,"* says St. Paul. *"Then we will know and love clearly."*

We bless ourselves - in the Name of the Father, the Son and the Holy Spirit – in the name of the great mystery of God's Being, revealed by Jesus.

The full revelation is something to look forward to. In the meantime we can learn much, by suspending our curiosity and in prayerful faith leaving ourselves open to the powerful love of God. He loves us much more than we can love Him. We are the adopted sons of God, brothers and sisters of Christ, and it is the action of the Holy Spirit that will gradually transform us into Christ, make us all *'one Person in Christ'*, as St. Paul says.

In this Love we will begin to love the Father with the same love that Christ, the Word incarnate, has for His Father. We will be lifted up to a new way of loving, greater than any that is possible in the purely created order. We will learn our true identity in Christ, become more like Him, share fully in His God-Life, and be lifted into the inner life of God Himself, burning in the great joy of the love that exists between Father and Son, in the Person of the Holy Spirit.

It is, indeed, something to look forward to.

The Beatific Vision is the term the Catholic Church uses to pinpoint the teaching.

Evil

How can a good God create a world in which evil so obviously flourishes?

There can be no dodging the question. It must be answered, if we are to have any peace of mind, if we are to be reassured that God is indeed good, that there is no duality of good and evil in His nature. At times in the past people have believed in a superstitious way that the Creator is a mixture of good and evil, have ascribed wilful maliciousness to spiritual powers that rule the world, e.g. the mythological gods of ancient Greece and the duality that affected the Catharist sects of the Middle Ages.

A Christian cannot entertain such an explanation. God alone is perfectly good. He is pure love. The world is a reflection of His goodness and love.

THE NATURE OF GOOD AND EVIL

But if God is perfectly good, and created the universe out of this goodness "and saw that it was good" (Gen. 1:3-23) how is it that evil entered into the universe? Surely a truly good God, totally in charge of the universe He creates, would have ensured that no evil would ever afflict it?

This is how we humans may view the matter. It seems very simple: a good, omniscient God, creating the universe out of pure goodness should have made it with built-in protection. But He did not, for horrors of sickness, pain, death and natural calamity exist. Worse than this, His creatures, made in His image and likeness, are prone to inflict malicious hurt upon each other. We, His creations, with a capacity to know and love and a limited power to make things, have a tendency towards evil.

So, while courage and love of truth and beauty do exist, along with a marvellous creativity of spirit, some men and women are corrupted by a range of evil attitudes: pride, envy, greed, hatred, malice and lust, resulting in murder, fornication, adultery, child-abuse, torture, extortion and cruelty - on such a scale that upon occasion one might be tempted to think that there is little goodness in the world. There is, of course, but even the majority of us (hopefully) who attempt to live good lives, are aware that we are not perfect. In fact, we can be downright bad at times, if we are honest, despite good intentions.

The Christian faith, with its root in Jewish history, provides the only rational, acceptable explanation, viz.: God created the universe, a perfectly good product, but it could go wrong, and it did, because men chose to be their own tin-pot little gods: i.e. our representatives chose "to eat of the fruit of the tree of knowledge of good and evil" – no apples involved! "Knowledge of good and evil" is the desirable fruit.

ADAM & EVE - A MYTH?

Some people are inclined to view the story of the Garden of Eden, along with Adam and Eve and the Serpent, as yet another myth, to be consigned to that part of our childish memories where we store Hans Christian Anderson, Aladdin and a Thousand and One Nights.

Pinocchio's growing nose and ultimate transformation into a donkey illustrates the consequences of lying debauchery, and to this extent illustrates a truth about human nature; but we cannot for an instant imagine that Pinocchio is a real individual.

Similarly, the Gods of Ancient Greece are Homer's imaginative attempt to explain the capricious elements of earth, fire and wind, and Aladdin panders to the perennial wish of men to win the lottery or have magical control over the world, with a genie of the lamp to fulfil dreams of wealth and power. This creative mythology tells us much about ourselves - even if it is only that we have a need to have things explained, create or find a pattern to the universe and human behaviour, which will, of course, only truly satisfy if it is true.

So what is different about the Adam and Eve story? Why should we believe that this is true?

There are other attempts, in cosmological mythology, to explain the origin and nature of things, as in Hinduism and the ancient gods of Egypt and Babylonia. What makes the God of the Jews so special, so believable? Why should we trust the creation story as recounted in the book of Genesis?

Partly from an analysis of the story: realising that the authors are trying to convey a series of truths in the only way imaginable at that time, using rich metaphor and symbol. The writers relate, after all, something that is utterly unimaginable and unknown to man - information regarding the unseen God and His actions as Creator of the universe, whereby He creates the physical universe *ex nihilo,* from nothing, where there was nothing, and sees that it is good. He creates mankind in his own image and likeness. He tells men clearly and unequivocally that there is only one condition attached to the maintenance of their special status: they are not to eat the fruit of the tree of life "the tree of knowledge of good and evil".

The fact that they are able to disobey is because they are true, living likenesses of the living God, with intellect and will, with real freedom to choose, regardless of the consequences.

The consequences of disobedience are dire: the gift of unending natural life is withdrawn. Mankind opens the door to death and suffering. It is Man's fault that this is so, not God's. Men - the family of men - have abused the great gift of freedom.

Acceptance of the story is reinforced, for me, by the beautiful, unforced economy of the language used. The Hebrew words *adamah*, meaning creature of the earth and *eve*, mother of the living, contain their own message, and "the tree of knowledge of good and evil" easily conveys the superior status of judgement and knowledge that the first men wished to attain.

This is the only proposed explanation of creation and the origin of evil that makes sense. The language may be mythological and figurative but the meaning is clear and truthful.

The use of powerful symbol is the only way in which such a mystery can even begin to be understood. *Adamah*, or Man, with a real freedom of choice, choose to make himself, rather than God, the judge of what is right and wrong: and through this act of pride sin and death entered the world.

We may reject this explanation if we wish. There is no compulsion to believe. But if we do we have no explanation of evil, and must live our lives in partial blindness, and die in blindness - in a worse state than a blind dog, for the dog is blind by birth or accident, while we, if we fail to discern and accept truth, regardless of the type of language in which it is presented, choose to remain blind. I repeat: there is no other acceptable explanation for the existence of evil.

My final reason for accepting the basic truth of this account of creation and falling away from friendship with God is based upon my acceptance of Christ as true man and true God. It is in the light of this gift of faith that what once seemed doubtful is recognised as totally truthful - reliable and in accord with reason because God, revealed in Christ, guarantees that it is so.

EVIL AS A LACK

Essentially evil is the lack of something:

Hatred is the lack of love, war the lack of peace, pain the lack of good health, death the absence of life.

It is a negative state, but has parlous, noisy effects: the snarl of anger and hatred, the destruction and violence of war; the putrefaction and stink of death; the hurt and anguish of betrayal through lies and lack of love.

We all know something of evil and its catastrophic results. But where does it come from?

Initially from mankind's betrayal of itself as depicted in the Book of Genesis. No use complaining that the situation would be different if we had been the first men and women. We can be certain that this is not the case. God deals with the human family on a cosmic scale, through aeons of evolving time, and we can be certain that our remote ancestors were no less in character than ourselves. Had we been the first men we would have behaved exactly as they did.

But did we humans do this to ourselves, without any assistance? No. The Genesis tale tells us of a spirit of evil that tempted the woman, and through her the man.

EVIL AS AN INTELLIGENT FORCE

"Tosh!" You may be tempted to exclaim. If so, look at the monumental scale of evil in the world: millions of people dead through war, disease and natural calamity. Such cosmic evil must have a cosmic source.

We could guess and speculate about this until the pubs close and the Universe explodes in a final big bang – and some of us probably will: those of weak mind and unsure disposition. The rest of us, who sincerely seek reliable guidance and find this in the Son of Man, Jesus, the New Adam, will know with absolute certainty that cosmic evil does exist. Jesus tells us that evil on this scale exists not in some abstract entity but in the form of malicious personal evil, a being whom He calls the Devil, a monstrous angelic presence who "roams the world like a raging lion" seeking whom he may destroy.

I would prefer to avoid acknowledgement of the existence of such a power. I would prefer that there was no spirit of evil. But evil is there, and its existence must be explained. We must know the truth.

The thought of a spiritual being with superior intellect and will twisted by hate is obnoxious. Jesus, the only reliable source of such information, tells us that there are a number of such beings, possessing powers of mind infinitely greater than ours; originally created by God, also in His image and likeness, but greater than us by virtue of their angelic, spiritual nature; beings who deliberately chose to be separate from Him, chose power for self, hatred rather than love. Such hatred is hard to imagine. But it exists.

"Rubbish!" you may cry! If this outline of the nature of evil were mine I might well support your position. But it is not my outline. It is Christ's; and we ignore what He says at our peril – to the grim satisfaction of those malicious, pride filled, evilly motivated spirits who actively seek the physical and spiritual death and despair of each one of us. The devils are happy to see our disbelief, maliciously pleased to see that we are prepared to share in their blind pride. Our pride in self, in our own personal judgement, a relic of man's first sin, makes us easy meat, whereas real humility, an awareness of our identity as created beings, acknowledging a creative and loving force beyond and above us, is indestructible armour.

But be not afraid, death has no more dominion over us. Evil has been put to flight – through the power of the Holy Spirit of Christ, sent out over the world by Him and His Father, protecting us and giving to us participation in the divine life of Christ through baptism and the gift of faith. All that we need to do is believe, and lead our lives in love and faith. You don't believe? Nothing I can do about this; you probably would not believe even if someone came back from the dead. I wonder where I have heard that before!

It is a dreadful truth that some, through pride and fear, and dullness of hope and heart, will actually refuse to believe in the love that God has for them. The clouding power of evil is great, until dispersed by an act of faith. After this the devil is reduced to a snarling menace, kept at bay by faith and love: the true spirit of love and obedience which evil cannot endure. Listen to the Man. Be wise. Be happy.

SUMMARY

It is part of the Christian faith, and the experience of many millions of people, that God is infinitely good, possessing within Himself no shade or shadow that is not perfectly loving, for He is love, as His beloved disciple John says.

Of course God knew, or more properly 'knows' (for He views events outside the restrictions of time) that men, given a true likeness of Himself, including real freedom, would rebel (will rebel). Of course he knew of the dire consequences - the suffering and death mankind would bring upon each and every member of the human family, but could He permit the foreknowledge of such evil prevent and negate His intention, His life-giving plan?

Certainly not, especially as He also knew that he personally would enter His created world, become a full member of the human family, and as proof of His love subject himself to the same terrible conditions that all men experience as a result of the sin of Adam.

In justice the gulf created between God and Man had to be bridged by men, but by nature we were inadequate to the task. Only God could repair the breach caused by such disobedience, but reparation was due from man.

In Christ, the new Adam, a man who is also God, the atonement was made - the at-one-ment - and we are offered a share in His divine life - a much greater life than mankind was first given.

Do we begin to see a plan emerge? Method in God's madness? Sense being made out of our nonsense? A greater gift being given, despite our foolishness? I hope you do. It is the truth, not because I say so, or Christians say so. It is the truth that God reveals, through His Christ, a truth of redemption that Christ even now is putting into effect. All honour and praise and thanks to Him, throughout eternity.

One final point. Most people will recognize the evil that men inflict upon each other. They will accept that individual people are responsible, and not blame God. Some people cannot accept that God is free of responsibility for natural disasters that occur on a grand scale, where hundreds of thousands of men, women and children are killed by flood, earthquake and disease.

It is natural to believe that a truly loving and omnipotent God would not inflict suffering on such a scale. The truth is that He does not.

The human race has inflicted such events, such possibilities, on itself, for our rebellion affects the entire universe, not just mankind. Order still exists in the universe, but it is affected, and the process of creation continues, afflicted by the angelic powers that God employed in its creation and continues to employ in a process of development that moves towards perfection; and some of these angelic powers, those who have chosen evil, are still able to exert influence. These are the demons that Jesus tells us about.

So the whole of creation groans in travail, as St. Paul tells us in his letter to the Romans (v.22), caught up in the consequence of our original sin, moving towards the re-creation under a final dispensation brought about by Christ, God incarnate.

So when we are appalled by knowledge of the death of hundreds of thousands of men, women and children, millions throughout history, we simply have to accept that this is the consequence of men's action in the 'Garden of Eden' and of the angelic rebellion that preceded it, both cosmic events with cosmic repercussions. After all, rationally considered, the death of one small child through aids, cholera or being crushed by a lorry is just as horrible as a thousand crushed by an earthquake or drowned by flood or cyclone. The scale may threaten to overwhelm us, but the effect upon each individual child and the suffering and sorrow that is experienced is just as appalling as the death of one innocent baby.

Only in Jesus, at the moment when this suffering and distorted world is remade through his death and resurrection, will we see the fulfilment of God's marvellous plan.

If you don't believe this you have nothing, literally nothing, to look forward to, except perhaps a short period of continued personal existence. Those who live in the faith, hope and love of Jesus are assured of an eternal destiny of life and love.

Life & Death

Strange, is it not, that on a day to day basis we can take the gift of life for granted? Only when it is suddenly removed from someone we love do we fully appreciate how fragile is the hold we have upon it.

We are so embedded in life that we tend to assume that it will continue, tucking away into the back of our mind that all people die. Perhaps, also, it is such a great mystery that we cannot imagine finding a totally satisfactory explanation of how we come to be and why we will die.

We understand concepts of fertilisation and generation of life in a biological sense. Less thoughtful people appear to believe that the gift can be explained merely in such terms, especially as processes of artificial fertilisation become ever more refined and we witness embryos frozen and transplanted after years of arrested development.

Medical science can give the impression that the whole process is almost mechanical, simple biology. To many it would appear that man is in charge, in total control, that we are Lords of life and death. We are not, of course.

Even should biological engineering develop to the ultimate point where artificially produced semen and ovum are combined to produce sustainable life, men can not be credited with the creation of life. They would be, as now, pro-creators, at another remove.

In theory it is just possible that biochemists will achieve such a remarkable breakthrough. It's unnecessary of course. The world that God has made is awash with semen and female eggs. But let's say that medical scientists achieve the unnecessary.

What they would have achieved would be man-made replication of existing life-making processes. The true creator of life will honour His commitment, for God does not give a gift in order to withdraw it because of mankind's foolish arrogance.

When God the Creator gives a gift it is given for all time, all eternity. Such is His nature. All of His acts are eternal, perfect and unalterable.

"Ah but...!" I can imagine some exclaim. "Men would have done it! They would have created life!"

Not at all. They would simply have recreated the conditions required for the generation of life, and just as men and women come together in the pleasurable act that creates life naturally, and perhaps unthinkingly claim that they are sole creators, medical scientists might make the same claim, erroneously, for we are merely pro-creators, i.e. creators on behalf of the Creator and Father of All.

God is always present in each creation of a human being, fully responsible for it. He did not merely establish a biological process and remain aloof.

You don't believe? You don't believe in God the Creator of life? You believe that the process is totally automatic, a mere biological happening?

'Tis a foolish act of unbelief. I shake my head sorrowfully, along with the psalmist, and join with him in proclaiming, "The fool says in his heart, 'There is no God!'"

It is a foolish and insupportable statement, to state categorically "There is no God. No Creator.".

(Excuse this little detour from my main theme.)

It would at least be rational to say, "I do not *believe* there is a God", and then try to give reasons for unbelief; and when you are confounded by the impossibility to then appeal to the unknown, saying: "God, if you exist let me know that you are." It is important to clarify the issue, and it is the experience of many that such a request will be answered, though it needs repetition, for God will not give the gift of faith in answer to an idle thought.

The earnest and inquiring person will receive an answer, though you should be warned that it may be confirmed during moments of great distress, for we are the type of created being who only appears to recognise our total dependence upon the Lord and Creator of life when artificial supports are knocked away and we are left barren, naked and hurting in our soul.

When this happens be of good cheer, for He truly is a God of love, loving each one of us personally with a great and consuming love, that fire of forgiveness which Christ could not wait to see cast over all the earth (Lk.12.49).

Excuse this little detour. Back to the main theme.

LIFE

What is life? We need to think about it.

A piece of grass is alive. A bird or a fish is alive.

Human beings are alive.

Each has different characteristics. Plants seed and grow, rooted in the earth, warmed by the sun, moving upwards towards the light. There is no capacity for lateral movement, except when moved by the wind.

According to the philosophy favoured by the Catholic Church, based upon Aristotle's thinking as adopted by Thomas Aquinas (1225-74), every individual example of created life has an *animus*, an animating principle of life, or soul. Yes - a piece of grass, or a chrysanthemum, has a soul - as has an alligator or an elephant - and a human being.

The central quality of a soul is that it animates matter which would otherwise be inanimate, in a variety of forms, each with limitations and possibilities. Whereas a piece of grass is restricted to growing upwards, attached to its roots and moving in the breeze, an eagle floats and soars in the air, while the antelope leaps over rock and crag and the salmon slips and churns through water.

In addition to the power of movement a remarkable number of animals appear to have an additional capacity. They are able to think, or at least relate to the world about them. In varying degrees they - we - have intelligence.

It is a continual curiosity to us that other animals have a power to perceive and understand, to react and communicate with each other, and with us, to a limited degree. It is a mystery. We can understand something of how they function, but not everything; though there can be no doubt, in the mind of a fair and honest human, that their intelligence is inferior to ours.

It is stretching credulity to an intolerable degree to believe that a monkey, given time and a typewriter, could tap out "Macbeth". In fact, it is nonsense. A chimpanzee just does not have that kind of intelligence. Animals other than ourselves cannot ask questions such as, "How did I come into existence?" or "Is there an overall Creator?" - never mind answer them.

It is clear that there is a fantastic difference in quality between the soul of man and other animals. Whatever about other animals the animating principle of life of a human being is of a non-material character (viz.: through our senses we can acquire a very good image of a rose, but the rose itself, being material, remains outside the mind).

Our human capacity to know and love is a reflection of God's nature, his capacity to know and love. We are made in the image and likeness of God, mainly in our soul, that animating principle of life. Each one of us is a combination of spirit and matter, a spiritual and physical entity, and it is the soul that gives form to the body.

The body can disintegrate but the human soul cannot be destroyed. When death occurs, i.e. when my personal knowing, loving and animating principle of life ceases to animate the atoms that form my body, I, that centre of knowing and loving, continue to exist.

All created life is surrounded by the unseen glory of the Creator: *"Think of the flowers; they never have to spin or weave; yet, I assure you, not even Solomon in all his regalia was robed like one of these."* (Lk.12.27)

We are surrounded by the same glory. The trick is to recognize it, in the way that a flower cannot.

DEATH

Death is not something that I can accept placidly, with a shrug of the shoulders and the thought, "Oh, it just happens. It's natural. You can't change it."

Such phlegmatic acceptance is beyond me. Death is the ultimate evil in the natural order of the universe – along with pain and suffering.

I wish to know why a good and benevolent God should permit such evil. I would not if I were He, and I am sure that most share my opinion. But I do not wish to attempt an explanation here. *(See: Evil: Page 299.)*

At this point I merely wish to examine the phenomenon of death, register that it exists.

To the Christian there are two forms of death: death of the soul and death of the body.

Death of the human soul is the condition whereby the person can not and will not participate in God's love; ultimately hell. Death of the body we are all acquainted with – though not yet by personal experience if you are reading this!

When death occurs the body decays and corrupts, gradually turns to dust. There is no escape. There can be no argument. It will happen, despite the efforts of some deluded humans to avoid the condition by having their bodies frozen in the hope of some scientific antidote of the future. Such attempts to avoid mortality would be mirth making except that they illustrate much frailty of mind, vain hope and delusion, among fellow humans who have failed to accept basic and essential truths about the nature and the meaning of life. I do not rejoice to see such delusion.

Death is truly a dreadful and horrible thing. When one contemplates the corruption of the body of a loved one (or even of oneself): the eyes that smiled and flashed with love and laughter and intelligence, there can be no joy - not humanly speaking anyway.

There is a universal tendency to believe, because life is such a precious thing, because people are so beautiful (even when we are a bit ugly!) that there must be something beyond this experience, something that will preserve and extend the value and beauty of the person. The impulse to believe in some sort of after life has created notions such as Heaven (perpetual existence of the disembodied soul) and various theories of different types of reincarnation (returning to life as someone or something else).

Notions such as these tend to be so vague and imprecise, so obviously the product of human speculation and, in some cases imagination, that I would have great difficulty in accepting and believing them with any degree of certainty. I would have, for example, great difficulty in accepting the possibility of reincarnation, in the form of another person, or an animal or bird (as Hindus, Buddhists and Jainists believe).

I have an awareness of my unique identity. I am just me, a recognisable personal entity, and I do not find it acceptable or rational that I can become an entirely different human person. People who believe that in a past life they were Napoleon, or a 13th century serving wench are delusional, quite clearly suffering from personality disorder. (If you think you are Mahatma Ghandi, King Tut or King George III, Martin Luther King, John Lennon or Elvis, please do not contact me!)

Yet the universal existence of a yearning for continuation of life, some form of immortality, gives rise to the suspicion that there may be something in it, and when I examine the problem more closely, realise that the soul or animus of a human being is something distinct from matter I appreciate that there are possibilities which I cannot reject out of hand, if I am wise.

What I lack is proper information from a reliable and authoritative source: one way or the other. What would be a reliable and authoritative source? Certainly not any further imaginative speculation by any fellow human being, no matter how gifted and apparently inspired and informed. I have had enough of that.

RELIABLE GUIDE?

The only source of reliable information would be God Himself.

Can I contact Him? Yes – but only in the Person of Jesus Christ. Of all the great teachers of men, of all the thinkers and philosophers and gurus only one person has ever said of himself, *"I am the way, the truth and the life. He who believes in me will not die. ..... I have come that you may have life and have it more abundantly."* The man who said this is either mad or is truly what and who he claims to be, God incarnate.

On reading about him in the gospels, and listening to him, and gauging what he says, and meeting his mind, I discover no sign of madness. Quite the contrary: such strength and wonder is revealed, such innate authority, that as I begin to know and recognise him I find myself filled with awe and amazement. He smiles upon me, and I can only worship (i.e. give worth-ship) and honour to a fellow man who is God.

He alone is the perfect guide, the person who gives to me, and all who believe in him, the only antidote to death: eternal life.

"This," he says, *"is eternal life: to believe in me and he who sent me...."*
It is a big claim – worthy of investigation.

Heaven, Hell & Purgatory
— and Limbo*?

If you have ever felt love for another person (or even the passing exhilaration and joy of a moment of personal or community achievement - of success) you will recognise the fact that at the highest point of awareness, of what gives meaning to our lives, we are made for joy and celebration. We are made for love. We pass our days looking for love, and we only find it intermittently, if at all, in this life.

Those who are alert and thoughtful must surely begin to suspect that we are made for something great, something awesome, though we rarely achieve it in this life - where passing moments of love and joy become memories, all too quickly.

Permanent joy and peace would be heaven, though cynics say that the idea of hanging around all day on a heavenly cloud does not appeal. Boredom would surely set in, they say.

They miss the point. Heaven is not like anything we can imagine. It is the actual fulfilment of every desire that we have had for love and joy. It is the fact of being possessed by and returning love, rejoicing in a fulfilment that is totally unimaginable, a sharing in God's inner life

---

* I will say little about 'Limbo'. No doubt such a state existed before the death and resurrection of Jesus. Heaven and earth had not yet been united by His action. There was a waiting 'time'. Now that atonement is made the state of limbo exists no more. Those old grannies of theology who worry and fret about the state of unbaptised children fail to understand the love that Jesus has for all his brothers and sisters. They should abandon theology and take up knitting.

of love - loving the Father of All through and in the power of Christ's love: unending bliss and joy - the heart's desire.

But heaven is not simply spiritual ecstasy. Total fulfilment will not be complete until we share in Christ's resurrection and the universe is remade.

If the final shape of Heaven is this, eternally caught up in the personal love that unites time and eternity, what can be the state of those who have rejected love, who have chosen evil?

As all of God's creative acts are eternal such people will never go out of existence. They will caught up for all eternity in the fire of the love that should be fulfilment but is to them shame, horror and awareness of love rejected, hatred and anger revealed in the light of love, suffering in the fire of a love that should be delight.

What a dread fate, deliberately and freely chosen, despite the goodness of life and the self-sacrificing love of Jesus on the cross, rejecting all that is good and holy, kind and loving[*].

We who are made in the image and likeness of God, in that we can know and love, are aware from time to time that we are not self-sufficient, that we need help from beyond ourselves. It is a healthy realisation, and if we accept the reality of our need, trust in God's goodness and kindness, as well as in the goodness and kindness of neighbours, we learn to live in hope and trust: learn faith and love, begin to move towards eternal love.

---

[*] Though I have made the point that all God's acts are eternal I cannot help feeling and thinking that the God of Love will bring to an end those who suffer in hell. Can God not change his mind? Is it only humans who have this capacity? Perhaps He will simply cease to think of such people, such fallen angels, and they will cease to exist. It would be the kindly thing to do. (God knows my thought. I hope He is taking note! Michael O'Shea – God's Counsellor? Wow!) I know that I am not being logical here, but I cannot help hoping, for I cannot bear the thought of men and women eternally suffering in hatred, rejecting love.

But many will not have achieved perfect, unselfish love before they die, will not be able to fully return God's love. They have not rejected love, are not in hell, though it may seem like it at times, until they are purged of their sins, their lack of love.

The Catholic Church defines this state as Purgatory, where people are caught up in Love, burn with desire for it, wish above all to live in it. It is a state to be endured rather than enjoyed: a painful purging of the soul. It may take place in this life, but also when we have left the body.

This fire of love is a torture, not in the same way experienced by those who have rejected goodness, but a suffering and a pain all the same, and it is the teaching of the Catholic Church that, as a consequence of the brotherhood of mankind, the prayers and love of those who are faithful affects those who undergo the cleansing fire of love.

"It is a holy and wholesome thought to pray for the dead, so that they may be released from their sins," writes a Jewish prophet of old. (2 Mac 12:46)

So, in the mystery of the fusion of human love with the divine we can help each other in this life and the next, expressing our love not only in practical, everyday concern for our neighbour but also through prayer for the departed, for those who are learning to love – all of us.

Prayer

"When you pray, go to your private room and, when you have shut the door, pray to your Father who is in that secret place, and your Father who sees all that is done in secret will reward you. ...... In your prayers do not babble as the pagans do ..... your Father knows what you need before you ask him. So you should pray like this:

> *Our Father in heaven,*
> *may your name be held holy,*
> *your kingdom come,*
> *your will be done,*
> *on earth as it is in heaven.*
> *Give us today our daily bread.*
> *And forgive us our debts,*
> *As we have forgiven those who are in debt to us.*
> *And do not put us to the test,*
> *But save us from the evil one"*
>   (Mt. 6, vv 6-13; similar to Lk. 11, vv 2-4)

"Ask, and it will be given to you;
search, and you will find;
knock, and the door will be opened to you.
For the one who asks always receives; the one who searches always finds; the one who knocks will always have the door opened to him.
Is there a man among you who would hand his son a stone when he asked for bread?
Or hand him a snake when he asked for a fish?
If you then who are evil, know how to give to your children what is good, how much more will the heavenly Father give the Holy Spirit to those who ask him!"
                    (Mt. 6 vv7-11; similar to Lk. 11 vv 9-13)

When we pray we are in very good company.......

These instructions by Jesus are, of course, for 'private' prayer, the preparation of the mind and soul for participation in the great Eucharistic prayer, in which the entire community offers praise and thanksgiving to the Lord of Hosts during the commemoration of the Last Supper, where the mystery is proclaimed and explained by Jesus: *"I am the living bread that came down from heaven. Whoever eats of this bread will live forever; and the bread that I will give for the life of the world is my flesh."*

The Jews then disputed among themselves, saying,
"How can this man give us his flesh to eat?"
So Jesus said to them,

"Very truly, I tell you, unless you eat the flesh of the Son of Man and drink his blood, you have no life in you. Those who eat my flesh and drink my blood have eternal life, and I will raise them up on the last day; for my flesh is true food and my blood is true drink. Those who eat my flesh and drink my blood abide in me, and I in them. Just as the living Father sent me, and I live because of the Father, so whoever eats me will live because of me."

We who are Catholic believe in the further explanation offered by Jesus, at the Last Supper,

Holding bread he said, *"Take and eat; this is my body."* Then he took a cup, gave thanks, and gave it to them, saying, *"Drink from it, all of you, for this is my blood of the covenant, which will be shed on behalf of many for the forgiveness of sins."*

We believe that at the consecration of bread and wine during the Eucharist, Christ becomes truly present, Body, Blood, Soul and Divinity, and that by eating and drinking, in obedience to Christ, we are taken into Christ's divine life, participate with Him in the life that He shares with His Father and with us.

There is no greater prayer. There is no greater reality, mysterious though it is.

Thanks

My thanks to George Rice, friend and neighbour, for correcting the more obvious faults of the half-remembered text of Joe's Latin discourse, and to Eithne Vogt and David Hough who read the text in draft and let me have valued reaction.

Also to Morris Rosenthal, from the United States, (www.fonerbooks.com/) for generously sharing information with a complete stranger about internet self-publishing and print-on-demand .... imagine how self-publishers of the past would have rejoiced at the amazing online self-publishing facilities that now exist – people such as William Blake, Stephen Crane, e.e. cummings, Deepak Chopra, Benjamin Franklin, Zane Grey, James Joyce, Rudyard Kipling, D.H. Lawrence, Thomas Paine, Edgar Allen Poe, Ezra Pound, Carl Sandburg, George Bernard Shaw, Upton Sinclair, Gertrude Stein, Henry David Thoreau, Mark Twain, Walt Whitman, and Virginia Woolf – poor lady.

So I am not alone, not a trailblazer, just an ordinary old guy fulfilling a modest destiny. Who knows – 'Brother Barney O.P.' might launch me to fame and fortune......? Pity I can't take it with me!

Dear Reader,

Thank you for reading this book – if you have.

You haven't! Good God! After the sweat and anguish of living it and writing it!

Right! Back to Page One, where Angel awaits, and, you never know, he might have something real to say, despite being a bit wordy - but don't you find this with most books, slow to start but after a few pages you get into the swing of it, as you begin to meet the author in the spirit?

So stick with Angel. It gets better once the action starts.

I just want to say to you: I'm an old guy now – 78 in December 2010 – so I may not be around too long. Should I last for a few years I have it in mind to complete a trilogy of Barney novels, all autobiographical. Don't hold your breath! Three-quarters of a century passed before I got around to writing this one - and even then I started in the middle of a trilogy - no logic!

'Brother Barney O.P.' is the middle of the three I have planned. *'Before Barney'* is to be the first and *'Beyond Barney'* the third. (I just love alliteration!)

That's the message. Sorry we can't talk, but there is an unspoken dialogue that exists between writer and reader. Should you wish to actually *say* something to me you can contact me via my website: www.o2cbooks.info - but make it before my one-hundred and first birthday!

At the start of the 'Addendum' part of this book I said, "Thank you for the hospitality of your mind"...

I really mean this. Thank you.

Yours truly,

Michael O'Shea

The Author

Michael O'Shea was born in Belfast in 1932 and spent his formative years there and in the County Down fishing village of Ardglass, where he now lives.

End Notes

1 Another event of great importance to 'Joe' took place at this one-day of prayer and spiritual recollection.
The priest giving it was Father Vincent Rochford, parish priest in the East End parish of the Isle of Dogs, and a CEG speaker. On this occasion, talking about Jesus telling the priests of the Temple in Jerusalem that the temple would be destroyed, but that it would be raised on the third day, Fr. Vincent made the point dramatically - by clutching his own body - that Jesus was referring to the temple of his body.
For the first time I became fully aware that Jesus had been and was a man, not just someone who could be described as 'God incarnate', a kind of historical icon
It was a profound moment of realisation.
Fr. Vincent was viewed as eccentric by some people. He said that in his parish the people lacked humour, to such an extent that when he made a humorous comment during his Sunday homily he was forced to lower a homemade placard over the side of the pulpit, displaying the word JOKE.

    Also, years before it was permitted to celebrate the Eucharist facing the people, he had hauled a massive slate tombstone from the graveyard into the church and erected it temporarily before the main altar, celebrating Mass there among the people – removing it before any visitation by his Bishop.

    A rebel man from County Antrim you might be tempted to say! No, a holy, enthusiastic priest, displaying his love for the risen Lord, with his entire mind and all his heart, waiting for the official church to catch up with him. A great man among many.

2 Frank Sheed was a major influence upon all CEG speakers, and a great stimulus to coherent thought and expression.
He was an Australian, had a Law Degree and was one of the first Catholic laymen with a Doctorate in Theology. A fabulously cogent and entertaining speaker, Frank could have made a fortune at the Bar. Instead, he made theology the focus of his life, and in addition to his CEG work in London and New York he and his wife Maisie Ward established the Catholic publishing house of Sheed & Ward in those two cities.
I am among a large number of people who owe much to Frank Sheed's trenchant, reasoned presentation of basic theology. He could refine ideas with vivid imagery, but imagination was always the servant of reason.
His great skill with words is illustrated by his subtle translation of *"The Confessions of St. Augustine"*. Some say that Augustine's Latin prose is limited. Frank Sheed's English translation gives a gloss of understanding to Augustine's thought that other translators have yet to equal, and probably never will.
His own books *"A Map of Life"*, *"Theology for Beginners"* and *"Theology & Sanity"* provide a thinking man's guide to the meaning and purpose of life.

3 Cecily Hastings was widely learned, with a deeply generous spirit and marvellous powers of recall. Above all she insisted upon accuracy - as numerous students in the Theology Department of St. Mary's University College at Twickenham no doubt realised when she joined St. Mary's as a lecturer. With an Oxford double first in French and German she translated the works of eminent theologians Carl Rahner and Hans Küng into English. She also made great vegetable soup – brimful of goodness!

4 No such excuse is open to Jews born within the past couple of hundred years, no matter where they live – following the invention of printing.
The blindness that exists among Jewish people is amazing – that they should fail to recognise the identity of a fellow Jew.
Centuries of abominable and unchristian persecution of Jewish people, perceived as God killers, is, of course, a grievous barrier, requiring generous forgiveness.
Uncivilised and barbarous so-called Christians - in name only followers of Jesus - seem to have listened to a mob in Jerusalem shouting "His blood be upon us!" rather than to the Man himself, "Forgive them what they do!"
When I receive the Body and Blood of Jesus in the Eucharist I am proud that I receive the life blood of the Messiah, the saviour of the world. In a very real way I live with Jewish blood, eternally given for the life of all.
 It is tragic that Jewish people, individually and collectively, appear not to be able to open their minds to even the possibility that Jesus came to offer eternal life to all who listen to him, all who genuinely search for the truth.
It is a dangerous thing to drown out a call that may indeed come from on high.

5 I have been re-reading the Qur'an, to make sure of my facts, and 50 years after my first reading I am even less impressed.
It's a heterogeneous collection of sayings that are supposed to be the direct word of God. All I can say is that this God seems to be pretty incoherent, really mixed up. Sorry if this annoys members of the Muslim faith, but that's my genuine impression.
I am carefully excluding any reaction to current violence carried out by Muslim extremists, and my personal aversion to attitudes adopted by the leaders of countries such as Iran.
This is a theological matter.
In October 2007 138 Islamic leaders wrote to the Pope and other Christian leaders, offering peace between Islam and Christianity, saying of Christians that *"we are not against them and Islam is not against them - so long as they do not wage war against Muslims on account of their religion, oppress them and drive them out of their homes".*

Ehem! Where are Christians waging wars against Muslims on account of their religion? Nowhere in the world! A large number of Western countries invaded Iraq and Afghanistan for reasons that have nothing to do with religion: *i.e.* deposing an undoubted tyrant and opening up oil supplies. *Nothing* to do with *either* Christianity or Islam. The Pope and the Archbishop of Canterbury did not bomb Baghdad.

These Muslim clerics present Islam as a religion of peace, but many of them openly approve of persecuting and killing former Muslims who convert to Christianity; and in many Muslim countries there is a total prohibition against building Christian churches and schools, whereas Mosques are freely erected in countries with a Christian heritage.

Further, the Qur'an, believed to be the unalterable Divine Word of God, proclaims that Jews and Christians should be destroyed:

> *Surah 9.30: And the Jews say: Uzair is the son of Allah; and the Christians say: The Messiah is the son of Allah; these are the words of their mouths; they imitate the saying of those who disbelieved before;* **may Allah destroy them; how they are turned away!** *[from Islam]*

In addition, the Christian belief that Jesus (Isa) is the Son of God, and has revealed the Trinitarian nature of God, is unacceptable to Muslims:

> *Surah 4.171: O People of the Book! Commit no excesses in your religion: nor say of God aught but the truth. Christ Jesus the son of Mary was (no more than) an apostle of God, and His Word, which he bestowed on Mary, and a Spirit proceeding from him: so believe in God and His apostles.* **Say not "Trinity": desist: it will be better for you: for God is One God: Glory be to Him: (Far exalted is He) above having a son.**

It would seem that, despite the wishes of a few Islamic clerics, echoed by many, many peace loving Muslims, I am sure, there *is* a great gulf, not because of Christian intransigence but because of Islamic teaching.

I note this situation with dismay.

Only if *all* Muslims decide to accept theological differences with respect, and truly live in peace, abandoning the basic Muslim prayer of the Surah about Christians: *'may Allah destroy them'*, will reconciliation come about.

Further, the attitudes of some of the signatories to the Islamic letter fail to raise my hopes.

Taissir Rajab Al-Tamimi, for example, a judge in an Islamic court in Palestine, and one of those who signed, has said in the past that, *"the Jews are destined to be persecuted, humiliated and tortured forever, and it is a Muslim duty to see to it that they reap their due. No petty arguments must be allowed to divide us. Where Hitler failed, we must succeed."*

This not the frame of mind that one would expect in a person seeking peace – of any kind.

Not all are like this of course. There are just as many good Muslims as Christians. The problem is with the Qur'an.

If you believe that it really is the unalterable word of God and you dedicate yourself to living it out fully, with all your mind and your heart and soul, and in action, you dedicate yourself to destroy all Christians and Jews.

It is not a religion to which I would care to belong.

The Muslim God is not one that I can believe in.

I do believe in the God who came and lived among us on this earth, who gave his life for love of us.

6 The Buddhist Society, Founded 1924, Patron the Dali Lama in 1961. The Dali Lama is a likeable man advocating a way of peace, but offering no solution to the problem of evil other than endurance; with no explanation as to how the universe might have came to be, and certainly postulating no purpose to it.

A purposeless world? I could not accept this, as every ordinary thing in the world seemed to have a purpose (if you could determine it) – except for suffering and death, which to me at that time appeared to be totally without purpose.

7 **Fr. Vincent McNabb O.P.**, Master of Sacred Theology and Professor of Philosophy was born in Portaferry, Co. Down on July 8, 1868.
Educated at St. Malachy's College, Belfast, he joined the English Dominicans and lived mostly in the Dominican Priory at Highgate, North London.
Ireland was his mother he said, England his sister. Each week, in addition to his life of prayer and pastoral care, he clumped in his thick working boots eight miles to and from Speaker's Corner, in all weathers, to speak for an hour of the things of Christ.
He died at Highgate on June 17 1943 with an extraordinary reputation for holiness.
Vincent McNabb was no 'ivory castle' saint. His life and personality greatly influenced Hilaire Belloc and G.K. Chesterton – he was at Chesterton's deathbed - and he supported proposals by Belloc and Chesterton for a world economic system to replace irreconcilable Communism and Capitalism. It was based on the encyclical *Rerum Novarum* (Of New Things) issued by Pope Leo XIII on May 16, 1891.
According to Distributism, the almost unpronounceable name used to identify the system, ownership of the means of production and distribution should be spread as widely as possible among the general populace, rather than being centralised under the control of a few state bureaucrats (communism) or wealthy private individuals (capitalism).
Distributism was to be to Capitalism as membership-owned Credit Unions are to profit-making Commercial Banking.
The collapse of Communism and the dominance of global capitalism and consumerism may ultimately cause society to seek something akin to the middle way they espoused. Not many at the beginning of the 21st Century would place absolute trust in Banks or Financial Institutions, no matter how grand they sound, nor yet in companies such as Enron in the US, and in the UK fraudulently price fixing companies such as Virgin Airlines and British Airways, plus over a hundred major British Contractors such as Balfour Beatty and Carillion, guilty in 2008 of defrauding central government and local authorities of British pounds in the tens of millions.

8 'Joe' too had questions about evolution.
How can one resolve the apparent conflict between the idea of a caring God and the spontaneous, bloody process of natural selection, the survival of the fittest?

The problem is only resolved by realising that the freedom He gives is absolute, without any reservation, and that God's creative activity does not merely relate to the physical universe.

The angelic rebellion confirmed by Jesus must be taken into account, for these angelic beings are also involved in the creation of the universe, bringing disorder where there should have been none, creating the struggle for survival realised by scientists such as Darwin.

Out of this cosmic, disordered struggle emerged mankind's primitive progenitors, and it is the Christian belief, revealed and confirmed by Jesus, God Incarnate, that at a specific moment in time God infused an added quality to a group of primates, creating *homo sapiens* - humans who, like Himself, had powers of intellect and will, the power to know and love with discrete intelligence.

According to Genesis these new creatures, made in God's image and likeness, were protected from death and the disordered cruelties of natural selection, in the 'Garden of Eden', but lost this protection through their own choice, 'eating of the fruit of the tree of knowledge of good and evil', making themselves the centre of moral judgement, as opposed to the Creator. As a consequence of being deceived into joining in the rebellion of the angels we lost our preternatural state and rejoined the struggle for survival.

Acceptance of this view depends entirely upon whether or not one believes the Christian teaching about the origin and purpose of the universe, summed up in the suffering of Jesus and His resurrection from the dead. We are free to believe or not, consistent with His continuing gift of freedom.

9 One day, at work, I received a telephone call from Cecily, who lived in the flat below. "I thought I better ring you before you heard on the news," she said. "It's about Sean. He was climbing in Glencoe, "- Sean sold books throughout the UK for Sheed & Ward – " and he has fallen 500 feet and been killed."
At that moment I had a fleeting vision of an angelic force catching Sean underneath his arms and carrying him safely away. The vision was like a brief cartoon, and I could not help but burst into laughter. The healing touch of laughter again? I could not help but believe so. *"In the eyes of the unwise, they did appear to die, their going looked like a disaster, their leaving us, like annihilation; but they are in peace." (Wisdom 3)*
I profoundly hoped that Sean's grieving parents, flown in from South Africa to bury their fine young son, would eventually see it so.

10 Peter was indeed a bit slow.
(The author identifies with the affliction.)
Because he was embedded in the traditions that existed before the coming of Jesus he needed a special vision on a roof-top about 'unclean meat' before he could accept that all things created by God are fit for human consumption. He also had to be confronted by Paul before he would accept that circumcision is not necessary in order to become a follower of Christ. Peter was a very traditional man, slow to learn. He was and is not alone:
Jesus groaned against the slowness of wit of the Apostles:
"Men of little faith ... do you not yet understand? ... How could you fail to understand?" (Mt.16. 8-11)
"You foolish men! So slow to believe the full message of the prophets!" (Lk.24. 25)
"He reproached them for their incredulity and obstinacy..." (Mk.16.14)
Quite a few priests and bishops, successors of the Apostles, fail to accept that they share the same root limitations, apparently believing that ordination and the 'laying on of hands' - the acceptance of an official position in the church - is a substitute for reason, perception and love.

11 Michael Bowen was and is a dedicated, caring priest, with a great sense of humour; up each day at the crack of dawn at that time, working through the day and teaching Latin to the St. Augustine's students five nights a week.

I was intrigued to discover that his grandfather was William Alexander, Archbishop of Armagh, Church of Ireland Primate, and that his grandmother, Cecil Frances Alexander, was the woman who wrote those memorable 19th century hymns, *"All Things Bright and Beautiful", "There is a Green Hill Far Away"* and *"Once in Royal David's City"*.

Michael himself went on to become Catholic Archbishop of Southwark. Something hereditary in the bloodstream? Too easy an assumption. Michael is a fine man in his own right, worthy through the gift of God to hold high office in the church. A private man, currently retired and living in the diocese, he will be mildly embarrassed by praise from an old and grateful pupil.

12 Despite Dominic's laudable aim a number of Dominicans were drawn into Papal Courts of Inquiry (Inquisitions) at this time, and were certainly guilty of infringing human rights, by depriving those found guilty of their property, but also, at times, of condemning the worst offenders to barbaric execution by burning, quite often instigated by local Lords and so-called Nobles, acting in collusion with what we would nowadays call lynch mobs.

Individual Dominican priests and some Franciscan Friars involved in these processes must bear the guilt, as must Popes Innocent III and Gregory IX, who instigated the pogroms, over-reacting against sects that threatened to subvert society by teaching with remarkable success the pernicious idea that the human body is evil, created by the Devil, and that only the spirit is good - even teaching that suicide is permissible, in order to get rid of the 'evil' material body. These beliefs were a widespread threat to mediaeval society, and provoked genuine fear and outrage; but the reaction was hysterical and out of proportion.

These 13th century activities should not be confused with the Spanish Inquisition that took place some two hundred years later, when the Spanish Dominican Tomás de Torquemada, in conjunction with Ferdinand and Isabella and with the nominal support of Pope Sixtus IV, living at a distance and unable to control such activities, mounted a vicious persecution of Spanish Jews, murdered at least 2,000 by *Auto de fé - Act of Faith! Burning* - and drove the remainder out of Spain, along with as many Muhammadans as they could find, all with the highest motive of keeping Spain totally Christian!

Torquemada, First Grand Inquisitor of Spain, was born at Valladolid in 1420 and died at Avila on 16 September 1498. He is rightly regarded by Jewish people, and by sane people throughout the world, with the same horror that normal people view Adolph Hitler and people of his ilk, those individuals whose perverted ideas of 'purity' of race, religion and political creed are in direct contradiction of the advice and information given by Jesus - the Ayatollahs of Iran, the present Government of Sudan, Stalin and his successors in Russia, China's communist rulers - as well as those with a primitive lust for power and wealth: the Generals in Burma, Mugabe in Zimbabwe – evil men hiding from the light, deceiving themselves and being deceived by the ever present power of darkness and hate, a constant menace to humanity: the power of evil that Jesus warned about.